UNDER ROSE-TAINTED SKIES

UNDER ROSE-TAINTED SKIES

Louise Gornall

CLARION BOOKS
HOUGHTON MIFFLIN HARCOURT
BOSTON NEW YORK

hmhco.com

The text was set in 10.75 Berling LT Std.

The Library of Congress has cataloged the hardcover edition as follows:
Names: Gornall, Louise, author.
Title: Under rose-tainted skies / Louise Gornall.
Description: Boston; New York : Clarion Books, Houghton Mifflin Harcourt, [2017] |
Summary: Will teenaged Norah, who is struggling with agoraphobia and OCD, accept
that she could be the right one for sweet, funny Luke?
Identifiers: LCCN 2016001081
Subjects: | CYAC: Agoraphobia—Fiction. | Obsessive-compulsive disorder—Fiction. |
Mental illness—Fiction. | Love—Fiction.
Classification: LCC PZ7.1.G665 Un 2017 | DDC [Fic]—dc23
LC record available at https://lccn.loc.gov/2016001081

ISBN: 978-0-544-73651-1 hardcover
ISBN: 978-1-328-74204-9 paperback

Printed in the United States of America
DOC 10 9 8 7 6 5 4 3
4500706373

Professor,
I wrote this book for you.
Thank you for helping me find my brave,
for showing me strength when adversity
was overwhelming,
and for always reminding me to breathe.

And Rach,
I know this was a tough one to get down.
I'm so grateful for all your support and encouragement, for
all the hugs and late night cups of coffee.
You never let me fall.

1

I'M GOING TO KILL the damn blackbird sitting on my windowsill, chirping and squeaking at the top of its lungs. It hops back and forth, wings spread and flapping, but has zero intention of taking off.

The point is, it can fly away whenever it wants. And it knows it can. It stops chirping, turns its tiny head, and looks at me. Smiling for sure.

Smug bastard.

I pick up my pillow and lob it at the window. It crashes against the glass then plops onto my window ledge, catching a pile of books as it dies a deflated death on my bedroom floor.

The blackbird is unperturbed, but it pales into insignificance as my eyes home in on my copy of *The Picture of Dorian Gray*. Its corner is now ever so slightly out of line with the books beneath it.

It's the Reader's Choice edition. Two hundred and twenty-eight pages exactly. Just like the five books under it. To the left is another pile of six books. They all have two hundred and seventy-two pages. The book on top of that pile is *Pride and Prejudice*, the Dover Thrift edition.

"Norah," Mom bellows up the stairs. "If you don't get your butt down here in the next ten seconds, I'm canceling the Internet service." I've been testing her patience for the last twenty minutes.

"I still have a stomachache," I call back. There's a pause, and I think maybe she's giving up on the idea of making me go outside.

"I don't care if you have the bubonic plague." Pause. Inhale courage. Exhale guilt. "If you're not down these stairs in the next eight seconds, you can kiss your Internet connection goodbye." Her voice cracks, but wow, she's really taking this whole "tough love" approach seriously. I don't think she's an enabler, but ever since she watched Doctor Motivator and his know-nothing special on mental health, she's been grappling with her conscience.

I surrender.

To her, at least. I look back at the books, see a crumbling tower, a broken wall. Dr. Reeves is in my head, telling me to test myself, telling me to leave the discombobulated book as it is and observe how the world does not collapse around me.

I huff a breath, climb off the bed, pick up my pillow, and place it back where it belongs. It's one of four. They all sit angled, diamond shapes, on top of my military-smooth bed sheets.

Neck hot, fingers tapping thighs, six beats each, I leave the room.

But before I hit the stairs, that tiny corner, no longer in line with the other five books, is consuming me. Like that song you heard but can't quite remember the name of. Or that actor you've seen in another film but can't for the life of you recall which one. The thought is a fungus, a black mold rotting my brain. I ache. My teeth itch.

I stand at the top of the stairs, close my eyes, and try to make my mind go blank.

Don't go back. Don't go back. You don't need to go back. Clear your mind.

Here's the thing. The blankness in my mind turns into a piece of white paper, the white paper reminds me of books, and then I'm thinking about *The Picture of Dorian Gray* again. *Fuck.*

I march back to my room, push the book to its rightful position, and then hate myself.

The blackbird catches my eye. It hasn't budged. Bet it knew I would be back. I slam my fist into the window and shout, *"Boo!"* It shrieks and takes to the skies. I smile. Throw it a sarcastic five-fingered *sayonara* wave. It's a small but satisfying victory.

Then I see a boy through my window. He's stopped halfway up the garden path and is looking at me like I've lost my mind. He's carrying a box labeled *Bedroom*. I take note of bulging biceps testing the durability of his shirt-sleeves.

New neighbors.

Why has he stopped? Am I supposed to smile? Wave? Throw him a thumbs-up? I feel like an idiot.

It's awkward; we're both just staring at each other until a woman in a floaty summer dress sails outside. He's distracted, so I slip away.

Like a giant in cast-iron shoes, I make my way down the stairs. Eleven steps, so I have to take the last one twice. I have this thing about even numbers.

You don't have to take the last one twice, Dr. Reeves would say.

But I do, I'd tell her. Then she'd ask me why, and I would say, as I always do, Because that's the way my mind works.

2

COAT ON, KEYS IN HAND, my mom has a grin plastered across her face and I know my Internet connection lives to fight another day. Losing that would be like pulling the plug on my life-support system, shutting me inside a chest and dumping me in the ocean. But as serious as she is about testing the current limits of my comfort zone, I'm not sure her guts are steely enough to follow through with the threat. Not that I'm a brat who would make her life a misery if she did. What I mean is, she feels sorry for me. She knows I would be completely isolated without the Internet. The clunky plastic box with flashing blue lights is my friend. Sad, but true. It helps me keep a toe in real life.

Still, my stupid brain and its never-ending wave of paranoia won't allow me to push her empathy any further. So I'm here.

And we're going out.

Kill me.

"Got everything?" Mom asks, her voice all singsongy.

We're acting normal. A short-lived façade when I open my bag and Operation Check Contents begins.

1. Phone to call for help if we have a car crash/get mugged/drive into the path of a tornado.

2. Headphones to drown out the sound of people if we get caught in a crowd.

3. Bottle of water for if we break down and get stranded in the middle of nowhere.

4. Another bottle of water in case that other bottle leaks or evaporates.

5. Tissues for nosebleeds, sneezing, crying, and/or drooling.

6. Sanitizer to kill the germs you can catch from touching anything.

7. Paper bag to breathe into or throw up in.

8. Band-Aids and alcohol wipes in case open wounds should occur.

9. Inhaler (I grew out of asthma when I was twelve, but you can't be too careful when it comes to breathing.)

10. A piece of string that serves no purpose but it's been here since forever and I'm afraid the world will implode if I don't have it.

11. A pair of nail scissors for any one of a trillion reasons, most of which conclude with me being kidnapped.

12. And, finally, chewing gum to take away the sour taste I always get when the panic hits.

Normal takes a nosedive into my bag, sinks beneath the copious amount of clutter, and dies a slow, painful death.

I nod; my mouth won't move. My lips are numb. It's already started and she hasn't even opened the door.

"Ready?" Mom asks. Her voice is warped. *Ready*, a word that should only have two syllables, suddenly has fifty. I nod. Not too hard, because I'm sure any second now my head is going to fall off.

A crease as deep as space tears across Mom's forehead. This is as painful for her as it is for me, and I can't help thinking it would be so much easier if we just didn't bother. But I'm not allowed to think that. Instead, I'm supposed to remind myself that we bother because if I don't learn how to control my fears, I'm going to die cold and alone. Hidden in my room while strangers post messages of condolences on my social media and rabid cats eat my decomposing corpse.

Reassurance resides in Mom's emerald-green eyes and the slight nod of her head. She claps her hand into mine and starts chanting the words that never help.

"Just breathe: in through your nose, out through your mouth. Just keep breathing."

When the panic sets in, the ground transforms into wet cement. My feet feel like they're sinking into it as we tread our way to the car.

I keep my eyes fixed on my boots because seeing the vast space outside will finish me off.

I'm drowning.

"Mom." I snatch her arm, hold it tight to my chest like it's a buoy.

"You're okay, honey. We're almost there."

Insects are crawling under my skin. My bottom lip has fallen off. I don't remember swallowing a golf ball, but it's there, stuck in my throat, trying to choke me. I concentrate on putting one foot in front of the other as the September sun spews red-hot rays all over me. My steps are slowing; my knees are folding.

I'm fucked. At this rate I won't make it to the car.

"Keep breathing. Just keep breathing." Mom wraps her other arm around my shoulders, squeezing. She's almost carrying me, which is good, because my muscles have liquefied and melted clean away.

What feels like a lifetime later, Mom pulls open the car door and hauls my ass into the front seat.

I deflate. Shrivel up in my chair like a lump of dehydrated fruit. Exhaustion hits like a Mack truck. And then, just because this panic attack hasn't quite finished screwing me six ways from Sunday, the spasms start.

Dr. Reeves calls them tics. Arms jump, legs twitch. A tortured heaving sound escapes my lips and makes my skeleton jerk. I can't stop it. I have no control. My body does what it wants when the freak-outs take over.

At least I don't pass out this time. Passing out is the worst, especially if there's no one around to catch you.

Luckily, having no one around to catch me has only happened once. It was my very first panic attack and I was at school. Of course, back then I didn't know what a panic attack was and just assumed I was dying.

It was the weirdest thing. Mrs. Dawson asked me a question in chem class, something about the Periodic Table, and my mind went blank. Everyone's eyes were on me, I could feel fire around my neck, and my vision started to wobble. Like when the heat rises off the desert floor and smudges the landscape, everything was out of focus.

The next thing I knew, I was waking up in the ER, a train track of staples running down my forehead. Six staples. Things got really bad from there.

I spend the next twenty-five minutes of our journey

wrinkled up in my seat, too scared to look out of the window. Angry-girl music blasts through my headphones, but it does nothing to quiet the voices listing potential disasters in my head.

Mom pulls into a space outside Bridge Lea Medical Center, kills the car engine, and turns to look at me.

"Are you going to come inside?"

"I can't do it," I tell her, my voice weak and squeaky like a mouse's. I'm not being awkward. I'm done. Seriously. Beyond exhausted and numb from the neck down. I don't think my muscles could take my weight.

Mom submits in record time. Doctor Motivator and his know-nothing mental-health special can take a hike. Forcing your crumbling kid to move is near impossible for any parent with a soul.

Mom takes ten strides across the parking lot and goes to get Dr. Reeves from her office.

Today's therapy session will have to take place in the car.

Mom steps out of the door accompanied by the good doctor. Mom's hands are lively, jumping about in front of her, reinforcing the apology that I know she's spouting. As per usual, Dr. Reeves sets a hand down on my mom's shoulder, assuring her that there's no need to apologize.

Dr. Reeves is shorter than my mom. She's closer to five feet and built like a twig. A strong breeze, and the woman would blow away. She's smiling, drunk on life. She smiles a lot. A cynical streak expands under my skin. No one should be this happy at nine a.m. on a Monday morning. No one.

Mom takes a turn to her right and heads over to the diner across the road. Dr. Reeves fixes a narrow stare on me and climbs into the driver's seat. She straightens her pantsuit and places her hands, one on top of the other, in her lap.

"What happened?" she asks, her voice calm and soothing, like ocean waves on a relaxation tape.

"Couldn't do it." I can't look her in the eye. "I'm sorry, I just couldn't." She exhales a sigh. She doesn't like it when I apologize.

"Let's talk about why." She pushes her glasses back on top of her head.

"It's stupid."

"It's not stupid if it makes you feel afraid. Tell me what you were thinking about when it was time to leave the car."

Deep breath.

"I started thinking about your stairs." There are twenty-eight steps to Dr. Reeves's office. They wind, like a staircase in a fairy tale. Up and up and up into the lofty heights of heaven. They're bordered by two solid white walls and traced by a black cast-iron handrail.

She nods. She knows where this is going. We talk a lot about ascending. I have this thing about stairs.

"What about the stairs?"

"I don't want to say it."

"Norah, this is just you and me talking." She relaxes, leans back in the seat like this is the school cafeteria and we're about to start discussing the star quarterback's abs. "You can tell me."

Her voice is low, kind of hypnotic, teasing the answer from my throat.

"I was hanging around on the Metro, that social media site I was telling you about." She nods, and I bite down hard on my bottom lip. "And all these people started pinning notes to their profiles about this tragedy in Seto." She knows I'm talking about the earthquake in Japan. I can tell because for a split second, grief clouds her eyes. She's seen the reports, read the firsthand accounts, mourned over the thousands of pictures that have been published.

"So I started reading . . ."

Her mouth turns down into a frown. "I thought we talked about not doing that."

"We did. And I was working on it."

I was. Truly. Weeks ago we talked about staying away from things I couldn't handle until I learned how to process better. The news is easy to avoid—just keep the TV off and don't pick up any newspapers. But then I see words on my social media like *death* and *destruction*, and I have to know. I can't help looking. Like how a moth still craves a light bulb, even though it burns. It's a compulsion.

"There was this story about this woman, Yui, who worked on the ground floor of this office. She said that everyone on the first and second floors managed to get out, but everyone on floors three to five were trapped when the stairs collapsed and the elevators stopped working." I'm twisting my fingers into white knots, sweating as I try to imagine what would have been going through the heads of those poor people.

"Okay." Dr. Reeves puts her hand on top of mine. "Just relax. We're not up any stairs right now."

"I know it's irrational," I tell her, because I do know that. I know that you can't live your life waiting for disaster to strike. I know this. Hell, if we all lived like that, we'd stay stock-still our entire lives or be forced to roll around the streets in those giant plastic bubbles. But it's like my mind and my brain are two separate things, working against each other. I can't get them to cooperate.

The doc reminds me that fear and rational thought are

enemies. Then we talk about neural pathways and breaking thought cycles, medical jargon that amounts to *Next session, we're going to climb a flight of stairs.* Fun times.

With that, she makes a follow-up appointment.

I suggest Monday, same time next week.

She insists on Tuesday, in the afternoon.

She likes to mix up our psych dates a little, says she wants to keep a pinch of spontaneity in our meets; this way, my brain doesn't start relying on a routine. The doc climbs out of the car.

I'm already trying to invent a sickness that will prevent me from leaving the house next week.

3

HOME SAFE AND SOUND, at last. It takes less effort to walk the fifty yards to my front door. It's the going out that rocks my world, not the coming home.

Mom heads off into the kitchen. I consider disappearing into my room and slipping into a vegetative state, but I have a science paper due in sixteen days, and I'm not one to leave things until the last second/minute/week. Well, anything could happen between now and then. What if the computer and laptop break simultaneously and it takes an eternity to get them fixed? What if I lose fingers in a horrific sandwich-slicing incident? Or a tornado tears through our house and sucks up everything we own? You just never know.

I slink off into the study, push the power button on the computer, and the old gal starts up with a cough and a splutter. Sadly, long-term sickness does not mean a free pass from education, and for the last four years, Mom and the Learn Long Distance website have been homeschooling me.

Like I don't love learning. I do. I absolutely love it.

I almost wish I didn't. I never used to. It's all part of agoraphobia's dastardly plan to make me look like the most abnormal teen on the planet.

I work as fast as I can, mostly because this computer is practically steam-powered and the clunky buttons tick every time I tap them. This does not bode well for a brain that obsesses over patterns and numbers. Superhuman hearing detects the slight variation of sound with every keystroke, and I become frustratingly fixated on the fact that no two clicks sound the same. Then suddenly it's as if I'm Mozart, losing hours trying to type out Shakespeare sonnets to a tune. Thankfully, this is one of those quirky behaviors that's not always present. It comes and goes like most of my compulsions, depending on how stressed/emotional/sleepy/hormonal I am.

The printer spits out my pages. I grab them, stack them, and bang them against the desktop so they're all nice and neatly aligned. I want to clip them together so they stay that way, but Mom's usually well-stocked stationery caddy is missing paper clips. There was this moment during a math quiz last week when my mind started to wander and I inadvertently twisted them all into a model of the Eiffel Tower. Art isn't a required subject, but Mom gave me an A anyway.

I glance around the study, uncertain where she's storing stationery supplies this week. Could be here, could be the trunk of her car, could be in her bra or at the bottom of her Louis Vuitton briefcase. I reach for the top drawer of the desk. Hesitate.

Mom is a mess monster. Her bedroom looks like a battle broke out between a hurricane and a thrift store. There are cold cups of tea in there, playing host to entire micronations. My Spider-Man mug went in two months and ten days ago . . . I haven't seen it since. A shudder rips through me. When my mug finally does emerge, it will need to be destroyed in the fires of Mount Doom.

But that's her space.

Our compromise.

She fights her natural urge to leave things lying around the rest of the house and we keep her bedroom door closed at all times.

"Mom?" I wait a second, and when she doesn't answer, I head toward the kitchen, admiring the crisp white sheets and perfect type on my paper. Perfection is a feeling; you'll know it if you've ever questioned the competency of your penmanship before writing on the first page of a new notebook.

I can hear Mom talking before I get to the kitchen.

"Can't you send Maggie or the intern, what's-his-face?" She's on the phone, sitting at the table with her back to me. Her words are heavy, weighted down with worry.

I'm instantly concerned. So much so that I spend only a second thinking about how vulnerable she's made herself to potential intruders; I'm halfway in the room and she still hasn't noticed me.

"Things are a little tricky with Norah at the moment. I'm not sure I can leave her again," Mom says. Her shoulders sink to the floor.

This is the third new job she's had this year. Last year there were two new jobs. It's tricky finding a boss who can be flexible with our situation. I'm dependent, and her job requires travel. Her employers keep promising she can bypass the travel part, but she's so good at selling construction equipment, they end up changing their minds.

"Leave it to me," she says. I choose this moment to sit down beside her. She doesn't startle. Maybe she knew I was here the whole time. She hangs up, winces at me.

"Sneaking up on me?" she says with a smile.

"How did you know I was here?"

"You're my child. I always know where you are."

That catches my brain in a way it wouldn't for most, and I start wondering if there's any validity to this theory. She mistakes my silence for anxiety.

"I should have applied for that nine-to-five gig at the bowling alley." She rubs her face with both hands, pulls down her cheeks so I can see the pink, squidgy bit of her eyes, and blows a raspberry.

"You love your job."

"But I hate leaving you here alone."

"I'll be fine," I tell her. My fingers find a pimple on the side of my leg. I pick at it until it stings.

"Maybe I could call in sick and they'll have to find someone else to go in my place." She's not listening to me. She never does when this happens.

"Mom."

"Huh?"

"I'll be okay." The times when we get to switch roles are very few and far between.

"Norah . . ."

"Mom. I just need groceries. The rest I can do myself. I'll be fine. Promise." I'm oversimplifying. I dislike being alone, sure. At first, it's overwhelming, like trying to find your way out of a forest without a map. It's easier to explain away noises, and the dark is always a shade less severe, when you know someone is sleeping down the hall, but I'm not afraid. I don't know. Things are always much more manageable from inside this house. Plus, I've done it before and nothing bad happened. My head puts a lot of stock in that, keeps track and uses it as a benchmark for next time. Dr. Reeves explains it better, with a bunch more science and phrases like *eliminating the fear of the unknown* — which I'm pretty sure is the title of a *Star Trek* episode.

4

It's Sunday. Mom crashes down the stairs, dragging a suitcase behind her. It slams into a step, pops her on the butt. *She* slams into a step, collides with the wall. The whole descent has the elegance of an elephant performing *Swan Lake* on a pogo stick.

As a fangirl of anything sci-fi, Mom's almost always wearing a shirt adorned with an alien or a Captain Somebody of Something. Today is no exception. Some creepy green interstellar species is flashing a peace sign at me. Slung over Mom's arm is a garment bag that holds a designer suit for tomorrow's conference. She's only ever conservative at conferences. In real time, her hair is the color of a fire truck and she has a peace lily tattooed on her wrist.

Crash. Bang. Wallop. Down the stairs she comes. "Are you sure you don't need some help?" I cringe, watching the battle through my fingers.

"I got it," she says, touching down on even ground. I exhale, stop chewing holes in the side of my tongue. The bitter taste of blood hits the back of my throat. In the twenty seconds it's taken her to get from top to bottom, I've watched her trip and break her neck eight times.

"What've you got in there?" I flick my eyes toward the tattered suitcase. "Bricks?"

"Hardy. Har. Har." She snorts. It's funny because her suitcase actually is full of brick samples and various other building materials she's showcasing at the conference. "I can't believe I'm doing this to you again," she says, all joking a distant memory.

"I'm fine. I swear." I twirl, because nothing says *I'm mentally stable* quite like an impromptu pirouette. She's beating herself up. I can tell. The fight with her luggage may be over, but she's still wincing. "Mom, really, I'm fine. It's only for two days—"

"Less, if I can get away sooner," she interjects, dipping into her purse. She pulls out a compact, dabs her cheeks with pink powder. I smile to myself, recall the early mornings when I was still in school. We used to share the bathroom mirror. I brushed my hair while she painted her face bright colors.

Makeup days for Mom are almost nonexistent now. She stopped wearing it when I got sick and there wasn't much call for her to leave the house. Guilt is a squeezing sensation in the pit of my stomach.

She needs these trips, these brief moments away. She

needs to be with grownups every now and then. To feel social and not secluded. I'm secretly hoping that she'll go out, get drunk, and shamelessly flirt with some dark-haired, dark-eyed Latino who sweeps her off her feet. I've seen the staff photos on her work's website. Apparently, construction is where all the hot guys hang out.

"Okay." She snaps her compact shut. "Hotel, conference center, cell, pager—"

"Numbers are all pinned to the fridge."

She nods; a smile lacking any humor sits on her lips. "I'll call—"

"Before you go to bed and when you wake up. I know the drill, Mom. Go, have fun, stop worrying. PS: Did you pack that silky blue shirt? The one that ties around your neck?"

"It's not that kind of conference."

"I'm just saying, it's a cute shirt."

"Hush." She kisses my forehead and heads out the door. "Oh . . ." She turns around, slapping the heel of her hand against her forehead. "I almost forgot, Helping Hands is delivering tonight at six. They didn't have a slot open tomorrow."

"Six tonight. Got it." I tap my temple.

"Should I write it down on the fridge?"

"Go."

I stand at the door as she loads herself into the car. I test my toes against the step, inching my foot down, like the concrete is red-hot lava. I'm so focused on putting a whole foot flat, outside in the wilderness, that I almost miss Mom pulling away. She honks the horn, I wave, and she's gone.

My fingers curl into the door frame so tightly it's a wonder they don't pierce the wood. But I can do it, one whole foot outside my front door, without my chest getting tight.

The step has been in shadow. The cold of the concrete seeps through my sock and makes my foot feel wet. It's weirdly refreshing, like splashing your face with cool water. I close my eyes, take a deep breath, and am exhaling ecstasy when I hear a cough. My eyes pop open and he's there again. The new boy next door. Muscles still bulging under the weight of a new box, this time full of groceries. He flicks his head at me.

"Hi."

Like a rabbit reacting to the sound of a gunshot, I retract my foot, scurry back inside, and slam the door shut.

That was close is my first thought. Followed by *What was close? Pleasant conversation?* Ugh. I press my back up against the door and wilt to the floor. I instantly dislike that a stranger has seen my crazy side, not once but twice within a week. I curl inward, try hard to split the floor with my mind so I can seep through it.

Once I'm done reassembling my self-esteem, life goes the way it always does.

Technically, I don't have to study on weekends, but I do anyway. I'm learning to speak French for a trip I'll never take. I watch some TV, eat, sleep, build a pretty impressive yet rather unstable castle of saliva and peanut butter cookies.

I'm in the middle of licking and sticking a broken turret when my phone sings like a cuckoo. It's a notification from the Metro telling me six people are talking about *Dream Stalker,* this supposedly pee-your-pants horror movie that just came out.

It's forever my intention to avoid social media on weekends, but a morbid sense of curiosity, or a subconscious desire for S&M, always convinces me to open the application when it calls. It's like a siren's song.

I click the button and am bombarded with selfies of Mercy, Cleo, Sarah, and Jade getting ready for a night out at *le cinéma.* They're blowing kisses to the camera and then they're kissing each other, hugging, and voguing in a creative series of shots.

I scroll down, see more selfies of more former friends wearing makeup and looking much older since I last saw them in real life. Which was only four years ago but feels more like four centuries. Puberty: the ultimate makeover.

I push my hand against my chest. My heart suddenly feels ten times too heavy. I press down harder, trying to keep it from flopping out of its cavity and hitting the carpet with a ground-shaking splat.

I miss having friends. It seems babysitting your house-bound BFF loses its appeal when your body turns banging and an active social life kicks in. They never really understood it, understood me, when I got sick. We were only young, but I was surprised at how easy I was to forget.

I throw my phone on the table; it hits my cookie castle like a wrecking ball and totals the carefully constructed architecture.

It's only five, but I trudge through the kitchen and lock myself in the box bathroom.

The most underrated room in the house, the box bathroom is so small, I can't even spin a circle in there with my arms spread out to the sides. It feels like an afterthought, a room tacked onto the house once it had already been built. I like it. It's cozy. The walls are bright yellow, and the faucets are shaped like dolphins. Plus, I feel weighted, and right now climbing the stairs is about as appealing as climbing Everest in my underwear.

I run a bath, dump my clothes in the hamper under

the sink, and submerge myself. I keep my eyes open, staring through a milky mist at the ceiling above. The water is so warm it turns my pasty complexion red, but I feel cold to the bone. My body is covered in goose bumps. There's a sob stuck in the bridge of my nose. It stings, but I stay under the water so it can't escape without killing me.

The bath cools quickly, but I lie in it until my skin feels too tight for my skeleton. Then, with great reluctance, I climb out.

Depression can't come in, I think, drawing a glass half full in the condensation on the mirror. I'm already covering a multitude of colors on the mental-health spectrum. Depression can't come in.

The lines of my drawing drip and blend together. I can see myself in the glass. "You're not missing much," I tell my reflection, then I slap a preppy-pink blush back into my cheeks. "You're fine."

I braid my hair over my shoulder, pull on the robe that's hung on the back of the door, and step out into the hall, whistling while I walk, because everybody knows whistling induces an unshakable delirium. I should probably stop watching Disney movies.

I'm caught between the kitchen and the hall when a noise stops me dead in my tracks.

"Hello. Anyone home?"

My heart splutters to a standstill, and I slam my back up against the doorjamb.

The potbellied gremlin known as panic claws its way up my throat and clogs my airways. The cold air of the kitchen licks at the damp stretches of skin that my robe is too short to cover, but it doesn't cool me. Fire burns through my blood as the fear takes hold.

I can't see him because we own a fridge the size of Saturn and it's blocking my line of sight, but I can hear his heavy feet padding against the laminate.

Fuck. I can't feel my legs.

"I'm looking for Norah."

He's here to rob me.

"Norah Dean?"

I'm going to die.

My heart pounds against my rib cage; my knees curl in. I need help, I need help. I need stability because the floor is moving and I'm going to collapse, and then my robe will flop open, and then I'll lose my towel, and then . . . oh God . . .

"Yo." A shadow moves to my left. "Are you Norah?"

Can't. Talk. Need. Oxygen.

"I'm from Helping Hands. I've got a delivery for a Miss Norah Dean. That you?"

Helping Hands. I know them.

The tension in my neck recedes just enough so I can lift my head and look at the boy in my kitchen. A scrawny twig of a thing with a shaved head and ripped jeans. Just above the rips, about an inch below his side pocket, there are three skull patches, stitched on in no particular pattern, which bugs me way more than it should. He's chewing gum like a cow chewing grass and looking at me with a poised brow.

"Nice place you got here," he says. "Big."

It's not six o'clock. If it were, I would have been ready for him.

"Hey. You okay?" He extends an arm in my direction, and I avoid it as if it were a bullet. I have this thing about being touched. Unless it's Mom or Dr. Reeves, I can't handle it.

"What are you doing in my house?" Teeth clenched, I glare at his outstretched hand. He drops it back by his side.

"I'm. Here. From. Helping. Hands," he says slowly. "I have a delivery for Norah Dean."

"Yeah, I got that. What I want to know is why you're *inside* my house."

"Knock-and-no-answer procedure. I'm just following the rules." A grin stretches across his lips.

"What rule says it's okay for you to break into someone's house?"

"I didn't break in. I had a key." He pulls a clipboard out from under his arm.

"What?" He's lying.

"A key. You know, one of those little metal things that open locks?" He plucks a pen from behind his ear and holds it out to me. "I need you to sign."

"How do you have a key?"

"You gotta hand one over when you sign up for the service. Like I said, knock-and-no-answer procedure. If you knock and the client doesn't answer, you go inside to make sure they haven't kicked the bucket or fallen off a ladder and knocked themselves unconscious. Died. It's all in the terms and conditions." This guy has a real way with words. Mom's never mentioned this key thing to me before. Understandably, I guess. Still, looks like I'm going to be dead-bolting the door from here on.

Helping Hands Guy is getting impatient. He shakes his pen at me for a fourth time. I can't touch it. It's chewed and marked with fingerprints. The thing needs its own *Caution: Contaminated* sticker. Not that I can sign his paperwork yet anyway. I glance at the clock above the oven. It's just past 5:45. When people change plans, times, locations, it turns my brain into the aftermath of an egg that's been dropped ten thousand feet. He's early. I'm not ready. Not prepared. The need to defend myself is overwhelming.

"I would have been ready for you at six," I tell him.

"I'll make a note of that." He retracts the pen, uses it to scratch his scalp before tapping it on the paper. "Sign, please." I swear I see little luminous green blobs of bacteria peppering the sheet.

"I think I have a pen," I reply, hugging my torso as I scour the kitchen for a stray Bic. There's a Sharpie stuck to the notepad on the fridge. It will have to do.

"You don't look very sick," the guy says as I scrawl my name in thick black letters. It doesn't fit neatly on the little dotted line. My nails find a scab on my wrist and start picking as his eyes saunter down my scantily clad frame, lingering on my legs.

"How grossly inappropriate of you to notice," I reply, fighting hard to keep my voice even.

I'm not surprised by his comment. It's not the first time I've heard it. I mean, I'm pasty, sallow, reasonably tall at five foot six, and my mom would say as thin as a rake. Social Convention dictates that I must deny being pretty, but I am . . . pretty. It's one of the only things I have that makes me feel normal. Of course, I pervert that normality by embracing my looks. I'm supposed to pretend that I've never noticed my face. I see it happen on the Metro all the time: a person tells someone else that they're pretty, and they deny all knowledge, refute the compliment into oblivion, but hell-to-the-no am I ever doing that. This is mine, one of the only things about me that I actually like. I own it. And Social Convention will have to pry it from my cold, dead hands before I ever give it up.

The thing is, Helping Hands has a roster of house-bound clients who are all on the far side of sixty. And most are undergoing some pretty intense treatments. As far as looking sick goes, people generally think I don't. I have what Dr. Reeves calls an *invisible illness*.

"Much feistier than the norm," Helping Hands Guy tells me. I steady myself against the countertop, moving as slowly as I would if he were a lion and I were a lamb. I'm not sure how I'm supposed to respond, so I say nothing. He doesn't seem to mind. "Cool pictures." He nods in the direction of the two art nouveau prints hanging on the wall at the other side of the room.

"Thank you." I'm trying not to be hostile. It's hard. His personal comments are still circulating, and my mind has started asking questions that I can't answer.

"You paint them?" he asks.

"No." The pictures are originals. Given to my grandma the Christmas before she died by the artist himself, Franz Muto. He's not much of a big deal . . . yet. He's hoping that'll happen the day after he dies. My gran talked about

Franz all the time. I know I could elaborate on my sharp response, tell Helping Hands Guy half a dozen stories about these particular pieces of art, but my brain is too busy trying to work out what he's still doing here. I'm fixated on the idea that he's waiting for a tip. Trying to work out how much. Considering what will happen if he's not waiting for that and finds the suggestion offensive. "Yeah. Anyway. Good talk." He rolls his eyes at me. "I'll see myself out." Helping Hands Guy flicks his eyebrows once, and with that, he leaves.

Wait.

My eyes dart around the room like Ping-Pong balls.

Wait.

Countertop: clear.

Kitchen island: clear.

Floor: clear.

Where are my groceries?

"Wait!"

Panic turns my dart to the front door into a tangled stumble of lanky limbs. I thwack my hip on a chair and stub my toe on the baseboard.

Alas, it's all in vain. I fling the door open just in time to see Helping Hands Guy pull his truck away from the curb. The grocery bags lined up against the side of my house make a brief appearance in my peripheral vision. "Wait!" I scream, but my voice is drowned out by the sound of maggot rock music blasting from his stereo. And then he's down the road, around the corner.

Gone.

"Wait," I whisper to the wind.

5

YOU MIGHT THINK THAT now that sustenance has been thrown into the mix, my debilitating agoraphobia will take a back seat to my survival instincts. You'd be wrong.

I reach for the phone, stab in the number for Helping Hands, jaw clenched so tight it's a wonder my teeth don't shatter. It's 6:05. I already know no one will pick up because their office shuts at six on Sundays, but I plow on through because panic is a vast, solid mass inhabiting my mind and there is no room for common sense. I dig a nail into my thigh and scratch until I feel a sting.

The phone rings twice before an automated voice apologizes and tells me I should call back at seven a.m. tomorrow. I slam the phone down, making the vase of fresh flowers on the end table shudder, only to pick the phone back up again, sense still AWOL.

Dr. Reeves gave me her number six months ago, after our first appointment. She said it was for emergencies. I've never used it, mostly because I have trouble deciphering what your average Joe considers an emergency.

My thumb hovers above the number 2 button. We have her on speed dial.

I mean, there is next to no food in this house and Mom won't be back until Tuesday. Plus, there's this whole countywide bear warning since a couple of trash cans were wrecked during the small hours one night last week. We've been double-bagging our garbage as a precaution. All that food out there, sweltering in the sun. It's basically an invitation. This is an emergency. *It is.*

I hit the button and am greeted by voicemail.

Damn it. I slam the phone down for a second time, abuse that somehow it survives intact.

Then I start pacing. Up and down the hall, chewing more holes in the side of my mouth and tearing strips off my nails.

Pace. Chew. Pace. Chew.

I stop, steal a glance through the window and out onto the porch, where I can see the three brown paper bags. A packet of luncheon meat is starting to sweat; a carton of eggs is no doubt boiling in the still-blistering heat. Even in the early evening, the California sun is merciless.

A buffet of smells permeating the air, calling out to a bunch of ravenous brown bears.

I have to get the bags.

I march over to the linen closet. I need clothes, something longer. Something that will cover my legs. Something that will cover me, hide me, make me feel less exposed. I grab the first mass of wool I find and pull it over my head. It drops all the way down past my knees. Perfect. I shudder in the warmth of it.

There's a reason the whole imagine-your-audience-in-their-underwear thing works. It makes the speaker, the possessor of clothes, feel like the strongest one in the room. There's a vulnerability that comes from showing skin.

The sweater is one of Mom's eighties throwback knits that she keeps handy for laundry days and lazy days. It feels like iron filings scratching against my skin. Two giant teddy bears flashing serial-killer smiles are embroidered on the front.

I grab the broom from the closet and head back over to the door.

Just like fishing, I think as I kneel on the floor and stretch the broom toward the bags. Except I've never been fishing, so I have no idea what that's like.

Hard, if it's anything like this. I lie on the floor inside, manipulating the space so only my arms are exposed to the fresh air. I have trouble hooking the broom head around the bags. And when I do hook one, the bag is too heavy to drag.

I lose my grip on the brush handle for the one-trillionth time and it clatters to the ground. A whimper escapes my lips as I look hopelessly at the grocery bags: boulders, refusing to budge.

"Do you need some help?" I'm drenched in shadow, and boots with steel toecaps take three steps onto the porch.

Three steps.

That's awkward. He leaves his back leg trailing behind. I wish he would bring it forward and make it four steps even. My eye twitches.

"Can I help?" I can't look up to see who's talking to me because anxiety has my chin stapled to my chest, but when I flick my eyes left I can see his reflection in the window. It's New Boy from next door. He has dimples, and a mop of shaggy dark hair falls casually over his left eye.

His feet meet, four steps, and my focus is free, running wild like a liberated stallion.

"No. No, thank you." In context, this might be the dumbest thing I have ever said. "I mean . . ." Deep breath. "I mean . . ." What do I mean? I feel flushed, like I've just dipped my face in the center of the sun.

Another breath as I stand up, back up, and steady myself against the door frame. I straighten my sweater, pulling it down and trying to cover everything above the soles of my feet. No amount of hugging my torso can hide the two giant teddies.

I can feel his eyes on me. Probably curious about my attire. Definitely confused as to why I'm fishing for grocery bags on my front porch.

"Could you please pass me those bags?" I talk to my feet, suddenly wishing I'd painted my toenails when I'd planned to last night.

"Sure," he says. I lift my eyes a little, discover jeans ripped at the knees and a belt with a Superman buckle. My lips pull into a slight smile. Superman is my favorite superhero.

"You need me to carry them inside?"

"That's okay." I snatch the bags from his hands and pull them tight against my chest. A wave of relief washes over me, and I feel my shoulders slump.

"Thank you. Really. Thank you." There's way too much gratitude in my tone, but I can't rein it in.

"No worries," he replies. If he has questions, he doesn't ask them, at least not out loud.

A thousand years of silence pass between us. Cotton mouth sets in. My fingers find the seam of one of the bags and pick at it.

"Anyway." He clears his throat. "We just moved in next

door. Mom insisted I come over and say hi, assure you I don't drive a motorcycle or play the drums, that sort of thing." He laughs. I like the way it sounds. "You know how parents are."

"Yeah. Parents." I force a laugh too, and it comes out as a snort. I don't think I've ever felt more alien. Or looked more alien. Hair still wet from my bath, pale, shoulders hunched, gangly legs twisting inward. I wish he would leave. My heart keeps missing beats.

"It's Luke, by the way." He holds out his hand, retracts it when I clutch the brown bags tighter. There's a silver ring on his middle finger, and my eyes are drawn to it like magnets. It's gaudy. Thick and bedazzled with diamantes. It might be a football ring, which is kind of confusing because he seems a little too emo to be jock.

And then I am lost. My crazy mind forgets he's in front of me and starts trying to figure out if emo and jock can coexist inside the same skeleton. I feel my face crumple.

"Are you okay?"

Mental slap. I clear my throat, decide against trying to pigeonhole him.

"It's nice to meet you, Luke."

"It's nice to meet you too . . ." He pauses. Nothing happens again for the longest time, until I realize I've missed the most basic of social cues. Talking to boys is much harder than it looks on TV.

"Norah," I bark when it finally hits me. "My name is Norah."

"Well, Norah, I'm here to assure you that I don't play the drums."

Say something redeeming.

"Pity. I hope it's okay that I do. Really loud. Mostly on Sunday mornings."

"You do?"

"No." I smile. I don't know if he's smiling back, but I'm kind of hoping he is.

"You're funny."

"It's both a blessing and a curse." I definitely hear him scoff a laugh.

"So, I guess I'll see you around, Neighbor."

"I'm sure you will," I lie. He leaves, and I slither back into the safety of my house.

"Whoa." I exhale.

Something warm fizzes like seltzer in my stomach as I watch him through the window, drifting down my driveway.

6

THE GROCERY-BAG DEBACLE and an overabundance
of human contact has straight up sucked out all my energy. It takes a lot of battery power to keep your mind and
muscles on high alert like that, so I drag my burned-out
body to bed. I collapse on my mattress, and, like a cotton
cloud, it swallows me.

The hours roll on by as I watch soap-opera reruns. I
don't sleep. Oh no. That would be way too simple.

Instead my brain turns to porridge. My eyes mindlessly
follow the characters moving around the TV screen, even
after they've lost definition and morphed into brightly colored blobs.

The moon crashes back to earth, and the sun assails
the sky.

I'm watching threads of bright yellow light forcing
their way through the cracks in my curtains when my
phone rings. Through gritty eyes I see Mom's ID flashing
on the screen. It's 6:00 a.m.

"Norah, honey?" Mom's voice, soft and sweet, comes
over the other end of the phone. I'm barely conscious, but

my brain, always firing on full, catches the faint wail of a bullhorn buried beneath the sound of calm.

Something is wrong. This is the same tone she used when I came home from my first day in second grade and she told me Thumper, my poor pet rabbit, had succumbed to a stroke.

"Mom, what's wrong?"

"Did you get any sleep?" *Small talk.* That's it. All the signs point to tragedy.

"No. You?"

"Some."

I count out the following fifteen seconds of silence in my head.

"Mom. Is something wrong?"

"Don't freak out," she says, and my heart charges. Like someone just zapped a million volts through my body, I sit upright. My free hand grips my sheets. A vocal tic rolls up my chest, pushed by pressure, until it flops from my mouth and I moan like Frankenstein's monster.

"Hey. Come on," Mom says, her tinkling-bell tone now reinforced with sheets of steel. "Take some deep breaths or you're going to pass out."

"Tell me what's happened."

"Remember perspective? You're talking to me right now so it can't be that bad, right?" she says.

"Mom."

"Everything is okay, baby, I promise."

"Mom!"

"There was a small collision."

My mind morphs into those giant, foamy waves you see in disaster movies smashing hard against rocks.

"Norah, listen to me."

I can't.

She's saying things, but I can only hear the sound of squealing brakes and crunching metal. "Are you—" I cut her off while she's mid-rant about some dick driver who ran a stoplight and plowed straight into the side of her ancient Ford Capri. "Are you okay?"

I stumble out of bed. Like I'm trapped in the middle of a tornado, spinning, trying to find a glass of water, trying to find a paper bag, trying to find my bearings, which I'm pretty sure are whizzing around my room independently of my body.

"A little scratched up. But the doctors are taking great care of me."

"You're in the hospital?"

That's bad. Hospitals are for sick people. This is bad.

My brain shuts down; my muscles stop working. My legs crumble beneath me, and my knees slam into the floor.

"Norah. Norah, what was that bang? Talk to me."

I crawl along the carpet, all breathless and sweating like the chick trying to escape a psycho in a horror movie. I squeeze myself into the small space between my bed and dresser where I turtle up, put my head in my lap, and try to space my breathing. My fingers find an old, flaking scab on my knee and pick it until it bleeds. I need the sting to bring me back, force me to relax, but it doesn't.

"Sweetie, listen to me. I'm fine. I. Am. Fine."

I cannot compute "I'm fine." *Hospitals are for sick people.*

"Mom," I say through bursts of sobs. Tears roll over my lips. I get splash-back every time I blow out a breath.

"Have I ever lied to you?" she asks.

I don't answer. She's trying to overthrow the anxiety with facts.

"Norah. Have. I. Ever. Lied. To. You? Answer me."

"No." I have to listen now. It's been said. It's out there. An alternative thread of logic that I can't ignore. Sometimes I imagine my mind is an arena, and there's a droid in there, stomping around, looking all high and mighty, fending off anything logical that tries to invade its space. But then, every now and again, common sense sneaks in. It too is a droid. It carries a sword to cut things down.

"Trust me now, okay? It's nothing serious," Mom says, overenunciating every word. "I'm all right. You're all right.

We're all right. Say it with me." She begins the reassurance spiel again, but my lips aren't quite ready to make real sentences.

She chants the words three times before I find my voice and join in. The heel of my hand drums against the side of my head, trying to make the words stick.

"I'm all right. You're all right. We're all right." I sound like I've been swigging liquor for a solid week.

"Baby, it's going to be okay. I'm going to be home soon. The doctors just want to keep me for a few days, a week, tops." A small collision. They don't keep you in the hospital for a whole week following a small collision. They turned my gran out after only six days, and she'd had a fricking heart attack. There's more to this.

"Are you hurt bad? You can be honest with me. I can handle it," I lie.

"Nah, baby. I promise. They're just being thorough, probably taking advantage of my insurance."

She's not going to tell me why they want her to stay in so long. She's trying to protect me. I may never know the full extent of her injuries, and while I'm 100 percent certain this will save my sanity in the long term, right now it sends me into a spin.

My breath hitches. This can't be happening.

I wince and let my body sink lower. Pressing my back against the drawers, I bring my knees up to my chest and hug them tight. I like how sturdy the wood feels against my back. I like how small I feel squashed against the floor.

"Norah," she snaps; it feels like a sharp slap. "Listen to me. We're not freaking out about this, right?" I nod. Pointless because she can't see me. "I'm safe here. You're safe there, like always. You don't have to leave the house. You don't have to do anything but sit tight and make believe this conference is lasting a little longer than expected. You're all right. Say it back to me?"

Mom refuses to hang up the phone until she can hear steadiness in my voice. I'm not so selfish that I can't fake it and let her get back to her sickbed. She's tired. I can tell by the croak that starts to punctuate her words.

"Dr. Reeves is going to come over today, okay?" she says. "Just to make sure you're all right. You're not alone, Norah. We wouldn't leave you alone, okay?" I hum, let her know I'm listening, but between me and myself, I can barely understand a word she's saying. She tells me she loves me and that we'll talk later.

My cell goes dead and I am plunged into silence. It's so quiet, I can't hear anything, like when you're submerged in the sea.

I'm not all right. It doesn't matter how many times I tell myself I am; I'm not. My common-sense droid has put up an amazing fight, but he is defeated, lying in pieces on the arena floor.

I'm shutting down. My mouth is numb. A black frost creeps in around the edges of my vision.

7

MOSS HAS STARTED to cover my skin by the time this panic attack is spent.

I have to get up.

I'm sticky and there's this residual tremor jit-jit-jitterbugging its way through my muscles, but it's time to stand and retake control of my limbs. I need a soundtrack, some droll overture played on the world's smallest violin, as I pull myself up and force my knocking knees to take the weight. It's like finding your strength after an intense bout of flu. I wobble across my bedroom, clinging to everything I pass, trying to make it to the kitchen because it's a couple of degrees cooler in there and/or, at the very least, I can climb inside the gargantuan fridge and ice myself off.

Except when I make it to the kitchen, there is no air and I still feel like I'm being crammed into a closet. So I keep going, forcing my legs forward until I reach the front door.

The two locks that I rely on to keep me safe turn into

twenty as I scramble to lift latches, turn keys, slide bolts. There's so much clicking. *Click-click-click*ing. I want to scratch away my scalp.

At last there's a *pop*, and I pull the door open. The air hits me like cold water, and my whole body sighs a sigh that I'm pretty sure can be heard on the other side of town. Tension falls off me, the same way it does when you climb into a hot bath after a hard day.

It's never made sense to me, how I can crave fresh air and be so afraid of it simultaneously. Dr. Reeves tells me it's not supposed to make sense. She says a study at her former hospital revealed more people were afraid of public speaking than of dying. Imagine that. A bunch of well-educated folks believing that talking out loud for ten minutes is more frightening than falling asleep for forever. The brain is basically an evil dictator.

"Morning."

I'm so deep in thought, I don't see him. My bones leap from my body and I brace, shoulders rising, back arching like a spooked cat's, a heartbeat away from hissing. New Boy is strolling down his driveway with a backpack slung over his shoulder.

Goddamn it. Why is he always outside? We never saw the former residents of number 26. Mom would often tease that they were vampires. Of course, then my mind got screwy and her living-dead joke stopped being funny. But New Boy Next Door, Luke, is like an unwanted relative, always showing up at the most inopportune times. I miss the days when I could have a panic attack in peace. Then he smiles at me and I forget why I am frustrated. His smile makes the summer seem insignificant. I can't stop staring.

"How's it going?"

"It's going okay." My voice is small, barely there. He'd be forgiven for thinking I had strep.

"You heading to school?"

I nod. A lie. It's automatic, a defensive thing born from years of saying no and then fumbling around for an excuse as to why.

"Where do you go?"

Ah. This could get complicated. The problem with lies is they like to hang around in packs.

The countdown clock from some cheesy game show starts *ticktock-ticktock*ing in my ears. There are two schools in our district, Cardinal North at one end of town and Fairfield South at the other. We're slap-bang in the middle. He could go to either.

"Cardinal," I say, my hands balling into fists. I actually was a student there for a few weeks and they did say I could go back whenever I was ready, so that's not totally a lie. Plus, Fairfield is some big deal in high school football and he was wearing that ring.

"Sweet. It'll be good to see a face I recognize around the halls."

Crap.

"You need a ride?" A waterfall of gold sun is raining down on him and obscuring his features.

"I'mnotgoingintoday." Conversation has never sounded so much like machine-gun fire. I choke out a fake cough, take a deep breath. and throw myself on the mercy of syllables. "Sick day." *Cough-cough-cough.*

"I'm sorry. That sucks."

"It's just a cold." I wave a nonchalant hand. "I'll live."

He opens the passenger door of a shiny black pickup truck and slings his bag in the front seat. I glance over my shoulder, ponder if this is my cue to go inside because we're done talking, but when I look back, he's walked up to the hedge that separates our houses.

"So what say you, Neighbor? Are they going to eat me alive over there?" He's smiling, but my Spidey senses tingle. I think there's some real concern in his question.

He's wearing a Transformers T-shirt and the same ripped jeans he had on yesterday. The ring is gone, and a black, braided cord is wrapped around his wrist.

I think maybe the girls will write poetry about him,

tattoo his name on the backs of their hands in ink, and circle it with red hearts. At least, that's what I would do. I don't know about the guys. I haven't really been around any since testosterone commandeered their spindly bodies and molded them into men. TV would have me believe that the new kid always gets his ass kicked on the first day, and how he deals with that determines the rest of his school life. Or is that what's supposed to happen on your first day in prison?

I've forgotten what we were talking about.

"Hmm." He strokes his chin. "A prolonged silence. That can't be good."

Sarcastic slow clap. Good job, Norah. Way to make a new friend feel secure. Well, not friend, exactly. At least, not yet. I wonder if he thinks we are. Probably not after this. Unless . . .

I'm doing it again.

"No. Not at all," I argue, hopefully before he's concluded I'm ignorant. I should explain that overthinking is how I function. But of course I don't, because I want him to think I'm normal for as long as possible. Instead, I pretend that saying *no* is enough. "Everyone is really nice. And your Transformers T-shirt is very cool."

"Interesting," he says, squinting at me.

"What is?"

"Fashion advice from a girl who wears a giant teddy bear sweater to go grocery-fishing on her front porch."

Pins and needles. Red hot. All over my body. I twist my fingers into knots, can feel the steep decline of a shame spiral tugging at my ankles.

"I have to go."

"Wait. Norah. That was supposed to be a joke," I hear him say as I slam the front door shut.

I'm dissolving. I feel like I've been scrutinized, judged. Like I was wearing a T-shirt with the slogan *I'm Odd* written all over it. Worse than that, I feel like I said the wrong thing. This is why my Metro page goes weeks without an update, because I'm awkward, and awkward people always say the wrong stuff. I have this thing about looking stupid, which, only after I've hidden back in my house, I realize I might have just exacerbated.

Resting my forehead against the door, I stare at my curled toes, wishing I were normal, when a folded piece of paper pokes its way through the mail slot and flitters to the floor. I push my ear against the wood, listening for sounds outside, but I don't hear anything.

I crouch down, stare at the paper for a long time, like maybe it's an animal lying in the road and I'm trying to decide if it's dead. No envelope. Just a single yellow leaf folded into a square. I reach out, don't pick it up, but peel it apart with the very tips of my fingers, right there on the floor.

Neighbor,

I heard you were good at jokes. Maybe you could
teach me how sometime?
PS: Do you like the Transformers movies?
PPS: My favorite is the first.
Luke :)

Hang on a second.

The sound of overworked cogs is crunching in my ears. You see, for the last sixty seconds, I've been breaking out in goose bumps, shrinking inside myself, convinced that he'd be laughing at me and prefixing my name with words like *crazy.*

I fall back on my butt, smack my spine against the radiator, but the pain doesn't register because I'm too busy wondering why he's reaching out instead of building barriers between us. And, because *crazy* isn't totally inaccurate, I'm admiring his penmanship. He writes in really straight lines, even though the paper is plain, and all his letters are the same size.

For the rest of the day I do the usual: build things out of various foods, watch television, read, line up the slightly out-of-sync corners of my DVD collection. I learn how to order a sandwich in French. Just. The whole time I'm doing stuff, my head is foggy, distracted by something I can't put my finger on. It's like that feeling of forgetting something you know you were supposed to be doing. I consider an Internet search of my symptoms, but the brain-tumor diagnosis of last spring is still fresh in my mind, so I decide against it. If it bleeds or makes you feel dizzy, the Internet will tell you it's cancer.

It's hormones.

Hormones have me in a chokehold. I know this because when I finally sit down and turn on my laptop, I don't research medical journals or even check my social media. Instead, I Google *kissing*.

At first it's a cute thing. I watch black-and-white filtered videos of cuddling couples hugging and rubbing noses in striped sweaters against fall backdrops. They hold each other tight, mashing their mouths together like the world is about to end. It makes my heart hurt.

I've never kissed a boy.

I grab the sanitizer from my bag and smother my hands, just so I can touch my fingers to my lips while I watch.

I've never wanted to kiss a boy before.

Kissing wasn't a thing when I was thirteen. We hadn't gotten there yet. We were too busy battling Pokémon and reading Harry Potter. And, well, I got sick right before the want-to-kiss thing kicked in. Now, the thought of someone touching me, with hands I can't be sure have been washed, is as terrifying a prospect as a plane crash. I'm not sure of statistics, but I'm pretty certain there's only a small portion of people in the world who will ever be able to understand what that feels like.

I lick my lips, rest my chin in my hands, and without so much as a flicker of the heebie-jeebies, I'm wondering if Luke holds hips or butt when he's making out.

I settle on butt, think maybe if you have pockets on the back of your jeans, he'll slide his hands in there.

Alas, three videos later and I'm struggling to maintain. I've stopped sighing wistfully and dreaming up "Dear Diary" moments as the romanticism dies a slow, agonizing death at the hands of my OCD.

The thing is, this one guy licks the tip of his girlfriend's nose. Her nose. That thing on your face that snot seeps out of. *Snot:* that mucus shit that is basically a fishing net for bacteria. Does nobody even do science anymore? My lunch turns cartwheels in my stomach as I watch him shove his tongue in her mouth and they continue trying to devour each other.

All I can hear now, in stereophonic sound, is the slurping, squelching, and popping noise of spit being swapped.

My fingers hit the keyboard and I start researching like a scientist on speed. Suddenly the only thing I want to know about kissing is how much bacteria there is in saliva.

I pull up pictures of petri dishes under microscopes. Discover microscopic buds of fuzzy pink stuff living under your tongue, and civilizations of invisible white stringy things snaking around your tonsils.

My hands get hot, and my palms collect a lake.

I fidget, can't sit still as I read about the millions of microbes and invisible-to-the-naked-eye beasties that might be hanging out in a person's mouth at any one time.

Nope. No way. Game over.

I slam the lid of my laptop shut.

I'll just have to come to terms with the fact that I'll never kiss anyone. Ever.

8

It's five o'clock, and I'm reaching into the fridge for a block of cheese when there's a knock at the door.

Stealth mode engaged, I abandon making what would have been the world's most perfect sandwich and creep up the hall, eyeing the door like whoever is on the other side is going to burst right through it.

We have a stare-down then, the door and I. It's pretty intense, just short of an evil sheriff hiding in the shadows, chewing on a matchstick.

Another knock.

Without moving my eyes, I pump a blob of Purell into my hands and rub it away. Because I'm sure the only thing on any home invader's mind, after being polite enough to knock first, is a sanitary victim. I roll my eyes so hard they almost fall out of my skull.

"Norah. It's Dr. Reeves."

My shoulders fall down from around my ears and I exhale. "Just a second." I sprint over and unbolt the door.

Dr. Reeves stands on the porch wearing a perfectly tailored tweed pantsuit despite the blistering temperature.

"How are you doing?" she says, smiling at me like I'm a box of abandoned kittens. It takes every ounce of restraint for me not to throw my arms around her neck and wail like a child.

"I'm good." My head is nodding too hard, but I can't make it stop. "Really good. Great, in fact."

Her eyes narrow. My lies are made of glass and she sees right through them.

"I mean, at first I was a bit . . ." I twirl my finger around my temple and make cuckoo noises, keeping it light because I'm eternally embarrassed by my breakdowns. "But I'm feeling much better now. Can I get you something to drink?" I say, traipsing back up the hall, forcing her to step inside and follow me.

"I can't stay long," she says, and it's a balloon bursting behind me, or nails being dragged down a chalkboard. My jaw tightens and I wince. It's unfair of me to expect her to want to be here after hours. She has a family to get home to. We never really talk about her personal life, but I did discover that she has a son in middle school. Still, I wish she would stick around. Not even to talk, just to kind of sit in a chair doing puzzles in her pajamas, like Mom. This house is too quiet. I swear it feeds off silence. When I'm alone, it always seems bigger.

"But," she adds, "I am just on the other end of the phone. Do you still have that number I gave you?"

I don't spit out the not-much-point-if-you-don't-pick-up comment that's trying to claw its way across my tongue. Being a bitch is something that often happens when I'm forced to endure things I'm afraid of. It's my least favorite stage of anxiety. The first time Mom tried to get me out of the house I told her I hated her. Ugh.

"You sure I can't get you a drink?"

"Norah."

I'm not listening. I head over to the fridge and pull open the door.

"We've got some Pepsi? Sunny D? Or I can make coffee." I point to the little silver machine on the kitchen counter. A fine layer of dust dulls its chrome finish. I think it's been used twice in the four years we've had it. Mom likes herbal tea.

"Norah. I can't stay." She throws that sympathetic smile my way again. "But, listen, I have Wednesday morning free—"

"Wednesday?" Wednesday is almost two days away. There is a whole Tuesday to consider.

"I would call tomorrow, but I have patients all day. I could perhaps have a colleague of mine—"

"No!" I yell. It comes out with the velocity and surprise of a sneeze. "I mean, no, thank you." It wasn't my intention to snap, but if it's not someone I know, I won't open the door anyway. "Did Mom tell you when she was coming home?" Paranoia has joined the party. It's not that I think Mom lied to me, but she might have buffered the truth if she thought she was protecting me. I hate that my mind insists on questioning my own mother.

"She said it could be a couple of days, maybe a week. Did she not tell you that herself?" Busted. This woman is to mental illness what Sherlock Holmes was to mindbending murder.

"She did. I just . . . I couldn't remember exactly what she said." I feel dirty.

"Norah, she isn't keeping anything from you. She told me she wouldn't do that."

I bite my lip to keep it from curling under. "I just wish she were home."

"Of course. That's normal. Anyone would feel that way."

I nod. Our conversation has run dry. Dr. Reeves's eyes flit around aimlessly, land on the note from the boy next door for a second before finding me again.

I'm not making this easy for her. *Mental slap.* I look away, focus instead on the contents of the fridge.

"So, I can still call you on that number you gave me?"

"Of course."

"Even if it's the middle of the night?" I turn the carton of orange juice in the fridge so the label is centered, facing out.

"Anytime. I mean it."

"Thank you. And thank you for stopping by. I really appreciate it."

"Coffee date? First thing Wednesday morning?" she says as I walk her back to the door.

"I mean, I'll have to check my schedule, but I'm sure I'll be able to fit you in," I tease. She quirks a skeptical eyebrow, and, with a smile, she leaves.

It starts to get dark sometime around seven and I switch all the lights on in the house. From the outside, I imagine it looks like I'm storing the sun in here. The Trips, a New Age kind of couple who live across the street, will be shoving more of their "Save the Environment" leaflets through our door tomorrow morning. Don't get me wrong, I'm deeply concerned about my carbon footprint, but I've watched enough horror movies to know that when I'm home alone, I'm 98 percent less likely to die if the lights are on.

Mom calls just before eight, and we stay on the phone for over an hour. She keeps asking me if I've eaten properly, then starts encouraging me to try the antianxiety meds I've had in a drawer for six months.

"This is the perfect opportunity," she says. "You'd only have to take one, then lie back on the couch and let yourself drift off to sleep."

I have this thing about swallowing mind-altering medication.

It makes me gag the second it touches my tongue. Like it's coated in superglue, it physically won't slide down. I don't think doctors are trying to take over my brain or anything. And I'm not one of those people who think medicine poisons your body and you should try natural remedies first. I can't take the herbal tabs either. It's the idea of relinquishing control that makes them too sticky to swallow. I'm too wrapped up in worrying about everything that could go wrong while these tablets have me half drunk. You know which guy is dying first if the zombie apocalypse happens? The one lying on his couch too spaced out on meds to run.

I say good night to Mom when she starts yawning, then grab a blanket and collapse on the couch. My eyes stalk a pair of sewing scissors on top of a box at the side of the patchwork armchair. These will be my weapon of choice should a home invasion occur. I'm so set on this idea that I push the coffee table back two inches so it's not in my way. My mom would ask why I don't just move the scissors closer if it makes me feel safer. And I would tell her that I can't do that because being too prepared is like tempting fate.

I need to go to sleep. I need to stop thinking. Just for a second.

9

I WAKE WITH A START, cold and drenched in blue light from the standby screen on the television. At first I think that's what woke me — it's blaring and I am the kind of girl who stirs at the beat of a butterfly's wing — but then I hear a voice.

Some guy shouts, *"That's not good enough!"*

My eyes pop, homing in on the sewing scissors, despite the fact that the voice is muffled enough for me to know it's coming from outside. From sleeping beauty to ninja in less than five seconds, I sit up, leap over the back of the couch, and make like a bullet to the front door.

I know it's locked. I checked it four times before it got dark. But my fingers find the bolt anyway and push on it. It can't slip any farther into the latch without breaking free of its metal bonds and slamming straight into the wall, but I don't stop pushing.

"Three years. *It's been three years,*" the voice keeps repeating. He says it in bursts of two. Quieter the first time, louder the second. "Three years. *It's been three years.*"

Hush. Yell. Pause.

The voice belongs to Luke. I can't hear anyone else talking, responding. Curiosity pulls me to the porch window on tiptoes, and with bated movements I peek around the edge of the curtain.

A security light shines on Luke pacing up and down his driveway, talking on his cell. I duck back the second I see him because he's shirtless, a bare torso covered in mounds of taut muscle. A pair of plaid pajama pants hang off his hips. He looks like he paced right out of the pages of a magazine. My face heats up. I feel like I just tripped in front of a roomful of people. The thing is, despite the overwhelming embarrassment making my cheeks blister, I want to look again. So I do.

This time, his back is to me. He's walking down the driveway. Stealth becomes secondary to getting my face closer to the glass.

Hush. Yell. Pause.

His perfectly square shoulder blades jump when he raises his voice. A fist snatches hold of my stomach and squeezes.

Hush. Yell. Pause.

He exhales a sigh strong enough to make the trees bend backwards. Something is tearing him to pieces. He shakes his head, grabs a clump of his hair, and clenches his jaw.

"I can't do this right now." He ends the call, jabbing his thumb into the keypad.

I think maybe he turns to stone then, because he doesn't move for the longest time. Just stands at the end of his drive, stock-still, arms hanging heavy at his sides, staring at the ground.

My fingers itch. I wish I could reach out, put a hand on his shoulder, and ask him if he is all right. A side effect of worrying about everything and everyone; I cry at least once a week over things that shouldn't concern me.

Minute after minute crawls by. My legs get tired. I stop caring about staying hidden and take a seat on the sill. Of course, when he finally does turn around to head back to his house, the first thing he sees is me doing my best puppy-in-a-pet-shop-window impression. He looks straight at me, and I'm forced to reanimate my ninja fu. I throw myself onto the floor, my body crashing against the wood laminate. I'll have bruises tomorrow.

I stay crouched and as close to the wall as I can. I hope he doesn't think I was spying. I mean, I know that's what it must look like. And, okay, perhaps I was a little. But beyond the minuscule amount of curiosity, it was all concern. Oh God. I hope he doesn't think I just sat there staring because he isn't wearing a shirt.

My pulse drums out the passing minutes, my thoughts

running wild. What must he think? *Weird girl from next door, sitting like a flower in the window, watching me.* I need to explain that I was worried and evaporate out of existence simultaneously. But I can't do either of those things.

So instead, I wait. I wait for an entire lifetime, curled up in a ball of cowardice on the hall floor, until a burst of courage manifests in my chest and I check to see if he's gone. I cling to the sill and pull myself up.

Shit. He's not gone. He's gotten closer. Moved, in fact, to the foot of my porch. I jump back, startled. He's looking at me, all bare chest and raised eyebrows. I'm not quite sure what to do, but my hand is up and offering him a half wave.

He lifts his phone, grimaces, and mouths *Sorry* at me. His signature smile is nowhere in sight.

I wave away his apology, hamming nonchalance like a seasoned Oscar winner, even resting my hand on a jutting hip—a position that feels too odd to maintain, so I let my hand drop back down almost immediately. He jogs up the porch steps, stands right up to the window. I take two strides back.

"At least I don't play the drums, right?" he jokes in hushed tones, but his voice is strong regardless. It carries, crystal clear, through the glass and straight to my ears. There's still no smile.

His chin hits the ground and he stares at his bare feet. My breath catches on the window and fogs up the cool glass. It's not right. Some things are just supposed to be. Like Harry Styles and his floppy hair. Or Captain America and his mighty shield. Luke New Boy Next Door should never not be smiling.

Twitching fingers tap out beats of eight on my thighs. I'm dying to open the door and ask him if he's okay, but I can't. I pick idly at a new scab on the top of my leg. Anxiety has created a million reasons why I can't. My heart is fighting back, but failing miserably.

Open the door. He looks so sad, like a kid lost in a crowd.

Do not open that door. It could be a ruse. There is no one awake to hear you scream.

Open the door. Are those tears in his eyes? Serial killers don't have sweet smiles.

Do not open the door. Remember the story of the homicidal maniac who used his not-so-broken leg to lure victims? Better to be safe than sorry.

This argument rages inside my head until I can taste fire, and smoke starts pouring out of my ears. When, at last, common sense kicks in, I could spit. Worry is such a drama queen. It takes the smallest thing, makes it so big and bulky that you can't see the obvious anymore.

I don't have to open the door to ask him if he's okay.

There's a tremor in my throat. My voice isn't confident like his. It's rarely strong enough to work its way through air, let alone barriers. So, using my finger, I write letters in the steam on the window.

Are you okay? Suddenly, spending three weeks last summer learning how to write backwards (and speak Elvish) doesn't seem like such a waste of time.

The glass squeaks as I draw the lines, and he looks up. A small, not-quite-at-full-power grin pulls on his lips. His left eye narrows and he gives me that look, the same look you give a crossword puzzle when you can't figure out an answer.

I curl inward and my heart tries to thump out the same beat twice. Maybe I shouldn't have asked. Or perhaps I should have plucked up the balls to open my mouth instead of doodling on the window. I punish my finger by popping my knuckle.

He nods once, throws a half wave my way. "I didn't mean to disturb you," he says.

"You didn't," I whisper, but he's already turning around.

He makes it back to his driveway in twenty-six steps and one small leap over the boxwood hedge that separates our houses.

I zombie-shuffle to the front room and flop down

on the couch. I'm more thought than flesh; a thousand questions flop down with me and make the room shake like an earthquake is running right through it. New Boy has been living next door for a week and my circuits are fried from trying to figure out what he's thinking. I mean, I watch MTV, so I knew this was a thing. Boys and girls: same species, two completely different planets. But this teamed with my super-ability to overthink—it's just too much. I don't like this feeling of always messing up. I don't like that scrutinizing has tripled in productivity since he moved in. I know it's me, my issue, my problem, which is why I decide I'm going to avoid him from here on out.

10

It's WEDNESDAY. AS PROMISED, Dr. Reeves drops by for a coffee. She stays forty-five minutes. We talk about what I'm eating and how I'm sleeping. I decide not to tell her I spent yesterday in my pajamas, building castles out of cookies and spit.

After we're done discussing Mom, the weather, what the world would look like without worry, she reminds me how to breathe, which is much easier to forget than you'd think.

She's gone approximately six minutes before I hear the squeak of the letterbox.

Neighbor,
Impromptu Eric Rhodes Day party at my house
Friday night, 7:30 p.m. Hope you can make it.
Parent-free place! There will be beer! Thank you,
Jesus, for weekends.
Luke :)

Oh. God.
This is not good.

This. Is. *Not*. Good.

Beyond the fire and brimstone, everyone has their own idea of hell. Shopping, doing Common Core math, fish-nibbling-at-your-feet spa treatments, or having to spend an eternity surrounded by people who click pens.

I screw up the neatly folded note I just found on my doormat and hurl it down the hall. I stare at it, lying in the middle of the floor, a ticking time bomb loaded with perfect handwriting. Then of course I stomp over, snatch it up, and dunk it in the trash, because I can't handle both impending party and mess stress right now.

I do laps. Walk in circles around our kitchen, being careful not to step on the pale beams of light the mid-morning sun is throwing through the window.

A party. With beer. Next door. This is my hell. We are at DEFCON 1. I can't think of anything worse. Oh no, wait. Yes, I can. A party with beer next door and me being home alone.

There are going to be people from my former high school fifty yards away. Tons of people. Flooding out of his front yard and into mine. I know my high school career was shorter than the lifespan of a fruit fly, but what if someone remembers me? What if someone remembers this is where I live? What if they want to come over? What if they want me to come out?

My head is about to explode and decorate the kitchen with pieces of petrified brain.

Drunk teens spewing vodka shots in Mom's rose-bushes, trashing the street, probably getting high. The police will come. I saw something like this unfold in a movie once.

"Norah. Norah!" A familiar voice infiltrates my cyclone of despair.

"Mom?" I look down at the phone receiver in my hand, Mom's tinny tones still emanating from it.

I don't even remember dialing.

"Mom. Mom." I jam the phone against my ear. "Mom. He's having a party Friday night. What do I do?" If she were here, I'd be clinging to her shirt collar.

"What?"

"It's Eric Rhodes. There's going to be beer."

"Sweetheart . . . Eric Rhodes is . . . dead."

"What? No." Frustration makes me flap. "I know that." Eric Rhodes, the founder of our small town, has been dead about a billion years. This coming weekend is something we do to celebrate his birthday. No, not we. Not I. Not ever.

My tongue is twisted up, feels ten times too big in my mouth. It's probable I'm not making much sense. Panicked, not to be confused with intoxicated, though the two often present as something very similar.

I take a breath. "The new boy next door," I say like a kindergartner learning language. "He's having a party Friday night. He invited me. There will be beer. He said that, wrote it on the invite . . . in perfect cursive."

"You got asked to a party?" my mom exclaims in a voice that implies she's going to magnet my invite to the fridge door the second she gets home. She's completely missed the point.

"Mom."

"Right. Sorry. They've got me on some crazy painkillers over here. An hour ago I swear I was floating above my bed." She giggles.

Oh. This is so not good. Well, at least not for me. For her it sounds pretty euphoric.

"Mom, you'll be home by Friday, right?" Oh God, please let her tell me she'll be home by Friday.

Pause. Longer pause. My hair is going gray.

"The doctor that came to see me this morning—he said I might be here until Monday."

My nails dig into my palm. I squeeze until the taut flesh on my knuckles feels like it's going to split. "He went on and on and on and on about putting pins in my bone. Said something science-y about my wrist healing wrong," Mom slurs, and she either swallows water or slurps back some drool. I jam my fist into my mouth and bite down. I absolutely refuse to whimper into the phone.

My mom is hurt. She does not need me to fall apart. Plus, I don't want to freak her out. She sounds pretty jazzed, and I remember reading about this girl who had a heart attack and died while she was high. That probably works differently with medical highs. Legal drugs. Pain meds . . . but then, you can get addicted to pain meds. I hope that doesn't happen—

"Sweetheart? Are you still there?"

Mind melt. There's too much to think about.

"I'm here." I slam the heel of my hand into my forehead, the equivalent of spanking my brain for misbehaving. "My head's a mess. I don't know what to do about the party?"

"Well, I think the first thing you need to do is take some deep breaths." She tries to walk me through what a deep breath should sound like, but all I hear is her hyperventilating. Think Darth Vader in labor. Still, it works because my OCD uses my lungs to correct her off-kilter pace.

"Remember what Dr. Reeves says about being unable to control everything? Norah, honey, my sweet baby girl, I'm afraid this is beyond your control."

The beyond-your-control speech is my least favorite of all the pep talks. It's the hardest one to corrupt. It's immortal, the adamantium of arguments. There is no "but . . . but . . . but"–ing my way out of this one. Sometimes, things are going to happen and the only way out is through. Like childbirth; it doesn't matter how afraid you are, that baby has to be born.

I sit on the kitchen floor. Mom's voice turns to whale song as she talks me down off this impossibly high life ledge. At least she's a smart stoner.

We talk for two hours, and she convinces my broken mind that I am safe. Even if the party turns into the hybrid love child of rush week and spring break, it won't affect me if I just stay locked in my room and ignore it. This is a wave I have to ride, but at least I can do it buried in a blanket fort.

It's a good talk, a little wordy, a lot off-topic. But when the advice comes, it's easy, obvious. Like always. And, like always, by the end of it, I'm wishing I could have slowed my mind down sooner and processed this like a normal person. That's the dream.

"One last thing before you go," Mom says. "A boy asked you out?"

I look over at the trash can, envision the crumpled piece of paper turning to rot in yesterday's garbage.

I don't know.

There was no time to analyze that. But there should have been. There should have been excitement. Excitement should have been bigger than fear. I wonder how many of my former friends would have been freaking out over being invited somewhere by a boy instead of sinking in possible party-apocalypse scenarios. Depression blows on the back of my neck, and I feel cold to my core.

It can't come in.

I force a smile and clear the clump of sadness from my throat. "I mean, *technically*, yes. But it's a party, with lots of people. So does that *technically* mean he's asked out everyone he sent an invite to? There are many subcategories to consider."

"Wow. Dating has subcategories these days?"

"Of course. God, Mom, sometimes it's like you're a dinosaur and we don't even watch TV." She laughs. Really laughs. It's hard not to notice that she enjoys the normal snippets of conversation we share. So few and far between, they really stand out.

I spend the rest of the day trying to finish an English paper.

Yeah, right.

The flashing cursor on my blank page blinks at me with a sense of urgency. I'm supposed to be dissecting the morals and motives of Lady Macbeth, but my brain is too stewed to translate Shakespeare.

I'm forever an overachiever . . . unless there is something else to think about. You can chart my bad months by checking out my report cards. Like the semester Mom thought we were going to have to move and my GPA slipped to a 3.0.

I'd love to see out my homeschool career with a 4.0. It sounds odd, cruel even to suggest, but shining in one of the recesses of my mind is the idea that being intelligent will force people to see past my crazy parts. Maybe even make them obsolete. I don't know. That's probably dumb, but no one remembers Charles Darwin as the guy who suffered from panic attacks. Ludwig van Beethoven isn't the bipolar composer, he's the composer who was bipolar. I'm sure it's not as simple as all that. I just want to have proof that I can think straight, that I am more than the girl who believes that odd numbers will cause a catastrophe.

Unfortunately, right now studying is about as likely as skipping to the store.

Instead, I hack at my keyboard until my restless mind composes a passable tune before I drag my butt off to bed.

11

I LIE AWAKE WORRYING about the party all night, like it's some crazed serial killer terrorizing our small suburban neighborhood.

Anxiety has anchored itself to my stomach and sits like concrete on top of the cheese sandwich I ate twelve hours ago. From my waist down to my knees, everything has been twisted tight. It's all the pain of getting your period without actually getting your period.

My mattress is made of bricks, and my sheets keep snaking up around my body. I'm almost certain they're trying to strangle me.

At six thirty, I stop trying to sleep and drag my frustrated bones out of bed. I wrap my comforter around my shoulders and head to the front door. Sometimes, seeing beyond the confines of these four walls is a necessary evil. For me, this means spending a lot of time sitting in the hall watching the world wake up through an open front door.

The morning smells like cut grass and honeysuckle. I ball up in a cocoon as the rising sun paints the sky various shades of pink, yellow, and purple.

The clock is just kissing 7:00 when an olive-green Volkswagen camper turns into Triangle Crescent. It crawls along the curb, pauses for the briefest of seconds in front of each house on the other side of the road.

My mental camera is quick and candid.

I only have to look at it for a second, and every tiny detail about the foreign vehicle is embedded in my brain, from the license-plate number to the burnt-orange rust eating away at the rear-wheel arch. It cruises around the dead-end bend and back up the road, this time surveying the houses on our side.

The man driving has a thick brown beard and a mop of dark curly hair. There are tons of stickers covering one of the side windows. Souvenir stickers. The kind that are shaped like famous landmarks. I recognize the Empire State Building and Disney's princess palace.

The guy sees me, stops, and rolls down his window. He's all smiles as I slide back on my butt, ready to retreat and slam the door shut, when someone shouts, "Dad!"

It's Luke.

He's standing by the boxwood bush, body on display, waving both arms in the air like he's trying to park a plane. I look away, bite my bottom lip as the camper parks next door.

I didn't know Luke had a dad. That's dumb. I mean, obviously I knew Luke had a dad, I just didn't realize he was still around.

They collide in the middle of the driveway and wrap each other in a solid embrace. It's the kind of hug that makes me think I'm witnessing a reunion. I don't mean to stare, but my no-touch rule is craving attention, and I'm trying to remember what it feels like to hold someone without worrying what kind of disease you could catch.

I've arrived at Ebola. I'm so busy considering the science of spreading that I miss the moment the pair break apart. I don't have time to snatch my senses and look away before Luke sees me staring.

"Norah," he greets me, looking all kinds of sheepish with his chin tucked into his chest. His dad looks at me expectantly, then back at Luke, then back at me again. But instead of offering an introduction, Luke scuttles into his house. His dad follows, but not before throwing a confused glance my way.

Interesting.

My mind is a rabbit hole that I fall down repeatedly for the next hour. I wonder why Luke got squirrelly at the idea of introducing his dad to me. I blame myself, being scrunched up in a blanket and sitting in my hallway like it's the norm. What's left of my fingernails pays the ultimate price for my feelings of inadequacy.

Sometime after eight, Luke emerges from his house, twirling car keys around his finger and carrying his school backpack. I turn away, fix my sights on a monarch butterfly that's flirting with the flowers.

"Hey, Neighbor." My head snaps up. Luke is standing by the boxwood, smiling at me, almost a different guy from the one who was here before.

I summon enough enthusiasm to smile back.

"Hi."

"Don't suppose you need a ride to school?" He shakes his keys at me.

"I'm good. But thank you."

"Anytime." There's a brief pause during which I attempt to braid my fingers. "Did you get my invite?" he asks.

"Yes." It takes a huge amount of effort to stop myself from wincing. Or, you know, start weeping and begging him to cancel for the sake of my sanity.

"You're coming, right?" He laughs, all nerves. "You have to come. Yours will be the only name I know." He plucks leaves off the boxwood. I pluck threads from my comforter.

"It's not that I don't want to come." Awkwardness bleeds into my tone.

"Ah. You have other plans," he concludes with a nod of his head.

"No. It's not that at all." This is not an absurd assumption for him to make, but I raise my voice and respond like it is. Relief flashes across his face, and I lift my chin a little higher. "It's just . . . I still have this cold . . ." But that's not enough. A slight case of the sniffles doesn't stop normal teenagers from having a good time. "Then there's this important French assignment I have to finish . . ."

"I didn't think they were still teaching French at Cardinal."

Double crap. They're not. Cardinal is the third school in the state to swap French for Chinese. It happened the summer after I left. There was a ceremony. Police Chief Zhang Yong gave a speech about diversity that made Vice Principal Turner ugly-cry. I know all this because someone took her picture, posted it on the Metro, and the thing was circulated for what felt like half a century.

What a dumb mistake to make. I'm not thinking straight. The space outside seems to be swelling. My head is begging me to kill this conversation, slip back inside, and close the door. Like a toddler tugging on my apron strings, it's demanding, forcing me to think about everything. It wants me to slink back, seamlessly, into our routine. It's getting twitchy at the idea of human conversation or, worse, human contact. In complete contrast, the only thing my heart's wondering right now is: *How well do you have to know someone before you can call them a friend?*

"It's this extracurricular after-school thingy," I reply. Eventually.

"Ah. Well, in that case, *bonne chance.*" He speaks French? It's boxy, and clunky, and butchered by his American accent, but I'm pretty sure it was French.

"Parlez-vous Français?"

His eyes narrow. He clears his throat and snorts a nervous laugh. "This is kind of awkward."

"Oh. You don't speak French?"

"Busted." He grimaces and I giggle. Then he does something I'm not expecting and hops over the boxwood.

No. Don't come over. Please don't come over.

Yes. Come over. Please come over.

He's coming over.

I slide back a little on my butt so I can be more inside without shutting him out. I don't know. I feel safer this way. I sit up straighter, suddenly wishing I'd slept in pajama bottoms instead of board shorts. My legs look atrocious, too skinny, too pale, too covered in purple scabs from all the scratching.

Before Luke gets too close, I tug the comforter from

my shoulders and throw it across the parts of my body that I don't want him to see.

"You caught me," he continues, perching on the porch steps. "I can't speak French, but I've been there, so it still counts as cultured, right?"

"You've been to France?"

"Yeah. A couple of times. You?"

No. Never. Not once.

I hate him. I mean, I don't hate him, but jealousy squirms like a nest of snakes in the pit of my stomach. The fake smile I throw his way makes my cheeks sting.

I thought for sure I'd reached my inadequacy limit when he didn't introduce me to his dad. I was wrong. Feeling intimidated is nothing new to me, but this overwhelming urge to fudge my skill set just so I can impress him is all new. It makes me feel cold, uncomfortable, like I'm two feet tall standing in front of a skyscraper. I'm not going to lie this time. Lying just trips me up, but I can't say no either.

"I'm going to study architecture over there." That was the plan. That had been the plan since middle school. Since Mom bought me plastic bricks one Christmas and Gran helped me build a castle with them.

"Wow. Impressive." His eyes widen; he leans back,

looks at me like I just invented time travel. And for the briefest second I feel substantial, more than medical terms and mental health. Made of blood and bone, instead of just head-brain-mind. Then I remember that France is a world away and I can't even step beyond my front door.

I swallow back a lump of sorrow. "What about you? What do you want to do after you graduate?"

"Hmm." He looks at his dad's camper and contemplates. "I'm still undecided. As long as it doesn't involve travel."

"Really? Why?" Maybe that's too personal a question, but I'm having trouble understanding why anybody who can travel wouldn't want to.

He hesitates. "My mom's a flight attendant. We used to take a lot of trips. I guess years of jumping on and off planes has me craving something solid."

"What does your dad do?"

He glances at the camper again, grimaces, and I wonder what it is he sees beyond the aging paint job and souvenir stickers. What is it he sees in his memories that makes his face crumple in painful contemplation?

"He disappears," Luke mumbles. He startles at the sound of his own voice, the depth of his honesty, the revelation in his response. Something. The only thing I'm certain of is he's wishing he hadn't said it.

"Luke?" his dad calls from the front door. "Your mom says, 'Isn't there somewhere you're supposed to be?'"

"Right!" Luke leaps up, relieved, I think, that he has an excuse to escape further scrutiny. "I gotta get to school," he tells me, already sprinting back toward his truck. "But you'll give the party some more thought, right?"

I nod. He can't see me, but it doesn't matter. The only thing he's focused on now is getting the hell out of here. If Luke knew me better, he'd realize that it doesn't matter how far or how fast he runs away from his comment; he said it, and my brain needs to know more like the body needs blood.

12

FRIDAY HAPPENS, DESPITE my spending all of Thursday wishing for a Sleeping Beauty–style reprieve, for the world to fall into unconsciousness and wake up on Monday with zero memory of Luke's party or why it didn't happen.

That would be magical.

Alas, magic is for stories and shampoo that doesn't sting when it gets in your eyes. Mom calls just before breakfast, and for the first time since records began, I let the machine pick it up. My voice doesn't feel very steady, and there's a numbness lingering on my lips that I'm almost certain will warp my words. I don't want to slow down her recovery any more than I already have with unnecessary stress.

I remember once, when the panic attacks started happening more often, I asked her how she felt about the whole thing. She whispered, "*Helpless.*" Told me it was like watching her kid drown inside a transparent box that she couldn't break into. I cried that day, hated myself.

Besides, she's said all she can say and my brain obviously isn't willing to believe it. I have no choice but to handle this one on my own.

The machine chimes three times before the sound of her voice fills the house. It makes me smile. "Hey, baby. Just calling to check in. See how you're holding up. Hoping you're still in bed. I hate it when you don't pick up the phone. Call me back, okay?"

Three more chimes and the machine goes dead.

And then . . .

One second passes . . .

In a thoroughly predictable fashion . . .

Two seconds . . .

The message tone of my cell squawks from inside my pocket. It's Mom, saying the exact same thing, only this time by text. I knew she would. Texting works. I litter my reply with half-truths and smiling emojis so she can carry on recuperating.

Meanwhile, in real life, calm is trying its best to stay above the surface while I mope around the house, eyeing the trash can in the kitchen like it's a giant spider commandeering that corner of the room. The invite is still in there, so naturally the trash can has become enemy number one.

It stalks me incessantly. See, anxiety doesn't just stop. You can have nice moments, minutes where it shrinks, but it doesn't leave. It lurks in the background like a shadow, like that important assignment you have to do but keep putting off or the dull ache that follows a three-day migraine. The best you can hope for is to contain it, make it as small as possible so it stops being intrusive. Am I coping? Yes, but it's taking a monumental amount of effort to keep the dynamite inside my stomach from exploding.

The party isn't until tonight, 7:30, the invite said, but I decide to take action early.

It takes me less than ten minutes to turn my room into a bunker.

I close my curtains, use stuffed toys and two towers of six books, all of them 332 pages thick, to conceal any cracks. I grab a glass of water, then another — you've got to have a backup — and set them both on my nightstand.

I don't need snacks; eating is out of the question since my stomach is already too tight to fit food in. I put a new paper bag on my dresser, just in case, and break out my spare pair of noise-canceling headphones. Standing back, I admire the space I've somehow managed to make smaller.

I. Am. Crazy. I have to laugh at myself.

It's times like this when I'm glad no one knows the things I do to make myself feel safe.

I promise myself that I'm not going to hide in my room until it gets dark. Instead, I slip into the study, hit play on the stereo, and listen to Marie Miraz talk irregular French verbs.

"Do you understand?" Marie asks in the same condescending tone she's been using since lesson one.

"*J'ai compris,*" I tell her. She rambles on, instructs me to follow, but movement next door has caught my attention. Luke's parents.

His mom is on the doorstep in her nightgown. His dad, standing just outside, leans in and kisses her hard on the mouth. It looks as if he's leaving.

He *is* leaving, grinning from ear to ear as he trots off down the driveway. But she, Luke's mom, in complete contrast, is swiping what look like tears of anguish off her cheeks.

I shouldn't be staring.

I wish I could offer her a tissue.

I need to stop staring.

Right. I dash to the stereo, put Marie on pause, and flee the study.

For the following hours I ferment on the couch and try to submerge myself in talk shows. I'm cringing at the sight of jilted spouses beating up their toothless exes when I hear an engine growl outside.

Ignore it.

The car pulls up next door, and I find myself second-guessing the party's start time. It's just before four. They wouldn't start now . . . would they?

Ignore it.

But what if something is happening that I need to know about?

Ignore it.

Of course I can't ignore it, because there is a certain amount of safety in knowing everything there is to know about a situation. I mean, you wouldn't throw yourself out of a plane before making sure your pack contained a parachute, would you? I only need to hide from the party itself; the planning of it is fair game.

On bended knees, I make my way over to the window. A truck covered in dust with the words *Clean me* and a cartoon penis sketched on the side is parked in the road. Luke skips out of his house, greets the guy driving with a high-five. It's not enough. The driver, a casual blond mop of muscle and chiseled cheeks, pulls him in for a hug. They slap each other on the back, hard, and for a second I wonder if I might have missed one or both of them choking.

I kneel on the floor, peep up from beneath the porch windowsill, and watch as the two carry pieces of antique furniture out of Luke's house and over to the garage.

"What are they doing?" I ask the air.

It clicks when Luke's mom appears at the door lugging a big glass vase decorated with gold flowers. Blond Guy hurries over, grabs it from her, and pretends to drop it. Poor Luke's mom clutches her chest; a look of horror flashes across her face before she realizes he's teasing.

They're trying to avoid collateral damage from the party; locking all the valuables away in the garage so they don't get trashed. I don't imagine regurgitated beer is easy to get out of vintage upholstery, and I don't imagine they'll be able to replace that vase at the Shop 'n' Save either. That's pretty smart. This bodes well for me; at the very least, Luke is a forward thinker.

The two guys laugh and talk a lot. And they keep finding opportunities to punch each other. I see bear cubs play-fighting.

At 5:37 they crash in the front yard, lie on the ground, and soak up the late-afternoon rays. Luke pulls on a pair of aviators, and my heart sighs.

The animated conversation they're having dies when Luke's mom walks out of the house dragging a small suitcase behind her. The weeping woman from this morning is nowhere in sight. This woman smiles as if she were walking the stage at a Miss America pageant. She's wearing a

crisp black flight attendant's uniform and a coat of shim-
mering pink lipstick. She makes me think of Hollywood in
the fifties. Blond Guy whistles, and Luke promptly socks
him in the arm. She ruffles Luke's hair and gives him a kiss
on the cheek. I think I see her mouth the word *Behave* before climbing into a silver SUV. His mom is not only going
to be gone for this party, she's going to be thirty thousand
feet in the air. Noted.

A little after six, a beat-up Nissan chugs into view.
The guy driving is a toothpick with long black hair pulled
back into a ponytail and a pair of too-big horn-rimmed
glasses perched on his nose. I know him. At least, I recognize his face from my Metro feed. I want to say his name
is Simon, and a few weeks back he was photographed at a
football game wearing a Cardinal Cocks jersey and kissing
a redhead. It's possible we said hi while passing each other
in the school hall. But that was all so long ago, I can't be
certain.

He pulls his car all the way up Luke's driveway, and I
lose sight of him. Shame doesn't register as I crawl across
the floor and over to the study. The window there gives
me a panoramic view of Luke's driveway, so I can get a
better look.

Dr. Reeves says that I take note of situations like this
because it tricks my brain into thinking I'm being proac-

tive about a problem. I can't stop or control Luke's party, but watching things unfold, tracking activity, taking mental notes, makes me feel less like I'm falling into an abyss. And that helps.

More backslapping and shoulder-butting happens, then the three of them unload giant speakers from the trunk of the little car. It's like Mary Poppins's carpetbag. Stuff keeps spilling out of the tiny space.

Mrs. Mortimer, the leather-faced grizzly from across the road, comes out of her house as the three of them wrangle with wires and some expensive techtronic-type equipment. She folds her arms across her chest and throws disapproving glances at the boys. For a mortifying few seconds, I see myself, only with more hair and fewer face whiskers. Mom says the girls at the hair salon call her Moaning Mortimer. A shudder rips through me. I'm not old and bitter, though. I don't hate the youth or having fun.

"You're not angry, you're afraid," I remind myself just as Agnes Lop, Mrs. Mortimer's fence buddy, joins her on the driveway.

I don't suppose our street has ever seen a party. I mean, Rhodes Center, in the middle of town, has this free-for-all cookout to celebrate our founding father, and both schools throw a dance, but as far as private parties go, they don't happen on Triangle Crescent.

Triangle Crescent is mostly where people come to die. My mom calls it God's waiting room, with the residents having a collective age that predates religion. Luke and I are the youngest by about twenty years. I'm not bitching. Most of the folks around here are nice. At least they were the last time I left the house. On Saturdays I used to walk around the street listening to stories about absent grandkids and collecting free candy for a chorus of "Twinkle, Twinkle."

It's almost seven. The light is dying. Dirty blue and purple clouds bruise the sky. I've ignored everything in favor of watching the guys toss around a dusty old piece of pigskin. The faint whistle of my plummeting GPA can be heard in the distance.

I eyeball the open door of the study.

This will all be over tomorrow, I reason. I can quit worrying about it then and get caught up.

Guilt might be about to shake me into submission when I hear Luke laugh. I like the way he laughs. He puts his whole self into it, throwing his head back and holding his stomach while his entire body shakes.

They seem to be having a good time until a phone rings, *Tubular Bells*, and Luke pulls his cell from his pocket.

He stares at the screen and his two friends exchange a rolling-eyed glance.

Amy.

I don't hear him say it, but I can read it in the way his lips curl around the pronunciation of her name. The guy who I am now, like, 99 percent certain is called Simon dismisses the call with a wave of his hand. But Luke is already walking away, lifting the phone to his ear. Blond Guy shrugs — it's a what-are-you-gonna-do type of gesture.

Amy.

My interest evaporates. I slump back against the wall, bring my knees up to my chest and hug them tight. My teeth grate against the skin on the inside of my mouth, but I don't bite down.

Why does this name bother me? My straightforward-thinking brain wants to know.

My heart keeps tripping, but I'm not panicking. I know what panic feels like and this isn't it.

I wonder what Amy looks like and if she kisses with reckless abandon. I wonder if she can walk down a crowded strip mall holding someone's hand. I bet she can go out for dinner and not spend an hour trying to taste salmonella in her entrée. I bet she can go here, there, and everywhere without worrying about what might happen.

Right. I guess that's why it bothers me. It's like watching my Metro feed play out in my front yard. And probably, maybe, definitely, the new boy next door has me intrigued. But suddenly I'm not sure if that's even allowed.

I kneel up, take one last look out of the window. Luke has rejoined his friends; they have their arms slung over his shoulders, laughing. But not with him. Luke looks unimpressed, kind of like a guy who's just been ordered to run laps around a freezing-cold track. Maybe they're mocking him.

Are you okay? I think it a thousand times, even write it out once on the wall with my finger.

He shrugs when Blond Guy starts making whooping sounds. Then he looks up, glances over at my house. There's no way he can see me. He's looking in the wrong spot, for starters. But I turn to stone and try to wish myself invisible anyway. Then he looks away and they all head back inside his house.

13

I HAVE A PLAN.

It is a good plan.

A safe plan.

So why am I itching to leave my room? My palms are drenched. I rub them in circles on my knees, trying to dry them off.

It's ten thirty. I should have been trapped between my headphones, submerged in music for the past three hours. But I can't stop pulling my headset off. Even when it's on, I don't hear a single one of my six hundred songs.

My mind has always taken care of me, protected me from things that are daring, dangerous. It's how we've been for four years. Blissful. Working in unison, like an old married couple. So why is it trying to fuck me over now? Why does it want so bad to know what is happening at Luke's house?

I fix a stare at my door for the ten-hundredth time, slide my headset off again, and let it rest around my neck. Some thrash-metal rock god is screaming tortured-soul song lyrics at me, but I tune him out, try instead to hear through layers of brick and mortar for any noise escaping from next door.

It's all very quiet—aside from a throbbing beat, I mean. But that's standard, normal noise. I was expecting more sounds of chaos, screams, sirens, drunken teens fighting in the street. I start to wonder why the only thing I can hear is music. And not regular-person wondering. *Norah's* wondering, which covers every scenario from mass suicide to a police raid. Then I realize that maybe my mind isn't a traitorous snake hell-bent on betraying me. Maybe this is just my need-to-know preparedness, working some overtime. A 2.0 version, thirsty to figure out more.

That's got to be it.

Before I have time to talk myself out of it again, I'm heading to my bedroom door. Crawling, because crawling makes me smaller, smaller feels closer to invisible, invisible makes me feel safer. I open the door, wince when it squeaks, like Luke's party is at library levels of hushed and is taking place on my landing.

I head downstairs, take the last step twice, and walk over to the porch window. Butt on the floor, I push my back up against the wall. My heart hammers in my throat. The music swamps me. Some unintelligible tangle of notes, tangoing through the air. A bass line capable of causing earthquakes in Brazil. I feel the vibrations through the concrete, slapping against my back. They tap into my body and make my spine tingle. I close my eyes, see Luke on the backs of my lids. He's drinking beer from a red plastic cup. Laughing. His whole face alive from it.

I must fall asleep—at least, I've drifted into some form of unconscious state because I find my eyes opening at the squealing sounds of our rusty mail slot being lifted, and a stream of what I can only assume is drool is rolling down my chin.

I panic, free myself from the velour porch curtain that seems to have attached itself to my shoulder, and scuttle back, putting a good seven feet between me and the door. I'm breathing so hard, every inhale lifts my shoulders up around my ears. I watch, a little frightened, a little feral, as a folded letter flies through the flap and lands on the mat.

Luke.

I stare at the note. Stuck. Too nervous to reach for it, just in case he hears that I'm home.

Minutes later, the flap groans again. It lifts, and another note sails through the air and crash-lands almost on top of the first. Curiosity spikes. Fear takes a step back —long enough, at least, for me to remember where I am and what my name is. I wipe the spit off my face with the sleeve of my sweater and clear hair from my eyes just as a third note drops to the floor.

What is he doing? Besides writing me a novel.

The flap lifts a fourth time, but instead of paper, a voice floats through it.

"I know you were watching. I saw your curtains twitch."

Horror. Red hot. My jaw drops. "But I wasn't," I defend myself without thinking and then slap my hand over my mouth, wishing I could suck the words back in. He laughs. That's not fair. My eyes narrow and I glare at the door, turning toddler, my bottom lip curling under. I can feel a sulk coming on. Luke lets the flap fall, and it clatters shut.

Then nothing.

I turn an ear to the door, listening intently, hoping/praying/pleading that he'll leave, but I don't hear the sound of retreating steps. I don't hear anything. My teeth find skin at the side of my mouth and I start to chew. Not knowing is unsettling; unsettling lurks beneath my skin like an army of crawling insects. Not that it matters. As much as I want to ask if he's still there, my lips are too numb. I can't make them move.

Instead, I turn my attention to the pile of folded paper on the mat, and my fingers spider-march across the floor toward them. It takes me a second to get the notes in order.

Neighbor,
Bonjour! How's the assignment going?
Luke :)

Neighbor,
There are approximately one hundred people in my
house and I only know two of them by name. What
do I have to do to get you to come out here and
save me?
Luke :)

Neighbor,
Also, you never told me which Transformers movie
was your favorite . . .
Luke :)

A smile is spreading across my face. Unstoppable, like wildfire, making my cheeks sting. He's 10 percent human, 90 percent charisma. All he'd have to do is ask, and he'd know all one hundred names within an hour. But then, if that's not the reason he's over here, what is? I don't know if I dare believe he's left his own party because he'd rather be sitting here talking to me. But it's already up there, the thought, and I can't seem to destroy it.

I'm blinking hearts and holding back wistful sighs

when something starts jingling on the porch. A cell. Luke's cell, the same *Tubular Bells* tone as this afternoon. With my body behaving like a beached mermaid, I hook my fingers into the floor and drag my limp ass over to the door.

I hear movement, the crunch of a leather jacket. The ringing stops dead, but Luke doesn't say anything. It rings again. I push my ear up against the wood because maybe he's whispering to the caller. Still nothing. The phone doesn't ring a third time. Or maybe it does and he's switched it to silent.

I'm breathing like a claustrophobic trapped in a closet, my breath warm, splashing against the door and bouncing back in my face. My tongue twitches. Words suddenly have substance. They're rising up my windpipe, thick, like a rolling rock in my throat.

"I think . . ." I begin, but my voice needs more volume if it's going to get past the door. Filling my lungs with air, I try again. "I think somebody wants to talk to you?"

I reach a hand up; my fingers flirt with the cold, cast-iron door handle. But I can't make myself open it.

"Alas, I don't want to talk to them," Luke says in a fake, maybe-British, chewing-up-his-own-tongue type of accent. I can practically smell the beer on his breath. I retract my hand and bury it under my butt. I'm not opening the door. I have this thing about folks that are drunk. I'm not a stiff. I'm absolutely not the pearl-clutching kind. But I've heard stories. I know alcohol can corrupt even the most stable of minds, and what with my mind being about as stable as a piece of string, I figure it's safer just to avoid it.

I look back over my shoulder and my eyes trail off up the stairs. It would take mere seconds to scale the steps. I wonder if he'd notice if I disappeared back inside my bedroom. Who am I kidding? Like that's even an option. If I leave now, I'll have to spend the rest of the night trapped in a tiny mind maze, trying to figure out if he's still outside, fretting over what he's doing and if he's even still conscious. Not to mention the layers of skin I'd lose trying to scratch away that itch caused by the unsettling insect army.

And then there is this something, something small and awake inside me. Something that makes me want to smile, to wet my lips with the tip of my tongue and wonder how my hair looks.

"Hey, Norah." I hear his voice as if he were whispering right into my ear. I get so caught up in wondering how close we are right now, I forget to respond. He continues talking anyway. "Why are you always watching?"

"I wasn't." The words barge from my mouth, all balled

up in a big gust of breath and waving white flags. "I mean, I know you think I was . . . the curtains twitching and all that. The thing is, they're kind of heavy, the curtains are. They're made of velvet and they get clingy . . ." I can't stop talking. It's like running on a treadmill; my mouth is moving but I'm not getting anywhere. Verbal vomit is the evil twin of absolute silence. You can often find them both lurking around anxiety attacks.

"What I mean is"—I take a deep breath—"I fell asleep against the wall. The curtains got caught on me and were moving when I was." I point at the window, attempting to illustrate my defense to a boy who is sitting, blind on the other side of the opaque door. You'd never guess that my brain is what Dr. Reeves calls high-functioning. Sometimes, when it mixes with panic, I'd make a good computer. Other times, I'm not even sure I'd make good kindling.

"I honestly wasn't watching." I twist my fingers, hoping to wring some of the sweat off my skin. "Say something. Please. Say something." I close my eyes and whisper to the wood.

The silence is screaming; my eardrums are beginning to blister. He thinks I'm a weirdo. He's barely spent any time with me and I've already frightened him off.

"Luke! Luke!" A girl's voice charges through the dark

and, like a pinball, ricochets around the houses, the trees, and the old Victorian-style streetlamps of Triangle Crescent. "Luke. Where'd ya go?"

"Oh, shit. Not now," Luke whimpers.

"Friend of yours?" I ask.

"I'm being hunted by Amy Cavanaugh," he replies, puffing air like he's just run a marathon.

Amy. *The* Amy? Why does he say it so casually, like maybe I should know who he's talking about?

"I don't know who that is."

He snorts a laugh. "You're kidding. You must be the only person in school who doesn't."

Oh God. I do know her.

Damn.

I've seen her. Well, her posts, at least. They pop up on my Metro feed all the time. Amy "Queen" Cavanaugh, she calls herself. Her updates get starred quite a lot. Honestly, I thought she was some sort of celebrity. I didn't know she went to Cardinal; she must have arrived after I left. More lies. More damage control.

"Right! That Amy. Queen Amy."

"That's her."

"All that French work has fried my brain." I laugh off my faux pas. Then I wait for him to elaborate on his and

Amy's acquaintanceship/friendship/relationship. But he doesn't. I don't know if we're friends yet. I don't know if I can ask him.

Of course you're friends. He came over here to speak to you, didn't he?

Unless . . . *unless he only came over here to hide from Queen Amy.*

My heart beats against the back of my throat. Then I hear his leather jacket crunch again. Movement. He's standing up. I stand up with him. Palms pressed flat against the door, I almost crawl up the wood. He's leaving, and the thought is inducing panic. I didn't want him here, but now he is, and for the second time in two days, he chased away the dark shadow that makes me drown my body in black and curl up in a ball when I think of friends.

"Hey, Norah?"

"Yes." It hurts to talk.

"Do you think maybe I could come by tomorrow and we can clear up this Transformers conversation once and for all?"

"I've watched the cartoon but never seen the movies."

"Panic not." He's talking in that fake-British-Swedish-possibly-French accent again. "I'll bring them over."

Wait! What? That's not what I meant. Is it?

"I . . ."

"Luke? Where are you?" That voice again, shrill, shouting above the music and into the night. Queen Amy.

I cross my fingers and toes, secretly hope he'll ignore her and stay here a little longer.

"I guess I better go. Good night, Norah."

And then he's gone. I try but fail to count the steps I hear him take as he walks away.

I feel cold.

14

I T STARTS THE SECOND I begin the Green Mile trudge
back to my bedroom; so many thoughts, wrapped around
my body like iron chains. I have to use the banister to pull
myself up the stairs.

Musings, meanderings, conversations that haven't
even happened run in one continuous loop around my
head. With a texture like smashed glass, they're tearing my
brain to pieces.

I stop in the hall and study my gangly reflection in
the floor-length mirror. I want to see a svelte blonde with
big blue eyes. I want to see that girl in my social media
selfies, the one that smiles and never has to live up to anyone's expectations or explain why she is the way she is.
But all I see in my real-life reflection are blunt smudges
of shadow. Fragile. Upset. Weak. Thin. Afraid. Failing. And
tired. Above everything else, tired of battling with my own
mind.

They, the geeks that deal in brain stuff, they're the
ones who christened what I have an *invisible illness*, but I

often wonder if they're really looking. Beyond the science stuff. It doesn't bleed or swell, itch or crack, but I see it, right there on my face. It's like decay, this icky green color, as if my life were being filmed through a gray filter. I lack light, am an entire surface area that the sun can't touch.

Luke can't come back tomorrow.

I've done a total 180. This is not uncommon. Especially when I'm given some time to think, to blink away the rose-colored tint from my eyes.

I force a smile, think of Luke, think of cheesy ballads and toe-curling poetry. It was nice for a second. He made the crazy feel small enough to stamp on, but that's not enough. That is a fleeting feeling, easy to latch onto from behind a locked door. Unfortunately, I'm realistic. And I'm no James Bond. Eventually, he will want to step beyond the door or, worse, he'll want me to step beyond it. Or maybe he won't. Maybe Queen Amy will meet all his expectations, and then maybe he will forget about the weird girl that writes on windows and sits by her front door at the crack of dawn for no other reason than to watch the sky. If he comes back, if I let him in, as hard as I try, I won't be able to hide all the madness from him.

My body drops down onto my bed, the frame squeaks,

and I wonder for a second if it's going to collapse. It holds out, and I pat my mattress like it's done me a favor.

My head is a ball of wool after it's been mauled by a kitten.

On the backs of my eyelids, every time I blink, I see me telling Luke about my weird rituals, my routines, my intense thought processes, and then I watch him recoil like I have the plague or some sort of tropical disease that no one can pronounce. Uncertainty and caution is how you're supposed to respond to things you don't understand.

After some intense internal debate, I decide that his recoiling is something I think I could manage. But then there's the laughing. I mean, he can laugh. I laugh. My mind is ridiculous. The way it works. Like on the days I wake up and can't touch things with my hands because I happened upon news of a measles outbreak in the deepest, darkest regions of Outer Mongolia. Those are the days I have to use my feet to open doors and pick things up off the floor. It's humor that you'll never really be able to appreciate until you've spent an hour chasing a pen across the floor with pincer toes. But it is funny, the if-I-don't-laugh-I'll-cry kind of funny. It's the cruel laughing, the vicious-playground stuff I won't — can't — cope with. Like, what if he mocks me? I can imagine it, vividly, in glorious Technicolor, like the way it happens in films, with all the pointing and name-calling to boot. If that were to happen, I think maybe all my pieces would come unstuck and I'd be broken beyond repair.

15

I DON'T KNOW WHEN NIGHT turns into day. My room is still a fortress, light banished, all cracks concealed. I'm one Elizabethan gown away from being that princess trapped in a forgotten tower. There's something about the dark space that reeks of smug. It reminds me for the ten-thousandth time that letting my heart direct my head has amounted to an almost total loss of control. Or, in average-teenager terms, I left my room last night, and now Luke is coming by to lend me movies I'm not even sure I want to watch. Note to self: This is not a mistake I will make twice. Next time, I stick with the routine.

I grab my comforter, trip downstairs in the same drunken way a Slinky does when it picks up speed, take the last step twice, and crash onto the couch.

I'm not awake, not quite asleep, when there's a swift, sharp knock at the door and I almost fly through the ceiling. But instead of the usual *Who could that be?*, my head goes to *How do I look?*

That's new.

And a little unnerving.

I don't need a mirror to know I look like I've been dragged through a hedge backwards. To know my blue eyes have turned bloodshot and are undoubtedly framed by big black bags. I feel like I'm wearing a hat, which usually means my hair is so piled up on top of my head, it's possible a couple of crows are already nesting in it.

My body weighs a ton. Moving is like hurling a big rig across the carpet. I'm sluggish, shoulders hunched, heading toward the window at the sort of pace you might expect from an overweight snail and scoring friction burns on the soles of my feet. I wonder if Luke is persistent. If I don't answer today, will he come back tomorrow? Will he keep sending notes? What if he starts asking around school about me? What if he thinks I'm horrible, just being rude, ignoring his knock for no good reason? I shudder. This is the least welcome worry, but it's the biggest and loudest, trickling into my brain and seeking out space like water. I'm not horrible or rude. It's just complicated.

I tiptoe to the window, take a peek from behind the curtain. I'm hoping I can manipulate my neck to an angle where I can see the porch without putting my face through the glass. Turns out, I don't need to. There's a car parked out front. A sleek silver sports car with a red soft-top roof.

Thank God. It's not Luke knocking; it's Dr. Reeves.

Wait.

What? I do a double-take of the car. I completely forgot she was coming today.

I never forget about therapy.

Never.

This is brand-new too.

And even more unnerving.

The doc knocks again, and I'm forced to abandon reflection. I make a dash for the hall.

"Norah." Dr. Reeves startles when I whip open the door. The gust it creates sends her hair into a brown-fire frenzy. I snatch her wrist, pull her inside before any Lukes can jump out to say hi.

"Morning," I say, out of breath and straightening my shirt. The doc's eyes narrow and her head tilts a little to the left.

"Everything okay?" she asks. My eyes home in on her mouth. Or, more specifically, on the clump of hair clinging to her lip gloss.

"Everything is fine." I nod until my neck feels like it might snap. Her lips are a burnt-orange color. She doesn't wear this shade at the office. My fingers curl into fists and I pop a knuckle. I really need her to brush that hair away before it finds its way into her mouth.

"Norah, where's your head at?"

"Huh?" My eyes stay focused on her rogue tresses.

Would it be rude to mention it? It probably would be, so I won't. But there is so much gross stuff lurking in hair, on hair. She might want to know. She must be able to feel it.

"Norah." The doctor snaps her fingers a bunch of times, and I adjust my eye line to meet her concerned gaze. "Where's your head?"

"Nowhere." My knees turn in, touch, and I feel like I just got busted doing something I shouldn't. She takes a deep breath and opens her mouth but doesn't say a word.

Unfortunately for me, Dr. Reeves didn't turn stupid in her sleep. She allows the silence to stretch, questions me with her stare instead.

"Everywhere," I admit. "I can't focus." My eye starts to twitch. It tickles until I give it a scratch. Maybe this is it. Maybe this is what a breakdown feels like. "And you have some hair stuck to your lip."

"Better?" she asks, swiping it away.

I nod, feeling way more awkward than she ever has, ever will.

"I'm trying this new stuff," she tells me, pressing her lips together and making a *schmack* sound with her mouth. "The color is Autumn Mist. The consistency is glue. I think the best place for it is in the trash. Anyway . . ." She smiles softly. "I know there is more on your mind than a slight makeup mishap. Spill."

We make our way into the kitchen, her heels clip-clopping across the floor.

She makes a cup of coffee, the instant kind that sits in an unopened jar in the condiment cabinet. Then we both take a seat at the breakfast bar.

It all feels a bit tense, me at one side of the counter, her at the other. The space around us has somehow morphed into the shady interior of a police interrogation room.

"Talk to me. Talk to me as a friend," she urges.

"There's this boy," I say, voice shaking, words so dense they struggle to slide beyond my lips. The doc raises her eyebrows. Shock. That's fair. Nobody is more shocked by this development than me.

"He lives next door. I resolved to avoid him, but our paths kept crossing, and now I'm not so sure I want to . . . avoid him."

My face feels how Botox abuse looks. "I might be in a little over my head." I abandon my chair, stand up, and start pacing, which usually helps me think, but today it's just making me dizzy. I grab the hem of my shirt, search for a loose thread, and pull at it.

"Norah, we're just talking right now. Who knows, I may even be able to help you figure this out. At least let me try."

It's like smashing down a dam, opening floodgates, dropping a flame into a box of fireworks. My mouth opens and the words keep on coming.

"It's my fault. I watched him a couple of times and he saw. And then the groceries got left on the porch, but Helping Hands was closed, and so he passed them to me. So he must be nice, right? And then he wrote me some letters. Not love letters; stupid stuff. He's funny. And I lied about going to the same school as him. And about having a cold." Imagine Hamlet sauntering about the stage, hand to heart, delivering an epic monologue. That's about where I'm at right now.

Dr. Reeves just lets me talk, doesn't even attempt to slow me down or stop me. She does this thing where she pushes a thumb up under her chin and strokes an invisible goatee with a hooked finger.

At first I thought it signaled her tuning out my incessant ramblings, but then she explained that she was taking mental notes. She says she doesn't like to interrupt my stream of panic because she knows my mouth is directly quoting my mind and she wants to hear exactly what is going on inside my head. I think she's brave.

"I can't tell Luke why I lied. Can I? How can I be his friend? I'm afraid he'll laugh at me. He came over to talk to me about France." Dr. Reeves always smiles wide when

I mention France. "I couldn't tell him I can't go there. But when he talks, he doesn't think about the things that are wrong with me because he doesn't know. Which is bad, but I like it. I think I'm his friend. I think we're friends. And then he goes and invites me to this party. Obviously I can't go to that either, but not that obvious because I think something inside me wants to go to the party." I slap a hand down over my heart and clutch at the skin because that's where I'm hurting right now. "I'm curious. And not just curious because my mind is trying to compute the millions of ways everything could go wrong. This is different. Persuasive. Powerful. It convinces me to leave my room. My room. My fortress. It talks me into getting closer to the music. And then he's at my door. Luke is. He writes me more notes. And suddenly he wants to come by today. He seems interested. So why does he leave when Queen Amy wants to talk to him? She's everything, and she's not hiding, so it makes sense that he would want to talk to her. She is probably normal. I'm so afraid he'll mock me."

And then silence. Eardrums everywhere rejoice.

I'm shaking. I don't cry, but I want to. Instead, I take a breath, suck all the air right out of the room and fill my depleted lungs with it. It feels good. Cold, the same way eucalyptus does when you inhale it deep. And freeing, like my entire torso has been wrapped in a bandage that suddenly unraveled.

"I've spent all night losing my mind. Can you please help me?"

"Of course, but first, let's get you something to drink," she says, clip-clopping over to the fridge.

I watch pearls of condensation roll down my glass of orange juice as Dr. Reeves takes a sip of her coffee. If it tastes bad, I can't tell. Beyond the slurping sounds, I can hear the wheels of her mind turning. I can't look up and meet her eyes because I feel all kinds of naked right now.

"You remember when we talked about neural pathways?" She draws on the table with her fingertip. A tree with squiggly roots sprouting off in all different directions.

"About how the brain learns and how it ties instances together so those things then become associated?" It's no coincidence that she's still drawing roots on the tree that I'm pretty confident we can now label *Norah's Brain*.

I nod. I remember this conversation. I remember breaking out in hives after hearing the conclusion. It's about changing the way I think. Which sounds so simple, but whether I like to admit it or not, anxiety has become my best friend. It's a crutch that helps me hobble through life. It's the brassy bitch at school that I don't like, but being her BFF makes me popular. Or the school bully that I don't really want to be around, but being his friend means I don't get beat up. I don't know how to be safe without it. We're buddies. It's like they say: keep your friends close, your enemies closer.

"We said we were going to try and change those pathways, right? Norah, the thing about cognitive therapy is, it relies on repetition. It would be fair to say that we can't create these new pathways, these new associations, if we're still clinging to the ideas that created the old ones, right?"

Of course she's right. Her brain's so big it's a wonder she can fit through doors that aren't double.

With two fingers, she starts rubbing away at the table-top, erasing some of the roots. "When we talked about how people perceive us, what was it we concluded?"

"I don't remember." I find a patch of skin on the back of my hand, start scratching, break flesh and feel blood, sticky, collecting under my thumbnail, but it doesn't hurt. I'm numb.

"Take a deep breath for me," Dr. Reeves says.

She wants me to draw a parallel between myself and a story she once told me about a chick we've aptly named Perception Girl.

"It's not the same," I tell her, shaking my head. I can

hear Luke laughing as I try to explain to him why I can't venture beyond the front door. Why I count. Why I wash my hands a hundred times a day. Why I go days without eating and sleeping. Why I haven't spoken to another teenager in almost four years.

"What's not the same?" Dr. Reeves pushes.

"About the girl."

"What girl?" She's trying to pull words from my mouth and I've run out of ways to stall.

"The perception girl!" I yell. "The one that doesn't get laughed at." Perception Girl's job is to help me see what other people see when they look at me.

"Remind me. Why doesn't she get laughed at?" Dr. Reeves says, setting her cup down on the placemat. Except she doesn't get it central and I can see it tilting. It agitates me. I don't ask, just reach across the table and set the damn thing straight.

"Because she's sick. And people don't laugh at sick people," I tell her through clenched teeth.

"And what are you?"

"I'm sick!" I shout. But not because I'm angry. It's like I'm trying to make myself listen. No, not listen, *hear*. The same way a sergeant drills instructions into the heads of his platoon.

Or maybe I *am* angry. Angry that my mind can function so proficiently on one thing and remain completely obtuse on the next.

"Norah, listen to me. The general population doesn't want to laugh at a seventeen-year-old girl whose life is being held hostage by her brain. As a rule, people don't laugh at those who are suffering. And Norah, you are suffering."

"How can I expect people to empathize with a sickness they can't see?" Tears sting my eyes.

"You don't expect anything. You talk, you teach."

I shake my head, pull back my chair, ready to sit down, but decide I'd rather stay standing. More control. That's what I need. Somehow, height gives me this feeling like I have an advantage.

Dr. Reeves draws new roots on our invisible tabletop tree. There aren't quite as many now, and they're not so squiggly, not nearly as erratic. I want to believe her; I want to be able to hear Luke understanding as easily as I hear him laughing.

"I'm afraid," I confess in a whisper. I'm always afraid, but I don't usually admit it out loud.

"It's a huge thing," she tells me. "That's why you fight this therapy so much. Your brain is freaking out because it knows that to create new paths and form different ideas, you have to lend yourself a little to the unknown."

God. I wish she was more like the Jar Jar Binks of therapy and less like the Yoda.

"Okay." I sit down. "What if . . ." My words are muffled by a mouthful of shirt collar. What I really want to do is pull the whole thing over my head and disappear, but I don't. "What if he is a part of the asshole percentage and does laugh at me?"

Dr. Reeves picks up her cup, cradles it, and smiles. "I think you've answered your own question." She sits back a little in her chair. "I met a woman at a conference once. She told us this story about her daughter who was desperate to date this guy on the football team. He rejected her because he said she was too ugly. Two years later, she met a boy at college, and after she got her law degree, they married, had three children, and now live a happy little life in the suburbs. What's the point of this story?"

"Effect and outcome."

"Exactly. We can assume the best, but we can't choose how people perceive us. We can, however, choose how those views affect us."

I stare at the tree on the table, realizing I'm a hypocrite. I've judged Luke before he even had a chance to judge me. And then it happens. He knocks, the sound echoing around my house.

"You have more control over this than you think, than

your pathways are allowing you to believe." The doc stands. "And you're assuming you have to offload your life story right now, but you don't. You don't have to say anything you don't want to. You do a lot of things in your free time with books and movies and music and language. Invite him in, talk about anything else."

"But what if I have to fix his leaning coffee cup? Or what if he starts biting dirty fingernails and my stomach does that swirling thing? He's going to know I'm a freak."

Dr. Reeves shoots me a look that feels a lot like a slap across the face. "I thought we banned that word."

"I revived it."

"Well, I'm killing it. For good this time. Just . . . be yourself."

"That's horrible advice."

She laughs as Luke knocks a second time.

"I'll be right there!" I turn my hand into a megaphone and bellow down the hall.

"You know what I hate?" Dr. Reeves asks, glancing at her reflection in the fridge door. With her pointer finger she strokes the bridge of her nose, flicks the end a few times, then crinkles it up. "I hate my nose. It's huge. Takes up eighty-five percent of my face. It's bulbous and I wish I had the guts to get it fixed."

"What?" I try but fail to see the problem. Her nose

is small and cute, maybe even a little bit button. "No, it's not."

"Aha." She points at me; her mouth opens and a gotcha expression pulls at her features. "You can't always look at yourself subjectively. You need to remember that. Trust me when I say just be yourself." She walks over to me, exhibits an extreme amount of caution before resting a soft hand on my shoulder. "And don't forget, that number for my cell is still good, anytime. Okay?"

As I nod, Luke raps on the door again. I just stand there, staring past the table, over a vase of pink peonies and down the hall, which I swear has doubled in length.

"You might want to get that," Dr. Reeves whispers as she leaves out the back.

16

DR. REEVES'S PEP TALK is pretty good as sustaining fuel. My bravery is showing no signs of burning out as my butt reboots and I head over to the door.

It's different talking to the doc at home. I mean, I knew she was smart—her office walls are decorated with academic achievements and her shelves are lined with books she's written, cowritten, or consulted on. But in her office I can never be 100 percent there. Half of me is always too busy worrying about being out of the house to listen to her talk. Here, today, I noticed that she has the vivacity of the President of the United States in one of those doomsday movies, talking guys into sacrificing themselves for the greater good. I bet in her spare time she gives motivational speeches at "Be a Better You"–type conventions.

Deep breath. *The general populace is compassionate* goes through my head as I unbolt the lock.

Prove it. My mind mocks me.

"I'm trying. If you'd just let me figure it out," I snap.

"Norah?"

Crap. I resist the urge to face-plant into the door and

promise myself to never again let passion increase the volume of what are supposed to be whispered words.

"One more second."

Shoulder roll. Yesterday's deodorant is forced into action when sweat starts pooling in my armpits.

It's just one root.

One tiny root that I have to draw. And with that, I open the door.

He's remembered the DVDs. They're tucked under his arm.

"Hi." He grins, and I fall down dead.

He looks like the next big thing in boy bands. Planet-size green eyes sparkling beneath thick black lashes. He glances at me, and his smile is full of flirt. Whether that's intentional, I'm not sure.

He's wearing product in his hair, the kind that makes his curls look wet. A single unruly ringlet has broken free from the pack and dangles down the middle of his forehead. It would be completely inappropriate to grab hold of the end, pull on it, and let it bounce back like a spring. Right? Of course it would. I twist my hands together so they're not tempted to stray anyway.

He's wearing a white tee that clings to his torso like a second skin and an unbuttoned, baggy green shirt, sleeves rolled up to the elbows. And just to add serious insult to injury, he smells like a mouthwatering mix of winter and sweet spices.

Garbage. That's what I look like in comparison. Ten-day-old garbage that's been left to fester under a blistering summer sun. I didn't brush my hair. Didn't wash my face or scrub my teeth, and now I'm piling an unforgivable amount of pressure on a twenty-four-hour-old squirt of rose-scented Stay Dry.

Just smile through it. No. Don't smile through it.

I lift my hand to my mouth, use it as a shield. What am I thinking? I can't smile when my teeth aren't clean. And I drank orange juice, the one liquid besides coffee you can still taste on your breath hours after your first sip.

"Is this a bad time?" Luke asks.

I shake my head, try to run the fingers of my free hand through my hair, but they get caught up in knots. What is supposed to be a stealth maneuver turns into a brief tug of war that ends with a stinging scalp and a handful of loose hairs. I fight back a wince and scream *Ouch* internally.

"Should I come back later?"

"No!" I yell.

Waiting for him to show up has already liquefied most of me. If I have to wait for a second showing I might just dissolve entirely. There's no way my body can survive another wave of anxiety so soon. I'll just have to fix it. "Can you give me another minute? Last one, I swear." He doesn't have a chance to answer before I slam the door in his face.

I'm halfway up the stairs when I realize how rude that must have seemed. He's been here ten seconds and I'm failing miserably at being normal.

Freak. Not killed off. The exact opposite. It's very much alive and kicking, like a monster living off lightning.

I look at the door. It would take more time to go back and explain to him why I can't let him sit downstairs in my house alone than it would to just carry on. Screw it. I'll be five minutes.

I jet into the bathroom. My toothbrush lives in a plastic case in the cabinet. I brush fifty-two times, twenty-six strokes on the top, twenty-six on the bottom. I don't compromise on this. I can't. But I scrub in double-quick time, then cannonball back downstairs, taking the last step twice and narrowly avoiding a broken limb.

Without pausing for a breath, I fling open the door. I don't know if a small part of me is expecting him not to be there. But he is, exactly as he was the first time.

"Hi," he says again.

"Hi," I reply, fearless of morning-breath fumes rendering him unconscious. "How's it going?" My voice is weird.

I've adopted a Boston twang to my accent. I have no idea why. I've never been to Boston and I don't know anyone from there.

A cramp kicks in, sucker-punching me in the spleen, and I have to lean on the doorjamb, swallowing back air like a drunk sucking back whiskey.

"Are you . . ." he starts, stops, looks over at his house. "You know, maybe I should just come back later?"

"God, no. Please. I'd rather you didn't." I miss how ugly that sounds at first because I'm too busy working through pelvic pain, but I realize the second I see his face melting into misery. My jaw hits the floor.

"Ouch," he says and forces a smile that wobbles before it takes shape.

"Oh, no. No. I didn't mean it like that. I'm so sorry. I just meant . . ." Don't know how to explain. My brain has stopped turning. It's gotten stuck, like a scratched CD. "I meant . . . I meant . . . what it is . . . I was just trying to . . ." I blink. See my head burst and watch chunks of gray matter slide down the wall.

"Norah." Luke grins and something inside me sighs. "It's okay."

I'm not sure it is. I'm not sure I wanted the first time I have a boy over to turn into something I just have to get through.

I've no idea what to say now. Any armor I was wearing has started to peel off me. As thin and as brittle as snakeskin, it blows away in the wind. Luke looks down, stares at his Chuck Taylors. I stare at them too and am tackled to the ground by a burly wad of instant regret. They're laced differently. It's just one tiny bit, on the left shoe. Instead of going across like the rest of the lace, it crisscrosses. My nails hit my neck, and I try to soothe the sudden itch.

Don't think about it. It's irrelevant. Don't think about it. Totally unimportant.

"Coffee," I blurt out. And he startles. "I mean, coffee," I repeat at a regular pitch for regular people. "Would you like some?"

"Sure." He nods and I scuttle off into the kitchen. The rubber soles of his shoes, his laced-wrong shoes, squeak as he follows me.

Don't think about it.

Have you ever been able to not think about that itch? The one that blossoms right between your shoulder blades? The one that you can't reach? Impossible.

I can feel his eyes burning holes in my back as I root around in the cabinet for cups.

"How do you take it?"

"However it comes. I'm not fussy."

Oh, brother.

I'm not channeling the right line of focus to figure out how to work the coffee machine, so instead I grab the jar of instant.

"So, Norah," he says when I hand him the steaming mug. He chews his nails; they're brittle and broken. I watch his fingers, wince when they almost connect with mine. He doesn't seem to notice. "Have you lived around here long?"

"Uh-huh." I nod, would offer him more of an answer but all my brainpower is going into stopping my mouth from mentioning his laces. My eye is twitching under the pressure. It's like when you're a kid sharing secrets with your friends and you pretend to lock your lips. I'm doing that, except my pursed lips are actually pinched between my fingertips and I'm twisting them into a knot.

"How long is that?" Luke asks; he's not going to let me off easy.

"Seventeen years, three months, and two days," I mumble. He raises his eyebrows and whistles a long, high-pitched note.

"Here." I grab a chair. "Have a seat." I'm hoping if he buries his feet under the table I can stop thinking about those damn laces and start acting normal. Normaler.

Once I have a frustrating thought, I have to follow it through. Have to. No negotiating or forgetting about it. I can't shrug it off or come back to it later. It just keeps growing and growing; like a balloon being filled with air, it expands until the pressure becomes too much. It's my between-the-shoulder-blades itch.

Luke starts talking about something, music or movies. I watch his lips make shapes but don't absorb the sound.

"Norah?" He waves a hand in front of my face several moments later, and I am pulled sharply back into the here and now. I hear the drum of my fingers on the tabletop and flatten my palm immediately to make it stop.

I clear my throat, pick at a scab on the side of my finger until it stings. "What were you saying?"

He pauses, mouth open, laser eyes fixed on mine, trying to burn their way inside my brain. Even if they make it through they'll never figure me out.

"I'm going to go," he says, standing.

Fuck. Fuck and shit and hell. And some swearword that has yet to be invented to describe how frustrated I am with myself. I've totally messed this up.

"Luke," I say, standing too. I'm on the edge, toes curling over the side. I don't know what to say. So instead of talking, I chew my fingers.

"Is there something wrong?" he asks. He's not blind. He can see my meltdown as if it were bleaching my skin a bright color. Pink. Neon. If panic were a color it'd be neon pink and you'd be able to see its blinding hue from outer space.

I nod.

"You want to talk about it?"

"Not yet."

"Not yet? But later?"

"It's really . . . complicated."

"Are you going to tell me you have superpowers?" I can't decide if his smile is real or fake.

Tell him. Just tell him. *Tell him the whole thing.* You may be able to salvage something from this freak show of a situation.

"I'm awkward." Ugh. Even an admission that small tastes like vomit as it claws its way across my tongue.

"I know," he says.

"You do?"

"Well, you do spend a lot of time hiding behind doors." Don't cry. Even though your eyes are burning and there's a glob of hysteria wedged like a chicken bone in your windpipe. Don't cry. "You wanna know a secret?" Luke asks.

I owe him words at the very least, but all I can manage is a nod.

"I'm awkward too."

He's humoring me, and I'm blinking hearts again. He's

so nice, I desperately wish my mind would give him a break and stop second-guessing his sentiments.

"I'm going to give you some space. But we'll talk soon, okay? Maybe I can sit on your porch and you can keep the door closed." He holds out his hand for me to shake. I take a step back to avoid contact and stare at his palm like it's a loaded gun. He retracts it slowly, slips it into his back pocket. My teeth bite down on my bottom lip as I force my eyes to lift and look at him. I'm bracing, convinced I'm going to meet with animosity, but he doesn't look offended or angry or anything I'd expect. He looks kind of sad. Feeling sorry for me, maybe. Or maybe mourning a friendship that he's decided won't go beyond half a cup of coffee. Whatever. All this over a shoelace. Sometimes I wonder if I should be locked in a straitjacket.

"I'll see myself out," Luke says, heading down the hall.

The door clicks shut, and I wonder if I can buy a lobotomy on eBay.

17

I HATE YOU. I FUCKING hate you." I seethe at my reflection through tight teeth. Tears roll down my cheeks and drip, drip, drip onto my shirt, making Rorschach patterns that I don't dare try to decipher.

An urge that I haven't felt in a long time is burning inside my stomach. I take a deep breath, but air has the consistency of tar as I suck it back and choke it down. I lean on the sink, claw at the porcelain basin. It's no good. I'm spiraling and I can't stop it.

Panic is bad. Panic mixed with disdain for yourself is worse.

Maybe I can sit on your porch and you can keep the door closed.

It burns, makes my ears bleed. I wonder how many times he's said that to Amy.

Never. Not once. God. I'm such a freak. I want to climb out of my own skin.

The room undulates. There's no one here, but I feel like there are hands on me, pushing me around and around in a circle. My head throbs; my teeth start chattering.

Most of the time I can ride out a panic attack. I just curl up in a ball and wait for it to pass. There's something about knowing it will come to an end that I'm certain of. Despite the way my body behaves, it feels manageable. But when it's cut with anger or rage, something shifts, and control feels further out of reach.

I open the bathroom cabinet, grab the nail scissors, and wilt to the floor.

Maybe I can sit on your porch and you can keep the door closed.

"*Shh.*" I press a finger to my lips, try to quiet my head, but the whirring sounds persist. There's static rattling around inside my skull, mixing with Luke's promise to stay ten feet away the next time we talk.

I lean back, feel the coldness of the bathtub side seeping through my shirt. My legs part and my fingers glide over the inside of my thigh, tracing the lumps and bumps of tiny scars.

"Please stop." I bury my face in my hands, mash the heels of my palms against my eyes until I can see colored spots.

Luke walked away in sixteen steps. Eight perfectly tied-shoelace steps. And eight not. It's not the laces, not really. They were just a catalyst, a microscope through which I could see all the broken parts of me. Why can't I be normal? Why can't I think the way normal people do? I so desperately would have liked to have him as a friend.

I squeeze the scissors in my hand, remember the first time I sat here, almost three years ago. The first cut I ever made came from the fear of taking a physics exam. I'd already left Cardinal by then, had started homeschooling with Mom.

Most kids who enter an exam room are freaking out about failing, but not me. I wasn't afraid of that. Failing didn't even enter my head. The fear came from the intensity of it all. I kept imagining sitting still, under strict conditions, not being able to move, not being able to come and go as I needed to.

I mentally shackled myself to a chair.

And then the what-ifs started. What if this happened? What if that happened? What if? What if? What if? Too many questions that I couldn't answer. I just wanted silence.

It's weird, the release I get from dragging the tiny metal arm across my skin. It's like slamming on brakes for an emergency stop; my head will go dead the second I feel the blade bite into me. All the buzzing receptors in my brain will forget the panic and concentrate on registering the hurt, the blood. It's drastic, a last resort. But so easy. Like breathing, blinking. One beat in time. One quick slice, where nobody can see, and it all stops. This is not about dying. This is about trying to get back some control.

My hands tremble as I lift my sweater off my legs, hitch my shorts up, and pull the skin tight on my thigh. The scars from before have faded to little silver bumps that could easily be mistaken for snail trails. I inch the blade closer to my leg, blink away a fresh batch of tears.

Despite my dangerously fragile thought pattern, OCD insists on its sick sense of loyalty to even numbers. It won't let me make a fifth mark, so I run the blade along one of the four existing scars. A well of blood springs to the surface, and I go slack.

It works like a shake, a slap, an injection of an anesthetic. I picture it like a never-ending tug of war between panic and calm. Self-harm is an impartial observer that steps up with something sharp to sever the rope. The minute the cut is made, both teams fly back, collapse to the ground on top of one another, exhausted.

The thing is, now that it's done, I want it to go away. I don't want to see it or feel it or acknowledge that I needed control so badly I cut myself. But I have to, every time I stand in the shower, or my jeans rub against it, or my mom walks by my door when I'm getting changed and I jump around like a jackrabbit to cover myself.

The blood tickles as it trickles down my leg. I reach back, grab the sponge off the side of the bathtub, and press it over the cut. The panic is dead, done. Disdain has tripled in size.

I can't win.

18

Iт's GONE DARK. I open my eyes when I feel a buzzing beneath my waistband. There's a chill on my skin that
reminds me I'm lying on a cold floor, wearing shorts, and
I left our air conditioner on. My mouth is a cotton mill,
drier than sawdust, like I haven't had a drop to drink in a
decade. I need water.

I'm about to stand when I feel that buzzing again. I
realize real quick that it's my cell and without a second's
more delay, I snatch it up and hold it to my ear. I don't
bother checking the caller ID. Don't need to. It could be
aliens trying to sell me apocalypse insurance for all I care. I
just need to hear another voice.

"Norah?"

"Mom." I'm hoarse.

"What's wrong with your voice? Are you crying?"

"No. No," I assure her. Words are sandpaper scratching
layers off my throat.

Suck it up.

I don't want her to worry. I want her to get well and
come home. I don't reach for scissors when she's around

to talk to, don't end up bleeding and passing out on the bathroom floor in a flood of tears. "I just have a bit of a sore throat."

"Could be allergies. Have you had the windows open?"

God. I miss my mom.

My body unfurls, and it's a wonder my bones don't creak. Muscles I didn't know I had are protesting about being mashed against the ground for hours.

I hoist my butt up. Blood is glue; the sponge between my legs is stuck to my skin. I don't peel it off because the cut will only start pouring again, and the last thing I want to do is deal with it.

I slump downstairs, take the last step twice, and collapse in Mom's recliner. The sponge stays. I'll rinse it off later but will never stop seeing it soaked in my blood.

Mom asks me about schoolwork. Even in the midst of her car-crash trauma, she's remembered my *Macbeth* assignment is due tomorrow. The ball shape my body is in tucks up a little tighter. I wish I could tell her that it's been sent back and I'm just waiting on my grade. But I can't. I couldn't write my own name right now, let alone one thousand, five hundred words. I force a hum, which she seems to take as a good sign because she doesn't push further. Why would she? I'm a great student; all my assignments are in early, never late. Not until now. I'm grateful when the conversation moves on and she starts talking to me about a TV show that she's watching. I pull the knit blanket off the back of the chair, drape it across my body, and sigh relief when she finally mentions that she's coming home.

I sleep away Sunday in a sorry attempt to forget about the angry sting that radiates down my thigh.

It's Monday, the beginning of a new week. A fresh start. A clean slate. The chance to do everything I didn't get to do on Friday . . .

Or not.

I don't remember the last time I felt this bad.

Wait.

Yes, I do.

It was the day after the last time I found solace in scissors.

Instead of embracing productivity, I act like a slug, dragging my butt around the house, trying to bury myself in a black oversize sweater. I'm in mourning mode. I make the couch my bed and fry my brain with daytime TV. Misery covers everything in a thick layer of lead, making even the simplest task heavy and hard work, so I just don't bother doing stuff. On the plus side, I've become a

pro at not looking out of the windows, having been transformed from diligent watcher to barely-able-to-hold-my-
own-head-up bystander in a single slice.

Dr. Reeves phones the house around lunchtime. At
first I let the machine pick it up, but then she starts mut-
tering about maybe, possibly, probably moving her last
client's appointment to Tuesday morning and signing off
early to come over and check on me.

Hell. No.

That would be the worst. I look like I just woke up
from a decade of being dead; smell a little like I have too.
There is nothing invisible about my illness right now. She
cannot see me.

I roll off the couch, crawl over to the phone, and call
back.

Faking perky is easy. I make up some BS about keeping my brain busy with homework and go all Stepford
Wives — excited over a cheese soufflé I just cooked up. Both
lies, but she's blissfully reassured within ten minutes, and I
resume living like a mannequin on the couch.

On the third morning, I wake up, open my eyes, and
snarl at the ceiling. An orchestra of blackbirds is fine-
tuning their vocal cords right outside the window. I turn
my head, snarl at them too. They're lucky I lost interest in
archery before I could buy a bow and arrow. Stretching

sleep from my limbs, I roll over and look at the clock above the fireplace. It's 11:00 a.m. Wow. I've really got to move. I don't want to—depression is a cold concrete slab crushing my chest—but Mom is due home today. The room needs airing, and I have to make myself look less like the living dead. She can't know how badly I've been regressing.

There was a time, back when my friends stopped calling, that I exchanged words for grunts and lived in my pajamas. I spent so long coddled in soft cotton, it's a wonder it didn't fuse to my skin. Pants were reintroduced into my routine at about the same time I stopped looking for control in a pair of nail scissors.

Still, I lie on the couch for another ten minutes, snuggling up in my blankets and listening to the sound of my stomach growling. It must think my throat's been slit. I'm starving, but my insides have been too tight, too sore, to eat anything. It's like recovering from a stomach bug. My internal organs feel delicate, like they've been bashed around. That's accompanied by a soft *swish* of uncertainty, but if I don't eat, my periods will stop. I don't want that to happen again. That's when Mom first called Dr. Reeves, and, besides making an appointment, she recommended these rancid shakes that I had to spend a week forcing down my throat.

Petulance makes cleaning up last a century longer

than it should. I stomp around with a piece of toast hanging from my mouth. Drag away one chunk of bedding at a time, back to my room, which has been sandblasted with sunlight and transformed into an oven. I tuck in the corners of my comforter with malcontent and beat my pillows to a pulp before laying them neatly back on my bed. A couple of bats fly out of my closet when I open the doors. It's a cave in there. In total contrast to the rest of the room, it's colder than a morgue, too out of reach for the sun to touch. I loathe every frozen fiber as I pull on jeans and a skinny sweater.

The mumbling of cuss words starts as I make my way downstairs, but I stop dead in my tracks when someone knocks on the door. They knock again.

"Mom." I figure it has to be her. I hope she hasn't been knocking long. Maybe I should have left the bolt off the door. I ski across the laminate in my socks, undo the lock, face exploding into a smile.

But it's not my mom.

"You don't go to Cardinal." Luke. I automatically take a step back and cower behind the sleeve of my sweater.

"What?"

"You said you went to the same school as me, but you don't." He doesn't sound angry, which I can't make sense of, because now he knows I lied to him. "I'm guessing you didn't have a cold the other day either." Twice. Now he knows I lied to him twice. "That was French you were speaking to me, right?"

"Did you . . . check up on me?" My teeth tear at skin on the side of my thumb.

"No." He holds up his hands like I just fired warning shots. "Of course not. Not at all. See, I made friends with this guy called Simon." The dude from the party, the one with the horn-rimmed glasses who drives a Nissan. I knew his name was Simon. I hold off on sharing this revelation. Now is probably not the time to be awarding myself Brownie points. "He remembers you."

"Erm . . ." I'm speechless because I've been caught lying, obviously, but also a little bit because I've been remembered by somebody other than my mom.

"He says he remembers you collapsing in class."

I clear my throat, stare at my feet and make my big toes touch. "Busted?" I'm hoping I look as adorkable as he did when I found out he was faking knowing French.

"Cute." He smirks. "Simon said that was four years ago."

"It's more like three years, ten months, and eight days ago," I correct. Because that helps.

"So it's all true?"

I nod. Bite down on the side of my mouth until the sting brings tears to my eyes.

"Okay," Luke says at last, but something else is on his mind. He starts fidgeting, shifting his weight from leg to leg and looking anywhere, everywhere, but at me.

"What?" I push as gently as possible.

"Are you sick?" he asks after a thousand awkward years have hobbled on by. Of all the ways I imagined my crazy coming to light, this wasn't one of them. "I mean, you don't have to answer that. I just have this hunch—"

"Yes," I interject. "But I'm almost a hundred percent certain it's not what you're thinking." Mental health is usually the last place people go when they think about someone being sick. That, and, well, I'm a tall skinny blonde with baby-blue doe eyes and have what my grandma used to call the sweetest smile.

I've heard *You don't look mentally ill* at least a half a dozen times in the past four years, a couple of those times from my former friends. I blame the media, stereotyping "mental illness" and calling every murderer since Manson crazy. People always seem to be expecting wide eyes and a kitchen knife dripping with blood.

"And what is it exactly that you think I'm thinking?" he asks, and I have to catch myself from crashing to the floor. People rarely challenge me. Or maybe they would if I let people get close enough to try. His eyes slim to slits as he watches me. Suddenly I have no idea what is happening in his head.

"I . . . I don't know."

"You think maybe I could come in?" He's wearing boots today. No mismatched laces to melt my mind. I picture us sitting, drinking coffee, me being normal and not doing anything to embarrass myself. Mom would freak, in the best kind of way, if she came home to find me chatting with a boy. "I don't have to," Luke says when the silence starts to stretch.

"No," I squeak, then push my fingers to my lips and feel my cheeks being swallowed by fire. "I mean, yes, you can come in."

19

My hand is shaking. I can barely keep Luke's coffee in the cup as I take it over to the table. "You're so nervous," he says when I set it down on the mat in front of him.

I shrink back inside my sweater. If he sees me squirm, he doesn't mention it—doesn't rush to rescind this line of conversation either. He still has those eyes, narrow and inquisitive, fixed on me. I wonder for a second if he's been taking how-to-study-your-subject lessons from Dr. Reeves.

I sit opposite him, feet on the chair, knees up to my neck, trying to shrink myself down as much as possible.

"I'm sorry I lied to you," I say, desperately seeking to squash the suffocating silence.

"No," he says. "It's okay. You don't have to tell me anything you don't want to."

I think maybe I want to tell him something, but I'm not sure what. There's a pulse in my tongue. It feels kind of eager and unpredictable, like if I start speaking I won't know when to stop.

I peek over my knee, look him in the eye, and he smiles a smile that could wipe winter out of existence.

"Why are you here?" I ask.

He keeps me speared with his stare, but in my peripheral vision I see his fingers twitch and dance around on the tabletop. He's bouncing a leg too. The vibration races through the floor. Nerves. Panic. Neon pink. I'd recognize it from a thousand light years away. Not on the same scale as mine, not even close, but I'm startled by it for a second. Sometimes I get so focused on how abnormal my reactions are, I forget a little panic is okay in certain situations.

"Honestly?" he says.

I nod.

"At first I thought you were cute . . ." He grins. I duck back behind my knees, but not from fear. I'm blushing, heating up the Earth's atmosphere by a thousand degrees and trying to stifle a snicker with the sleeve of my sweater.

"At first?" I question, lift my gaze enough to watch his mouth move. It'll be a while before I can look him in the eye again.

"I mean, I still think you're cute, obviously, but . . . I don't know. I'm intrigued. Curious about you. And . . ."

"And?"

"I wasn't lying when I said I was awkward."

"You threw a party and a hundred people showed up."
I don't know a huge amount about high school parties or,
as the kids on the Metro call them, *partays*. They're another one of those things that didn't happen until after I
got sick. Still, I'm pretty sure a full house means you're one
of the popular kids. And I don't suppose there's much call
for awkward among the elite.

"Yeah . . . and I ended up over here, talking to you."
As if on cue, the fresh slit on my thigh smarts. "I guess I
have a tendency to gravitate toward people on a different
wavelength," he says with a shrug.

"You think I'm weird," I reply, because my special
skills include sweeping away the words of a sentence and
finding a brand-new meaning buried beneath them.

"That's not what I said." He's adamant. And now I'm
curious.

"But what if . . . what if I *am* weird?"

He thinks about the possibility, and I scratch, scratch,
scratch the nape of my neck.

"Have you ever eaten a cream-cheese-and-applesauce
sandwich with mayonnaise?"

I throw up a little bit in my mouth before shaking my
head. I'm not sure where this is going, but I find myself
leaning forward. "Have you?"

"All the time. It's, like, my favorite kind of sandwich

in the world. Everyone who knows about it tells me it's weird."

"It's not," I say, defending him. The thought of him feeling even a little like me makes my heart hurt. Turns out, he doesn't need any reassurance from me.

"I totally agree. And you know what I realized?"

"What?"

"When people say *weird*, what they really mean is *different*. And difference has never been a bad thing."

He's smart. I like smart almost as much as I like funny.

"I think you'll be disappointed when you figure out what's going on with me." It's not that I want to rain all over his friendship parade. I don't. I just have this overwhelming urge to warn him that I can be hella frustrating to be around. It's not meant to sound maudlin. I'm not interested in him tuning up the world's smallest violin to play me a sad song. Fact of the matter is, people who depend on the level of perfection that I do are tiring. It takes some getting used to, and it won't ease up until I do.

He shakes his head at me and laughs lightly. "Are you always this pessimistic?"

"Like you wouldn't believe."

My words hang in the air like smog, so thick it's a wonder we're both still breathing.

"Norah, I just want to be your friend. Will you let me be that?"

"Yes."

His smile sets my kitchen on fire.

"Okay." He stands, slaps his thighs and fishes a tangled wad of keys from his pocket. "I gotta get back to school. My free period is almost over, but can I leave you my number?" he asks, already heading for the notepad on the fridge.

I can see what's happening, but I don't believe it.

A boy is writing down his number on my fridge. I swallow down girlish squeals and wait for him to finish. The first boy's phone number I've ever gotten is being written, on my fridge, right now. And there is no one around to tell. I kind of want to open the door and scream it to the street. But I won't. Who would have thought a bunch of digits could bring this much excitement?

We stroll toward the door in silence. "Chat later?" Luke says, stepping out onto the porch. He holds out his hand. "Are we still not shaking?"

I stare at his outstretched palm. I want to take hold of it, feel his skin against mine, but I'm already wondering when he last washed his hands. It's not fair of me to make assumptions, but I can't stop it. OCD destroys any romantic notions pressed flesh has to offer.

Deep breath. "Maybe . . . maybe next time you come

by, I can tell you why?" Wait . . . what? Was that me? Did I just say that? It sounded like me, but that's not something I would say. I touch my throat. I've no idea why—checking to see if it's still warm, maybe.

"Yeah?" He looks . . . excited.

I solidify, can feel butterflies beating their wings against my rib cage.

It's not too late to take it back.

But I don't want to.

This is new.

And a little unnerving.

Over his shoulder I see a yellow taxi pull up. Mom is sitting in the back, her eyes stretched wide open, trying to swallow the sight of a boy standing on our porch. I can't decide if what I smell is exhaust fumes or her burning curiosity. It's a wonder her face isn't pressed against the glass.

"Talk later, Neighbor." Luke sprints off down the driveway, hops over the boxwood bush as Mom climbs out of the cab. The slam of the car door echoes around Triangle Crescent.

Rachael Dean, a.k.a. Mom, is about as subtle as the *Titanic.* Not even a car accident can shake her spirit. Her bright red hair has been pulled into space buns on the sides of her head, and she's dressed like science fiction threw up on her. Cosmic print everywhere. She eyeballs me, scurries toward the house like she's being dragged by a Great Dane, her jaw trailing on the ground behind her. She looks well. Really well. The giant knot that's been in my shoulders for over a week unravels and my arms suddenly feel ten feet too long.

"Norah Jane Dean!" Mom is so excited. I'm really looking forward to showing her his phone number, just as soon as my muscles come unstuck. "Is that Party Boy?" Mom asks. I nod. "He's cute," she exclaims, turning around to wave at Luke as he pulls his car out onto the road. He waves back, then drives away.

"You okay?" Mom asks, nudging my shoulder. "You're looking a little pale."

"I'm okay," I reply, falling into her chest and wrapping her in a bear hug. *I think.*

20

*D*EAR LUKE . . .

I hit the DELETE button for the eleventy-billionth time. What is he, my lawyer? Nobody writes "Dear Anybody" in a message unless they're paying a ton for a Mr. Somebody to read it.

Luke . . .

And that's about as good as it gets for almost five hours.

I lie on my bed, staring at the ceiling, trying to balance Luke's phone number on the tip of my nose. Every time I exhale, it floats away and I turn trying to catch it into a game.

"Knock, knock." Mom pops her head around my door and I snatch the piece of paper out of sight. Mostly because I'm embarrassed by the meal I'm making out of this. "I think I'm going to call it a night," she says. "I can't wait to be in my own bed." She's all kinds of dreamy, imagining her fluffy comforter and soft sheets as she says this.

"It's good to have you back." I mean it. Listening to

her putter around downstairs has been music to my ears. "Good night."

She looks at me, uncertain for a second, and then her bloodshot eyes spot my phone on the floor. It slipped off the bed about an hour ago, and I've yet to pick it up, a what's-the-point attitude oozing out of my pores.

"Uh-oh." Mom steps into my room. "Did he not text back?"

"No." I sit up, clear my throat, and braid my fingers together. "But then, he has nothing to text back to. I didn't send anything yet."

"I see," Mom replies. She scoops up my phone and perches on the bed. The faint scent of industrial-strength disinfectant and antiseptic still clings to her clothes.

"TV didn't adequately prepare me for talking to boys in real life."

Mom winces. "Is there maybe something I should have done?"

"No!" I exclaim. "Not at all." What's she supposed to do? Tag on some boy advice after she's done convincing me there isn't about to be an apocalypse? Talk me through dating etiquette once she's finished assuring me I won't choke on my food? "You've done everything."

Also, let's be honest, two weeks ago, the likelihood of

me ever talking to another human being beyond her, Dr. Reeves, and the staff over at Helping Hands was slim to none. At least for the foreseeable future. Two weeks ago there was still an infinite amount of time to talk to me about boys.

"Maybe I can help now. What are you thinking?"

My face crumples and I give her that look, the one that says *Have you got a spare sixty years while I take you through the list?*

"Right," she replies, reading my mind. "So what's your biggest fear?"

"I have two."

"Hit me."

I count them out with my fingers. "I don't know when the right time to text is. Like, I'm thinking today is too soon?"

"Not at all. Did you not see the size of that boy's grin as he left? Any time would be a good time." When she smiles, her nose scrunches. I like the way her long-since-dead Southern accent wakes up when she says *boy*.

"You lie."

"Hand to God. That boy wants you to text him as soon as poss, I guarantee it."

"Huh." My eyes go glassy and I get lost in thoughts

of Luke and his smile, his eyes, his arms, the way his shirt grabs his body. *Click.* Mom snaps her fingers in front of my face.

"You need me to get you a cold compress to go with that swoon?"

"Har. Har." But in all seriousness, that might not be a bad idea. It's hot in here; I have to shed my sweater.

"You were saying?"

"Right, the second thing . . . I'm afraid of saying the wrong thing."

She starts chuckling. Not quite the reaction I was hoping for. "Hey. Why are you laughing?" I give her a slight nudge with my shoulder. "This is serious."

"Ahh, baby," she says, running her palm down my cheek and giving it a slight pinch. "You realize what this is?"

"Horrible?"

"Perfectly normal," she says, wrapping *normal* in air quotes. That's a thing we do a lot around here. Both Mom and Dr. Reeves are forever exercising their fingers to defuse the definition. "There's not a person in the world at your age who doesn't worry about this stuff. Bad news? There is no one answer. You just have to be yourself and do what you think is best." She kisses my forehead and stands to leave.

"That's it?" Normally her advice is more helpful, more
. . . *more.*

"That's it." She shrugs, and her palms slap down
against her thighs. "You'll figure it out. Have fun. Be yourself. That's all you need." Her tone is teasing. I'm surprised
she doesn't slip in a wink before she disappears down the
hall.

"Ugh!" I exclaim, feigning an aneurysm and falling
back on my bed.

Why do people keep telling me to be myself? Honestly. It's like they've never even met me.

Hi :)

That's it. After a millennium, an ice age, a fricking era
of dissecting dialogue, that's the grand conversation starter
I settle on. I hit send and a fizzing current zips through
my veins, making my body buzz. Excitement is electric. It
reminds me of this one Halloween night, forever ago, when
me and a couple of kids from school dared one another to
knock on the door of the abandoned house beside Bennick
Marsh. Legend had it a witch lived there.

My phone bleeps to tell me the message has been sent,
and without thinking, I throw my cell to the end of the
bed. I don't know, maybe my subconscious was going for
out of sight, out of mind. It doesn't matter; I retrieve it

a half second later because it feels like a galaxy too far away.

My heart is in my throat, my intestines all tangled up. I'm not sure anymore if it's nerves or excitement. Maybe a bit of both. I place my phone on my pillow, flip over onto my stomach, and lean up on my elbows. With hawk eyes I watch my screen fade to black, then start willing it to light up with a text.

It doesn't.

The second hand on my clock goes round and round and round, sending my head into a spin. Reluctantly, I stop scrutinizing the dial and collapse into the crook of my arm. I don't have the latest cell, one of those that tell you when a text has been read. I'm completely in the dark. An agoraphobic obsessive-compulsive's most favorite place to be.

I'm listing forms of torture that would be infinitely more merciful than waiting for a boy to text back when, at last, my cell bleeps.

My fingers are slicker than oil as I unlock my phone and punch buttons to find the message: *Amy?*

Ouch. At least the message I sent him was better than that. A picture of a monkey scratching its butt would have been better; almost anything else would have been better.

One Thanksgiving my mom bought a deep-fryer. On Sunday mornings, she likes to load it with everything she can find in the fridge, and the smell of greasy food floods the air. It lingers for hours, clings to your skin, your hair, and the fabric of your clothes. It's sticky and gross and the only way to get rid of it is a scalding-hot shower and plenty of soap. I need that sort of shower right now.

Deep breaths.

My brain starts pitching ideas: Don't freak out. He couldn't have known it was me texting. I didn't sign my name and he doesn't have my number. So how could he have known? But then, he was obviously expecting a message from Amy. Amy, the girl whose name keeps cropping up. Why doesn't he already have her number? Should I be texting a boy who wants to talk to Amy? Should I be texting a boy whom Amy wants to talk to? Am I going to become one of those girl friends? You know, a girl that is his friend and nothing more? And if I am going to become that, will I have to hear stories about him and Amy?

I chew on my nails, pick up my phone, heart thumping fast, and hammer on the buttons that spell out my name. This time it takes me less than a minute to write my message.

It's Norah.

My thumb dances around the send button until I utilize a burst of courage and punch it. It's gone. *Message sent* flashes up on the screen. I hope to God I'm not texting someone else's boyfriend. I've seen love-triangle fights go down on my Metro feed. It never ends well.

I wait for Luke's reply. I wait. And I wait. And I wait some more.

He doesn't text back.

I watch my phone until 5:00 a.m., occasionally illuminating the screen to make sure my signal bar and battery are both still full. They are.

It's possible I've ingested enough of my own fingers to call myself a cannibal. They're so chewed I have trouble straightening them. I very much doubt every girl my age does this. This is perhaps bordering more on my unhealthy levels of panic.

By 5:30, I'm begging sleep to drag me under.

21

I T'S ONLY 7:10 WHEN my cruel mind forces my eyes open. The sun is firing lasers through my curtains. I duck under my comforter, make a blanket fort to shield myself from the scorching rays.

Despite what was probably one of the most restless sleeps in recorded history, I'm comfortable. My mattress is a giant marshmallow today, soft and squishy. I bear down and sink into it.

I'm contemplating pulling a sickie, blowing off studying, eating, and talking, to stay here all day, when I hear clattering coming from the kitchen below. Mom is like a bird, up at the crack of dawn and always puttering around in the garden. She loves growing things. There are forty-eight different colors of flowers in our garden. Eight of them are roses. She keeps them in a pattern that reminds me of a rainbow. I would like to be able to go over and smell them one summer.

With reluctant fingers I reach up, snatch my phone off the dresser, and drag it beneath the blankets. A streak of pain, like toothache, flashes across my chest when I illuminate the screen and discover there's no text waiting for me. I close my eyes, try to convince my brain that, unlike me, Luke goes to sleep at night. He probably hasn't even seen my message yet. But it's like trying to convince a kid that Brussels sprouts taste better than fries. Pointless.

I'm mentally listing the benefits of being cryogenically frozen when I hear Mom talking and my eyes pop back open. It sounds like she's conversing with a second someone. Maybe I'm mistaken. She likes to listen to the radio. Could be that. I narrow my eyes, because that's what you do when you want to listen closer. There are definitely two voices, and one of them belongs to a guy. A burst of simultaneous laughter bounds up the stairs, confirming that it's not the radio. She has company.

I morph into Nancy Drew, slip out of bed, pull on a sweater, and carefully inch open my door. Mom is explaining the accident to someone. A cop or an insurance guy, probably.

"Wow. It sounds scary. But you're okay?" Luke. Luke is in my kitchen. Talking to my mom.

I choke. My head turns into a tumble dryer, spinning fast and ferociously. Any upset over his first text message, and the subsequent lack of, vanishes. I was expecting a little more time to prepare myself for his return. His return. Our chat. My explanation of why I can't shake his hand.

I slip into a trance, stare at my feet as I walk across the hall to the bathroom and brush my teeth. The conversations that happen in my head are unbridled. There is no line of questioning left uncovered. I lose count of how many brushstrokes I make and have to start over six times. When I'm finally done, my pearly whites are so polished they squeak against my tongue.

I dab my mouth with a cucumber-fresh wet wipe — I can't use the towel on my face on account of this article I read about bathroom bacteria that breed in fabric.

"He's nice. He'll understand," I tell my reflection.

And if he doesn't?

"Then it's like Dr. Reeves's story. I don't need him as a friend." I wish my bottom lip weren't wobbling when I said that.

As casually as I can muster, I trot downstairs, take the last step twice, and saunter to the kitchen. I'm trying to channel breezy, floating, pretending like I don't even care that he's here.

I hope he can't see the strain on my face.

"Good morning, sweetheart," my mom chirps from beneath her oversize straw hat. She's wearing the teddy bear sweater. "Look who I found while I was out weeding that pesky patch of daisies in the front yard." Luke jumps up from his seat, knocking the table with his elbow and making his coffee cup rattle.

"Hi. My classes don't start till ten. There's this school administration thing going on," he says. "I was hoping maybe I'd catch you hanging out by your front door." I stare at him. He stares back. Something about his stance makes me think of a dog with its tail between its legs.

"Well, if you'll excuse me, I have more weeds to destroy," my mom says, picking up a trowel and swishing it around like a sword. She trots past me, plants a kiss on my cheek before heading out the front door.

Then silence.

Amy. That's the name of the enormous elephant he's carted into my kitchen. I'm okay with that. The longer we spend talking about the text debacle, the more likely he is to forget about my life debacle.

The tornado in my head picks up speed and I have to scratch. I need to stay busy. The silence is a lit burner and my panic attack is already starting to bubble. I exhale a breath, head to the fridge, pour myself a glass of orange juice, and take a sip. It makes me cringe. Freshly squeezed citrus and recently brushed teeth do not mix.

When I turn around, Luke is channeling his inner

psychic and attempting to read my mind, again. I wonder if he realizes that concentration won't make my skull any more transparent.

Does he want me to break the silence? I hope not. I'd be more comfortable sharing a swimming pool with a gaggle of potty-training toddlers.

"About the text . . ." he says. Half my brain is with him; the other half is straightening a tub of butter in the fridge. "You remember me telling you about Queen Amy?"

"You said she was hunting you." Ugh. My voice wobbles nearly as much as my knees.

"Right. See, she just broke up with this guy, Derek, and, well . . ." He pauses, sits down, squirms in his seat. "She keeps dropping not-so-subtle hints that she wants to hook up with me." I glare at a jar of mayonnaise, try to melt it into mush with my mind. "She is one insistent chick."

If he starts detailing said insistence, I might have to pick up this damn fridge and throw it. At least, I would if I weren't, you know, teetering on the precipice of panic.

"You don't have to tell me this. It's really none of my business." I fight to get the words out.

"Thing is, she kept calling, so I blocked her number. Last night, when you messaged, I didn't recognize the digits and just assumed it was her, using a friend's phone or something." I turn to him, relieved, though I'm sure I don't look it. Holding off anxiety feels like clenching your teeth for a prolonged period. My face aches; pressure is building at the back of my neck.

"I would have told you this last night, but my phone up and died on me. I don't know what's wrong with it. Anyways, I just needed you to know that I don't go around giving out my phone number to every girl I meet." He puts emphasis on the word *you*, a sentiment that I'm sure would make me feel like a million bucks under different circumstances.

More silence. Stretching out forever.

There's nothing to think about. There's nothing to do. My head whips around the room searching for a distraction, which is when it hits me that I've forgotten to breathe. So easily done.

"Norah. You don't look so good," Luke says, the tempo of his words rising.

My heart stops dead. It makes me lightheaded, and I have to grab the countertop to steady myself. I'm free-falling.

"Whoa. Are you okay?" Luke panics, lurches toward me, and snatches my arm. His fingers close around my wrist.

His flesh, pressed against mine. His palm is warm, damp. I think of pores, open pores on my arm, and his sweat settling on my skin. He sees me glari immediately, and lifts his hands in surrende

"Norah, honey. Relax, take a deep bre swans into the kitchen, 700 percent casua loses his shit all over our linoleum.

"I'm sorry," Luke splutters. "I thought she was going to fall."

"Don't worry about it." My mom dismisses his apology with a flick of her wrist then continues to wash the soil off her hands in the sink.

The kitchen is turning. Words are melding into one.

"Do you need me to do something?" Luke can't stand still. He's looking at my mom like he might be getting irritated by her lack of haste. Thing is, when you've lived this a thousand times, it becomes less of a trauma and more of a scraped-knee type situation. "Is there something I can do?"

Go home, I think.

"Stop worrying, for starters. I'm not sure I can handle two anxiety attacks at once." She smiles, all warmth. "Why don't you take a seat?" Mom links her arm through mine and leads me to a chair. "This will all be over in a few minutes."

Why in hell's bells would she offer him a seat? This is not a play, a production. He's the last person I want around to witness this. But she is a lover, a Beatles song, one of ose people who collect inspirational quotes. She thinks that all my baggage shouldn't matter. She thinks people should see past it, should see that I am more than what is wrong with me. The clouds in her sky are always rose-colored, which I know is a beautiful way to be. Alas, I have a mind that muddies everything. My skies aren't so pretty; more tainted with fear than tinted with whimsy.

I cling to the tabletop; the room is tipping upward like the *Titanic*.

"Norah, your lips are going purple. If you don't take a breath, you're going to pass out," Mom says, kneeling in front of me and resting her hands on the top of my legs. She rubs circles. "Come on, honey. Take a deep breath." She shows me how and I copy her. The rhythm feels unnatural. My chest fights it, tries to go faster, tries to go slower. A bead of sweat trickles down the back of my neck.

It goes on and on and on. I think maybe a century passes before my body gets so tired of twitching it comes to a complete stop. I'm still, calm, in the same way an ocean is before a big storm.

I can hear Mom talking, but a bubble of awkward silence is expanding around me. My shoulders hunch over, my legs shake; my head sags and a curtain of blond hair flops forward. I hide my face behind it, wishing I could stay cloaked like this forever.

Luke's army-brown boots are in my line of sight. His left foot bounces. I attempt to think myself invisible. But that never works and I'm still here.

"You need some water?" Mom asks, standing and patting my shoulder. I nod. Can't talk. My mouth is so dry I'm afraid my throat will split. "Luke, can I get you another coffee?"

"No. Thank you." There's a quaver in his voice. He's going to leave. He's freaked out, like maybe he just watched an exorcism or witnessed an alien attempting to adapt to oxygen. Any minute now he's going to excuse himself, get up, and go.

"Right. Well," Mom says, driving a sledgehammer into the growing wall of tension, "I think I'm going to head back out into the garden. Shout if you need me."

I'm shouting, but there's no sound coming out. It's all internal, tumbling around my chest like a breeze trapped in a bottle. I don't want Mom to go, but the *flip-flop* sound of her sandals fades into the distance.

22

I DON'T KNOW WHAT to say. Luke apparently doesn't either. The silence descends again. I keep my eyes fixed on his feet, which stay at a standstill for the longest time. Then they move. Stand up and shuffle away. I bite down hard on the inside of my mouth. Harder and harder, until my eyes fill with salt water and I can taste blood, but the pain I feel comes from my stomach. A tortured twist that I want to push on until it goes away. I keep my head down, watch the empty space on the floor.

I scrunch my eyes shut and when I force them open, Luke's feet have reappeared, facing me, less than a foot away. I catch a breath, keep it trapped in my windpipe. He crouches, and, very slowly, like a rock sailing through space, his fist glides toward me, maneuvers its way past the blond curtain, and hovers in midair, just above my knees, right under my nose.

U OK? It's written on the back of his hand in big, black letters.

It's possible I began this sprint before the starting pistol sounded.

My head snaps up and my eyes land on his impossibly adorable frown, his hundred-watt smile turned upside down. I want to coo like you do when you see pictures of baby bunnies snuggling fluffy kittens. Instead, I nod, my dropped jaw flopping around.

"I'm sorry," he says. "I didn't mean to upset you."

"No." I don't shout, but I want to. His apology is beyond unnecessary. I hate that he's feeling guilty for trying to help. "It wasn't your fault." I consider elaborating but then bail, decide he's probably consumed enough craziness for one day.

There will always be an excuse.

I'm not sure exactly what he saw. I study his face, try to figure it out. I don't remember what I did, how bad it got. That happens sometimes; panic attacks have a tendency to suck away moments of my memory. I run a mental check. My throat isn't grainy like it gets when vocal tics put in an appearance, so hopefully I didn't make any starving-zombie sounds. My shoulders ache, which means there was probably some intense jerking around.

The good news is there's no drool on my shirt, so at the very least I remembered to swallow. *Sarcastic high-*

fives. It gets hard to look at him, and my chin starts to dip again.

"I'm so embarrassed." I don't know what else to say. I wish he would fill the room with words so I don't have to.

"You've got nothing to be embarrassed about."

Okay. I wish he would fill the room with words that are true.

"I really wish you hadn't seen that. I didn't want you to see me all freaking out, looking like I'm being electrocuted or something." I sniff, scrub stray tears off my cheeks with the sleeve of my sweater. I'm tragic, an unkempt gravestone, what a sorrowful Shakespeare sonnet would look like in human form.

"You've been trying to keep this a secret?" Luke asks carefully, testing his weight on my mind with only the tips of his toes.

"No. Maybe. I mean . . . yes. I did. I have. I was . . ." Everything seems so complicated, like a Rubik's Cube with twenty-six sides. No matter how much my mind turns over, my explanations won't make any sense. It's too much; there are too many facets.

"What if . . ." Luke sits back down in his chair. "What if I told you I've seen this happen to you before?"

He's joking, being ironic. I can't figure out how exactly, but there's a punch line coming.

"I'd tell you it was a case of mistaken identity." Knuckle meets teeth, and I start to chew, because although what he just told me is improbable, he's looking kind of serious.

"I have a confession to make," he says, hissing a note through his teeth like he's just been nipped under the arm.

Is this the irony? Is he about to fess up to being the serial killer/stalker/maniacal clown with a cleaver my mind wanted me to believe he was? He must see the look of horror wash over my face, note my features being pulled into a Munch-esque composition.

"Wait." Luke chokes out a nervous laugh. "That sounded a lot less creepy inside my head. Let me explain. Remember the day I moved in?" he asks, shifting to the edge of his seat.

That day. It was a Monday, a doctor's-appointment day. I remember labeled boxes, his boxes. I remember the blackbird bouncing on my windowsill. I remember the stack of books that left me feeling out of sorts.

"I saw you having a hard time getting across the grass to your car." He whispers it, like he's telling me secrets.

"You saw that?"

He turns a slight shade of pink, rubs the back of his neck, and stares out the kitchen window.

"I wasn't spying." For a moment he looks ten years

younger. "I was hoping to get your attention. You see, I thought we were flirting."

"Hang on a second." I'm confused. It's like being introduced to AP Calculus all over again. "You mistook an anxiety attack for flirting? How?" Trying to figure out which part of my harpooned-squid impression could be considered anything other than tragic.

"No. It was before that, by the window. When you waved at me."

Maybe he gets high. I wonder if he sparked up before he came over here. A bong for breakfast. If that's the case, he needs to leave. I'm afraid of all common-sense inhibitors.

"I never waved at you."

"Yes, you did."

"No. I didn't."

"You did. I was carrying a box to my bedroom. You knocked on the window and then waved at me."

The memory crashes into me like a runaway train, almost knocking me off my feet. That damn blackbird.

"You remember," Luke says. He must see the recognition flash across my face. Smiling, all smug, he sits back in his chair, folds his arms across his chest. Oh, breaking this to him is going to be sweeter than cherry pie.

"Um, sorry to burst your bubble there, Romeo, but I wasn't waving at you," I tell him.

"Yes . . . you were." But he's not so sure anymore. "Weren't you?"

I shake my head.

"Then who?"

A wicked smile pulls at my lips. Luke smiles too. "I was having a bad day, and there was this bird bobbing around on my windowsill outside. I knocked on the glass to scare it away—"

"You were waving at a bird?"

"Exactly," I say, working hard to stifle a giggle. He laughs and my knees go a good kind of weak.

"Well, this is awkward. Again."

"Is that why you came over to introduce yourself?" Anxiety is a million miles away as I flop back down onto my chair. Elbows planted on the table, chin resting in my hands. It's like we're old friends having a good gossip. He leans on the table too, folds his arms in front of him, wincing and groaning, before falling forward and burying his face in them.

"Yes. Of course it is. There you were, this cute girl waving at me. There was no way I was going to just ignore you." His words are muffled.

We're both laughing. This moment right here, this is the best normal moment I've had in the past four years. I want to put it in a box and keep it forever.

"Hey." He turns his head to look at me. The light pouring into the kitchen catches his eyes and makes them flash bright green. My heart squeezes. "Are you afraid of going outside?" All good things must come to an end. But I guess rarity is what makes a perfect moment perfect.

My turn to fold my arms, fall forward, and bury my face.

The word *yes* is so small and simple. I can say it in four different languages—including French. After mastering *Mom* when I was a baby, *yes* was the second thing I learned how to say. But right now, I've forgotten how, and all I can do is nod.

"I'm sorry," he says.

"What for?"

"I don't know. I mean, I've watched you go through that twice now. It looks painful and exhausting. It's not nice to see someone suffer so much, you know?"

The general populace is compassionate. Maybe that's not quite the bullshit statement I first thought it was. I turn my face to look at him. He throws a soft smile my way; I catch it and smile back.

"You don't like being touched?"

I shake my head. Pick at a scab on my wrist.

"But you're okay if your mom touches you?" There is no accusation in his tone. At all. His curiosity is just taking a gentle stroll around the mysterious workings of my mind, but guilt gurgles in my stomach anyway. It sounds awful, like I've concluded he's going to hurt me or something.

"It's not you. It's about feeling safe," I tell him. Hives and concentrated patches of heat are blistering on my body. "I mean, I guess it's about you a little bit . . . or anyone I don't know. It's confusing . . . complicated." It's like trying to talk underwater; nothing coming out of my mouth sounds like it should. "We're still working on figuring it out."

"Norah." Luke's hands go up. "It's okay. Am I grilling you too much?"

"No. It's just, my head works so fast sometimes. I want to explain it, but most of the time I don't understand it."

"You're shaking a little," he says, looking at my hands. I retract them, pull them back up into my sweater sleeves, and tuck them underneath my knees. "I know this is tough to talk about, but will you let me know if there's anything else you're afraid of? I don't want to scare you again." His voice is so soft, you'd think he was reading me a bedtime story. I consider offering him a list then remember he has a life to get back to.

"Everything," I confess in a whisper. "I'm afraid of everything."

He looks so loaded with sympathy there's a real danger of him joining me for a dip in my ice-cold pool of depression.

"You know what scares me?" he says, sitting up suddenly. Something in the air shifts. His voice is light. It makes the somber fog scatter.

"What?"

"Spiders. Not the small ones." He doesn't quite beat his pulsing pectorals. "The big ones. Anything equal to or more than the span of an Oreo." He shudders. "I can't handle them."

This guy makes me smile so easily. I have to wonder if his cologne is cut with laughing gas.

We sit at the table until nine thirty. Talking nonsense about movies and music. He likes horror, like me, and if anybody asks, he listens to all the latest bands, but secretly, his heart belongs to jazz. He talks about musicians I've never even heard of and does a pretty convincing playing-the-saxophone impression. He prefers comics to books, and when he graduates from high school he wants to study fine arts.

It's weird. I know he goes out, has friends, throws banging parties and the whole school shows up, but his mouth moves at light speed, like he hasn't spoken to a single soul in more than a million years.

"I gotta go," he says, glancing at the retro Casio on his wrist. "Need to drop my phone at the store before school starts, see if they can fix it. I might not be able to text for a while. Just so you know. I don't want you to think I'm ignoring you."

I wasn't thinking that—not until he said it, anyway. Doubt sneaks up behind me like some horny dude at a disco, its arm snaking around my waist, wrapping me in its cruel embrace.

I wonder if I'm ever going to see him again. The last hour and a half rolls through my head; everything I've said, done, is highlighted. I'm looking for anything that might have put him off coming over again. *All of it*, I conclude. Doubt hugs me tighter.

"We'll chat soon, though," Luke tells me. But all I can focus on is the lack of a specific date. When is soon? My mind is pushing the idea that soon is never. Is his phone even broken? My heart splinters, but I refuse to let the anguish creep into my face. I stand up, swallow down all the feelings. They taste like ash and scratch like nails.

"Catch you later," he says, signing off with a half wave.

"Bye," I tell him. And with that, he leaves.

I'm joined in the kitchen a few moments later by Mom. She's carrying a tray of scrawny, scrunched-up seedlings. They're exhausted, like the world was too much for their fragile little frames so they went to sleep instead. I can relate.

"I like him," Mom says, squirting the plant graveyard with some of her "special mixture." I'm not sure what she puts in it, but it gives her dying flowers a new lease on life. For another week, anyway.

I wonder if it would be safe for me to use in the shower.

I don't respond to her Luke comment. I'm too busy pondering whether or not I'm going to see him again.

"Are you okay?" she asks.

"I'm fine," I reply, fixing a plastic smile on my face. "I'm going to go and read for a bit."

I skip to my bedroom and turn into a troll the minute I close the door. My shoulders slump forward and my steps get heavy. I thump down onto my mattress, grab my laptop instead of a book. I'm not really sure why, but I scan through my search history and click on one of the kissing videos. Instead of the cute couple wearing matching sweaters and strolling through an auburn wilderness, I see me and Luke. There are none of my issues stacked up between us, stopping him from clasping my hand.

I spend the rest of the afternoon reading Plath and wondering if Mom will let me paint my bedroom black.

23

ANOTHER MONDAY MORNING ARRIVES, but, for the first time since June, it looks like it's going to rain. We're currently cruising toward the end of September, so you could say it's been a while.

I try but fail not to think about Luke and how it's been four long days since I spilled my secret . . . four long days since I last saw him.

After breakfast, Mom kisses me goodbye and jets off to work. Old habits die hard, and I tiptoe toward the porch window, teeth mashed together tight, because everyone knows that makes your movements more cautious. I peel back the curtain and scan Luke's driveway for his truck. It's still there. He hasn't left for school yet.

I exhale a breath that, by rights, should set off our earthquake alarm. "Effect and outcome," I remind myself, just like in Dr. Reeves's story about the girl who couldn't catch a break with the football player but still got her happily-ever-after.

My happily-ever-after isn't quite a husband, kids, and a house in suburbia. I just want some rain. See, when you live in a place that only puts out twenty inches of rain a year, it does become essential to savor every last soaking-wet second. Plus, I'm not skipping out on world-watching because I'm afraid of seeing Luke. This is the only outside I get to see.

Did I really just think those things?

Apparently so. And I must mean them because I'm already opening the front door. I slide down, sit on the floor, stretch my legs out in front of me, and wince at how pasty they are, like someone spilled milk. If I hadn't been traumatized by FakeTanGoneWrong.com, I would totally invest.

Gray clouds, thicker than smoke from a bonfire, clot in the sky. I breathe in the fresh air. Our front yard is a Monet. Not quite as colorful as the back, but still vibrant and beautiful.

Across the road, the Trips line their lawn with tubs and bottles. They catch the rain, recycle the water. It's why Mom won't drink anything at their house that's not boiled.

Malcolm Trip stands looking up at the sky, hands on hips, smiling like he just fell in love for the first time. He's draped in an eye-bleedingly bright caftan. Natural fibers, of course. It looks like a sack, makes me itch from all the way over here. He spots me and waves.

Mom says Malcolm reminds her of my dad, a.k.a. some

man who knocked her up at twenty-one and took off before I was even born. I've never met him, but he wrote me once. I didn't read the letter. Well, you don't look through a stranger's photo albums if you don't have to, right? You don't know the people in those pictures. Same principle. I don't know the man who put pen to paper either.

The rain falls slowly at first, huge drops plopping down on the ground, making the blistering concrete fizz. I love the way it smells. Hot. Like a coal fire the day after it's gone out.

In seconds the rain falls so thick I can barely see two feet in front of me. I lean my head back against the door, close my eyes, and listen to the sound of Triangle Crescent being cleaned, the water a soothing balm for everything that's been burned. Some of the splashes that hit the porch spray my bare legs and I shudder.

The pictures I love looking at the most on my Metro feed are the ones with almost-kissing couples standing out in the rain. Now, it's possible that's because my OCD likes the sanitation implied by running water, but beyond that, the part of me that cries every time I read *Pride and Prejudice* thinks it's wonderfully romantic.

I'm contemplating never moving from this spot when my phone cuckoos to notify me of social media updates.

Again, I've decided to stay away from the Metro until my mood lifts, or at least until I can figure out how to remove Luke from my mind without excessive intake of alcohol. It's all the sloppy status updates. Apparently everyone fell in love this weekend and all they want to do is talk about it. The fawning and excitement over their new romantic endeavors just reminds me that Luke witnessed the full force of my crazy before he left last week. I want to fork my eyes out. In other news, Cupid is an asshole.

With next to no enthusiasm I lift my phone. I'm about to dismiss the notification when the name on my screen catches my attention.

Luke has requested my friendship.

My thumb can't work fast enough. Pressing all the wrong buttons, I unlock my screen and open the page. His avatar makes me pause, push a hand against my heart to calm its erratic rhythm. The accept button is bright red. I push it and his page opens up automatically.

Cut to ten minutes later, and I can't seem to bring myself to snoop around. I feel like I'm going to touch the wrong part of the screen or drop my phone and star one of his posts by mistake. Hell, I'm afraid I'll exhale too hard and accidentally friend his mom. This is so unlike me. Usually I zip around the Metro like someone who's just gotten her learner's permit. I've never had a problem playing around people's profiles before. Maybe I'm having so much trouble because I know I'm prying. Prying with intent. Ugh. That sounds like a criminal offense. Something people go to prison for. I swear someone got arrested for doing that exact same thing on an episode of *Hollywood Cops* last week. Or was that supplying with intent? Intent to supply? Whatevs. This isn't going to happen. I need to regroup. Get some orange juice, eat some ice.

The rain has stopped, and the clouds are being torn apart by giant chunks of bright blue sky. It's a different color than it was before. Fresher somehow. Like it needed the twenty-minute reprieve to charge its batteries so it could beam bluer.

Across the road, the Trips emerge from their house and start carrying their buckets of bounty inside. That's when I spot the car.

My mind camera takes all the mental snapshots it needs.

As an avid unofficial member of the neighborhood watch, I pay attention to the vehicles that visit our little corner of paradise. Well, you have to be observant. What if a robbery was to take place and the police were looking for leads? What if my account of, say, a black Lincoln circling our road twice before disappearing was just the break in a case they needed?

Paranoia is like that kid in high school, the one who

runs up behind you and yanks your pants down around your ankles. Paranoia enjoys making you look stupid.

I've never seen this car around here before. It's on another level from Luke's dad's crusty camper. This car is compact, champagne gold, with a black roof that looks like it folds down. The kind of car that would cost you a kidney or the sweet soul of your firstborn.

The windows are blacked out. I'm ogling it with zero discretion when the driver's door pops open and a leggy blonde steps out. I'm not saying she's gorgeous, but the previously absent sun chooses this exact moment to explode in the sky.

She looks up, smiles gratitude at the burning spotlight, then slides a pair of huge white-rimmed sunglasses off her head and down onto her nose. Her hair matches the color of her car. She runs her fingers through it, shakes her head a little, and I have to remind myself I'm not watching a shampoo commercial.

She makes her way across the road toward my side of the street. This girl doesn't walk—she struts. Puts every inch of her body to work so her shoulders stay straight and stiff, but her hips sway from side to side.

I want to be her. I don't care how much it costs; I would pay it to have her tan and high cheekbones.

Blondie stops at the edge of Luke's driveway, reaches

into her purse, and pulls out a bedazzled compact. With a soft shade of pink, she traces the lines of her lips. My mouth does that mimicking thing, morphs into the same squashed O shape as hers because I'm concentrating too hard. Cork wedges signal her ascent up Luke's driveway and I feel myself shrinking.

I look down at my knees, try to get a handle on my thoughts, but they're running wild, making me dizzy.

Please let her be his sister. Please.

"Hi there." At first I think she's talking to whoever has answered the door. "Excuse me. Hello." Her voice is louder, piqued, like she's frustrated. I look up to see her standing by the boxwood bush, sunglasses raised, which catches me off-guard. It makes no sense. She's having to squint because the sun is shining in her eyes. Why wouldn't she just keep the sunglasses on?

"Is that a *yes?*" she asks. And I realize that while I was trying to figure out the sunglasses situation, she's been talking to me. I have no clue what question she asked. None. The shaving rash under my arms burns as I start to perspire.

"I'm sorry. I didn't hear you." My reply carries for about half a yard before it turns to vapor and vanishes.

"Huh?" she says, holding a hand behind her ear.

"What'd ya say? Wait." She thrusts her ear-trumpet hand at me like a stop sign. "I'm coming over."

Shit. Why do people keep making me converse? I just wanted to watch the rain. I think about protesting. Dream about protesting, because, let's be honest, there's more chance of hell freezing over than there is of that.

I clamber to my feet as she strides over the bushy barrier between Luke's house and mine, one shiny bronzed stem at a time. The boxwood must scratch her because before she heads over to me, she scowls at it, and I wonder how it doesn't burst into flames.

She gets bigger as she clomps closer. My heart jumps into my throat. I turtle up, withdraw as much of my body into my sweater as possible. My arms abandon the sleeves entirely and wrap tightly around my waist. But before the blonde can make it to me, Luke jogs out of his front door, school bag slung over his shoulder and what looks like a sandwich hanging from his mouth. I wonder if it's loaded with cream cheese, applesauce, and mayonnaise. We both look at him. He freezes when he sees Blondie, then his eyes travel a few inches farther, and he smiles when he sees me.

He looks so good in a button-down blue and white shirt, sleeves rolled up to his elbows, and a length of black cord around his neck.

"Never mind," the blonde says, turning around.

"Amy. What're you doing here?" Luke asks, dry-swallowing a chunk of bread.

Wow. My self-esteem, already beaten black-and-blue, coughs up a lung.

Queen Amy. Of course it is. Except for her hair being a little lighter, this is the chick in her Metro profile picture.

Amy holds out her hand to him. Luke rolls his eyes before grabbing it and helping her hop back over the box-wood.

"Morning, Neighbor." He's talking to me. I just about muster the strength to wave.

Amy clucks her tongue. At me, maybe? I don't know. And I don't care. Can't care. Luke is smiling at me, and it doesn't look forced or fake. It's warm, welcoming, exactly the same smile he flashed my way pre any mention of my mental health.

I get goose bumps, feel a warmth spread through the pit of my stomach.

"Anyways." Amy dismisses my presence with a flap of her hand. "I thought maybe I could give you a ride to school," she says, straightening her shoulders and lifting her chin so high it grazes the sky.

"Thanks, but I already have a ride," he replies.

"I know, but I thought we could go to school together.

Maybe grab a coffee before class?" She bats her lashes, puts a hand on his arm and runs it up and down, over his biceps. He looks down on her, and she wrinkles her button nose and flutters her lashes some more. "Please, just a quick cup?" The irritation that was crinkling his brow is replaced by indecision.

He's not going to refuse.

How could he?

Why would he?

It's not like I'm ever going to be the girl that runs her hand up and down his arm, cajoling him into going for coffee, right? And he knows it, must be thinking it. It's too much, the final nail in my inadequacy coffin. I'm done.

24

I SLINK BACK INSIDE the house and close the door. I'm angry.

Not at her, not really. Not at her, not at him, not at them. I'm angry at myself for wanting to touch him so badly and remembering that the last time he put his hand on me, I almost had a stroke.

The fear of going through Luke's Metro profile is dust. Curiosity is maniacal, controlling me from the inside. My phone is out of my pocket before my butt even hits the couch. I open his page, don't hesitate to scroll down the screen and find any "connection" announcements. As suspected, Amy "Queen" Cavanaugh is in the first group of connections he made. I hit her picture and it takes me to her profile.

Fate could save me from the torture I'm about to inflict. Her page could be locked and I wouldn't see anything but the promo stuff she pins.

Fate hates me.

Her profile pops up and I hit her photo tab. There are pictures of Amy sunbathing with her friends, riding horses, cuddling lions on safari in Africa. Pictures of dinners out, of pool parties and boat parties. There's even a photo of her sitting on the back of a motorcycle. I narrow my eyes, lift the phone for a closer look. The guy she's straddling in the motorbike pic looks like Grammy-winning rock god Brock Samson. No. Effin'. Way.

My self-esteem packs its bags and quits me completely. She's grinning like a Cheshire cat in every shot. Loving her life. Living it.

I blink green, breathe green, taste sour grapes on my tongue.

I don't know what has me more jealous, the Hollywoodesque life that she has or the fact that I never went horseback riding before I got sick. I didn't have time to catch a tan that wasn't filtered through windows. I never went to a concert, let alone snuggled up to a lead singer on the back of his bike. There was always going to be time for that later. Always.

My hands are shaking. I flick back to Luke's profile, blow up a picture of him, and spend a few seconds staring at it. My thumb touches down on his face. Maybe he was smiling at me because he felt sorry for me. Maybe it was just to piss Amy off. Maybe he wanted her to think there was something between us so she'd leave him alone. I pick at the cuticle on my thumb, peel it back and make it bleed.

I'm done with today, I decide, tossing my phone on the coffee table and curling up into a ball on the couch. I'm all pout, being devoured by my diva counterpart as I tug a patchwork throw from underneath me and cocoon myself in a blanket fort.

Except it's too stuffy. My breathing is coming thick and fast. It feels like someone's got a fire going under here.

It's frustration, is what it is. I can't close down and shut the world out like I could before. Great. Something else I can add to my ever-growing list of new experiences. Except this isn't one of those times when it feels like I just won a blue ribbon. Shutting out things is essential; it's my Swiss Army knife, my flask of water, the compass that points me home.

I'm pissed. I throw the blanket off. I may not have a horse at hand or a buff rocker and his bike, but the sun is blazing right now. There is no reason why I can't step out into the backyard and snap a selfie of me catching a few rays. I'm always whining about how pale I am. Maybe some color will make me look more alive.

Light bulb. Maybe I can use this urge, this growing mound of motivation, to create a new root, a different thought pattern. Right?

Right, I decide, and march up the stairs.

I know I have a bikini top somewhere. It doesn't look like Amy's; all white with a gold, half-moon-shaped, fancy-button thing on the front.

The first place I look is my underwear drawer. It makes sense I'd keep it here because a bikini top is not unlike a bra. I dig through bunches of socks, maybe a million pairs of tights, briefs that are anything but, and a couple of sports bras before I become acutely aware of how comfortable and safe everything I own is. Everything is white or black, no frills or patterns because that's what's comfortable. And I can't be worrying about itchy lace or a cutting thong while I'm trying to manipulate the big bad world.

God. That's a depressing thought pattern. How did I not notice that my illness has taken over my wardrobe too? I pick up a pair of once-white leg warmers that have gone a gross shade of dishwater gray. This. This drawer is a visual representation of my life, I think, as I volley the leg warmers into the trash can at the end of my bed.

I find the bikini top scrunched up amid thick woolen socks. It's plain black and clips around the back of my neck. I think I got it free with a magazine. I know I haven't bought one while I've been sick, and I didn't have any boobs to put in it before that.

Leaving the safe, warm fabric of my sweater, I slip the

top on, handling the clasp like I'm wearing Mickey Mouse gloves. I pull my hair back into a bun and head to the bathroom for sunscreen.

We have two different kinds stockpiled in the bathroom cabinet, one with SPF 20 and one with SPF 50. I read the backs of both bottles like they're how-to guides on defusing a bomb. I opt for smothering myself in the stronger stuff and head back downstairs fifty shades whiter than I was when I went up.

Several panic attacks and a perpetually tight stomach have seen me lose a few pounds over the past couple of weeks. I hug my hips, notice more sharp edges on my body than usual. In conclusion, I look ridiculous. Maybe I should skip sunbathing, I think as my fingers curl around the door handle. Who wants to see a picture of a bag of bones in a bikini anyway? *That's not a good enough reason for you not to try*, I can hear Dr. Reeves saying in my head. She would tell me, *Don't do this for the picture, forget that. Do it because you want it.*

Need it, I mentally correct as I pull open the door.

I'm a wave breaker to the wall of heat that hits me. It's so warm it sends a shiver down my spine. The sun is a slice of lemon. A soft hue, like fine smoke, blurs the contrast of Mom's blooming garden. The scent of flowers hums as it sails across the patio and nearly knocks me off my feet. For a second, I wonder if I've accidentally opened the door to an English country garden in the nineteenth century.

The space is big enough for a swimming pool. I know this because my grandma wanted to buy us one before she died. Alas, Mom said we didn't need it. At the time I thought it was because she hated fun. I later found out she'd had a chat with the Trips and they'd guilt-tripped her about our carbon footprint.

My mind is whirring, already building a case to keep me inside. I lift my eyes; there's not a single cloud out now. But I'm not really surveying the weather. I'm checking for planes because I've read about them falling from the sky. I eye the trees because I know they can topple over too. Earthquakes are what worry me the most. I can't see them coming. And then there's the spiders, and snakes. Anything that can force me to step away from the house to visit a hospital is a major cause for concern.

Thing is, my survival instinct seems to have been malfunctioning since the day this all started. It's pretty messed up, probably makes zero sense to a person with normal thought processes, but I'm not sure I could trust myself to leave the house for help, not even if my life depended on it.

My bare foot hovers over the mosaic flagstones that mark out our patio. I wriggle my toes in the fresh air, testing the outside, as if too much exposure will scorch my skin.

Fifteen minutes later, my toes are cramping and I haven't made it any farther. My heart's been hammering out Slipknot songs and I can't feel the right side of my face. I'm tired, frustrating myself to a dry whimper.

Screw it. Screw this. Screw thought patterns. Screw roots. Screw Amy's photos. Screw everything.

Life was never this complicated before life got involved.

I slam the door shut on the world outside, storm back through the kitchen and into the hall, where I'm forced to stop dead. The front door is wide open and Luke is on the porch. I can't be sure, but I think I see the smudge of a champagne car, careening away behind him.

The door is open.

Why is the door open?

My first reaction is to eye my surroundings. The door is open because someone must have come through it.

"Hi . . ."

"Mom?" I cut Luke off to call up the stairs. He stays silent as I wait for a reply. "Mom? Are you home?"

"Norah. Is everything okay?" he says after my second call gets no response.

"Why is the door open?" I'm twitching, scanning our

open-plan living room. I grab the throw off the back of the couch and pull it around my shoulders.

"I can answer that."

I turn to him, glowering, fully expecting him to cop to opening the door and invading our house.

"Before, when you went inside, it bounced back when you tried to shut it," Luke replies with a nonchalant shrug.

"No," I scoff. Ridiculous notion. He's made it up. "No. I always make sure it's locked before I walk away." It's routine, robotic. Like how a dancer remembers every single step in her recital.

"O-k-a-y," he says, drawing out the word. "But maybe this one time you forgot."

"No," I say, marching over to the door. At this point, I'm willing to believe witchcraft and wizardry are more responsible for this mishap than I am. I look at the lock, see that the bolt, the small sticky-out bit that's supposed to slot into a hole in the frame and keep the door closed, isn't poking out.

No.

I don't forget to check locks. The latch clicks, and, ever since Helping Hands dude came into my house uninvited, I hit the bolt.

This can't be right.

It's either black magic or broken.

But it is right.

I run my hand over and over it. My fingers disappear into the groove where the latch is tucked away. Because that's where it stays when you hold down the button and twist. The very reason we had it installed was that every time Mom went to collect the mail, she got locked out in her pajamas.

I remember doing that, holding down the button and twisting. Keeping the latch hidden away while I watched the rain, just in case some freak thing happened and I found myself outside, unable to get back in. I knead an eye with the heel of my hand.

"I can't remember checking it or throwing the bolt. Why can't I remember checking it?" My nails creep down my thigh and start scratching at skin. Another new/scary/terrifying thing to add to my list. Before long, I'm going to need a wheelbarrow to lug this list around.

"Norah. It's okay."

"It's not okay," I snap. How can it be okay? I don't forget to do things that make me feel safe.

I don't.

Except I did.

Who even am I?

25

Luke steps inside, arms open, but he looks less like he's trying to touch me and more like he's trying to round up a flock of spooked sheep.

"What are you doing?" I ask him, doubling over. I know there's a science to this whole head-between-your-knees bit, but all it does is make me dizzy, so as quickly as I'm down, I'm back up.

"Well," he says, dropping his arms. "I'm trying not to touch you but also kind of freaking out that you're going to faint."

"Faint?" What is this, a Brontë novel?

"You know . . . pass out, hit the deck, kiss the floor?"

"Yeah, but you said *faint.*" I lower my butt onto the bottom step of the stairs, breathing like I'm giving birth.

"Huh." Luke lifts his chin, tucks his hands behind his back, and starts strolling around the hall like a patrolling police officer in Victorian London. "You don't seem impressed by my outdated idioms."

My eyes follow him across the floor, but I keep the

door in my peripheral vision, hope it picks up on the I'm-watching-you shade I'm throwing its way.

"I prefer modern slang myself," I reply.

"Word," he says with a grin so glorious I feel sorry for anyone in the world who will never get to see it.

When you take in air too quickly, it tends to have a hair-dryer effect on your throat. Right now I could store sand in my mouth without compromising its consistency, but I'm not sure I can make it to the kitchen for a drink. I lean left, check the distance from the banister to the fridge.

"You need something?" Luke asks, killing the flirt that was apparent in his voice a few seconds ago. I can't ask him to get me some orange juice. Can I? No. It's too weird. He's not working a shift at a restaurant.

"No, thank you." I grab hold of the banister with both hands, squeeze it so tight I'm in danger of getting blisters. But when I heave my body up, my legs let go of a hell-no jerk. Luke lunges forward as my butt thumps back down, only this time I'm sitting on the second step from the bottom. That was embarrassing. And there's no Mom here to buffer the impending awkwardness. Luke buries his hands in his pockets, I'm assuming because he doesn't trust them not to reach for me a third time.

"Norah, not that I'm not loving this gallant display of independence, but could you please let me go and get you what you need? Please?" He might be about ready to throw himself at my feet.

"I could use a glass of orange juice," I tell him, but talk to my curling toes.

"Orange juice. Right. Where would I find that?" he calls as he heads off toward the kitchen.

"It's in the fridge."

"Okay," he says and then starts humming. I hear him opening and closing cabinets. "Hey, Neighbor, where do you hide your glasses?"

"Above the microwave," I reply.

"Gotcha. Is it okay if I pour myself one?"

"Sure." I smile because this must mean he's staying awhile.

Luke starts singing. Not lyrics, notes. A string of *la*s and *dee*s and *da*s as he strolls around my kitchen. I'm imagining him juggling tumblers like a bartender in LA, shaking the carton of orange juice to the left and then to the right.

A couple of seconds later he falls silent and strolls back into the hall.

"For Madame," he says, overenunciating. His fake French accent is adorable, almost as cute as his fake British. He hands me one of the two drinks he's carrying, studying the exchange carefully so we don't connect.

"Dinner and a show," I tease. "Now I'm impressed."

Maybe I'm not teasing so much as I am flirting. Talking while I glance up at him through my lashes and flashing a coy smile. I've definitely seen Mom work this face on Dave the delivery guy before. She makes eyes at him every time he drops off a box of sample rocks.

Luke throws me a one-shouldered shrug. "What can I say? It was only going to be a matter of time." He makes his way up the stairs, pressing his chest tight against the wall so he doesn't graze me. I flush when I realize I'm checking out his butt. Luke takes a seat on the fourth step, leans forward on his knees, and smiles at me.

"Shouldn't you be heading to school?" I ask, a little reluctantly.

"Nah. I can cut. I'll just tell them I had a medical emergency."

"You're going to use my medical emergency as an excuse to cut class?"

He shrugs again. "Cut class, maybe . . . but I'm kind of hoping I can use it to hang around with you for a little bit. Do you mind?"

Moral dilemma. Do I argue and tell him he should get to class, or do I keep my mouth shut and sit here drinking orange juice with him?

No contest. I bite my lip, trying to hold back the grin that's threatening to expand and swallow my face.

"So, have you ever met the Great and Powerful Amy Cavanaugh before?" Luke asks.

"No. Today was the first time."

"And how was it?"

I swish the orange juice around in my glass. The box claims it's pulp-free, but you can never be too careful. "Most people scare and/or intimidate me. She was no exception."

He gets lost for a second, staring vacantly at the swirling pattern on our wallpaper.

"How does it work?" he asks. "I mean, have you always been afraid?" I look at his face and see a bubbling stew of kindness and sincerity with just a dash of curiosity.

"You don't want to hear all this." I'm not sure if I'm saying that for him or me.

"Yes, I do. I want to know who you are."

I want to make progress. I want to, *should* do some explaining. It's not like it's a secret anymore. He's already seen me melt down a handful of times in our brief friendship, and he's still coming over, asking questions, sitting next me on a staircase drinking orange juice. That has to count for something. Plus, once I know how he feels, I'll know. Constantly trying to guess what he'll make of my so-called life seems to be destroying my brain cells. Literally. Mom and I were doing the crossword at breakfast this morning and I couldn't answer a single clue. That never happens, but I started sketching cartoon hearts and totally checked out.

The buttons in my brain that control the crazy must think it's time to open up too — at least, they can't seem to find a counterargument strong enough to make my mouth stay shut.

"I wasn't always afraid. I mean, sometimes I might have closed down a little, or preferred my own company to anyone else's. I wasn't scared, but maybe I was shy."

"Did something happen?" The one question I wish I could answer in the affirmative. Not that I want some tragic story to tell. I just mean, it would make it easier to explain to everyone else. There are no skeptical questions for the guy who developed a fear of reptiles after he was bitten by a snake.

"No. Nothing."

"So, you just woke up one day and were afraid to leave the house?"

The fingers of my free hand curl around the lip of the step. I hold on tight, worried the force of his question will blow me away.

"Wait . . ." he says, shaking his head. "That came out wrong. I'm sorry. I didn't mean for it to sound so . . . dismissive." Regret streaks his forehead, and a nervous hand, fidgeting around like it's forgotten what it's used for, slaps his knee. He's being sincere. I can recover.

"It's okay," I tell him, smiling. If I was brassy enough, I'd throw in a wink. "At least you didn't ask me why I don't 'just get over it.' Or, my personal favorite, 'Why don't you just not think about it?'" I click my tongue, fire finger guns at the empty space in front of me. "Sure. I'll get right on that," I say to all the hundreds of skeptical voices that seem to think I'm living like this for fun.

Luke tucks his hands between his legs, presses his knees tightly together so they make a prison, and I wonder if maybe it's because he wants to reach out and touch me. Save me from a different kind of fall.

"Does that happen a lot?"

"It's happened a few times. Friends—former friends —have said it before." I shrug. That was a day that started out with popcorn and a movie, but ended with tears and heartbreak.

Mercy Carr, a girl I'd only known since kindergarten, began the discussion before the opening credits had even begun. Mercy liked to talk with her hands. They began flapping as she casually mentioned that she and a couple of the girls were talking—a.k.a. questioning the legitimacy of what was wrong with me. Apparently they couldn't figure out why I didn't just tell myself not to be afraid. She compared my situation to her disliking the color purple. Then one day, her mom bought her the cutest pair of lavender capri pants and she got over her aversion. Just like that. I didn't see Mercy again after that. I didn't see any of my friends again after that.

"My grandma said it to me once."

Luke's eyes pop with shock. Mine did too at the time. I kind of expected Mercy Acts-Like-She's-Eighteen-but-Thinks-Like-She's-Eight Carr to question what she often referred to as my head drama, but when my gran did it, I died a little inside.

"Yeah," I say, smiling.

"Bet that was hard to swallow."

"Like nails coated in acid."

"Ouch."

She didn't mean to say it. Gran was like a replacement parent. My dad's mom, she never forgave him for leaving us. When I was growing up, she tried everything to get him to come back and take responsibility for me, even threatened to cut him out of her will. Which I assume is why a week later I got that letter.

"She freaked out one day when I passed out over black bits in my food. But she was actually kind of the shit."

I laugh because besides this one, almost every memory I have of her is funny.

"Oh, really." He arches his eyebrows.

"She was Katie Maine, of K. Maine Bath and Beauty products." At one time, her Sugar Sand Scrub was in every bathroom in America. Her beeswax lip balms bought Mom and me this house.

"No way. My mom has a ton of that stuff on her shelf."

"Yeah?"

He nods while taking a swig of his orange juice, and I hear his teeth click against the glass. I'm about to get all anxious about it shattering in his mouth, splitting and slicing through his strawberry lips, when he pulls it away and sets it back down on the step.

"She took good care of me and my mom." I think about the summer when I turned nine and she took us to Disneyland. She came on all the rides with me because Mom was too afraid. She lost her false teeth on the log flume. "She was super quirky and kind of impossible to stay mad at. And when all this started, everybody got scared, you know? It took a lot of effort and adjusting." My gran's heart was so big, I was shocked to discover that's what killed her.

We stop talking. He lets what I just told him sink in. The seconds drag on and my body starts to fidget, trying to get comfortable in the uncomfortable silence.

"My gran lives in Gray Oaks," he says, and I am beyond grateful that he's good at reading body language.

"Gray Oaks?"

"It's a retirement complex." Of course it is. The guys that name those places have less tact than a cold sore. "Whenever I go over there these days, she calls me Matthew."

"Why?" I ask, exercising caution because I've read about the damage dementia does. Assuming that's what she has.

"Her mind isn't what it used to be," he says. "And I guess I look a lot like my dad when he was younger." Right. Matthew is his dad's name. He touches the finger where the football ring was. Doesn't take a genius to work out that the gaudy chunk of jewelry he was wearing the first time we talked belonged to his father. There isn't much you miss when you're really looking.

"Last I heard, my dad was in the Alps, squandering his inheritance on a twenty-one-year-old blonde named Anika," I say. Nice. There are artists who work delicately, painting thousands of fine lines, and then there are artists who throw globs of color across a room in the hope that it will hit something. In this moment, I definitely fall into the latter category.

"Ouch. That's gotta sting," he says.

"Nah. I decided to take a pragmatic approach to the whole thing. I can't miss a man I never met, right?"

"Do you think maybe I could borrow your no-bullshit shield for school sometime?"

"Absolutely. I'll mail it to you. What's your address?" I reply. His grin is hella hypnotic. He doesn't seem to care that I'm not trained in the art of icebreaking.

"Luke, what did you mean when you said your dad disappears?" The question is out of my mouth before I realize the weight of it. It tumbles down the stairs like a boulder and smashes straight through the laminate floor. I fluster; my cheeks burn bright red. I was always going to ask, just maybe not now, when tact is in such short supply.

"Nice memory you've got there," he replies, all light-hearted.

I wince. "I'm sorry. I shouldn't have asked. When I start thinking about stuff, when my mind gets too busy, more often than not I forget to engage a filter—"

"Norah, it's okay," he interjects. "You don't have to panic. I don't mind talking about it. Besides, I think I owe you a little bit of background, right?" He smiles and I wonder if it's too soon to suggest we get married. "My dad has what my mom calls wanderlust."

"Wanderlust?"

"He likes to travel. Like, he *really* likes to travel." He's looking at me as though I should understand. I don't think he realizes how little he's said, but the puzzled expression on my face clues him in.

"This is going to sound so messed up," he says right before he jams his thumb knuckle in his mouth and starts chewing on it.

"Messed up is kind of my default." I smile, can't help it. Can't help noticing that he just inadvertently told me he doesn't see all the things that are wrong with me.

"So my mom's been a flight attendant all her life," he says. "She met my dad onboard a flight to Argentina when they were in their early twenties. He's a traveler. A real home-is-where-I-hang-my-hat type of guy."

"The souvenir stickers on his van?"

"All the places he's been." Wow. There were a lot of stickers. "My mom doesn't think he'll stop moving until he's been everywhere there is to be and seen everything there is to see." You can tell his mom said that. The words are romantic, spoken by a woman in love. His hands ball into fists; he pushes his knuckles together and they pop.

"Are you angry at him?"

"No. Not anymore, but I used to be." Luke turns his chin and looks at me, his eyes narrow, pain clouding the usually luminous jade of them. "It's a sickness. He tried to stay with us, build a home. Actually, he's tried it a few times, but he gets so depressed when he stops moving."

Huh. He's like me, only in reverse.

"So, your parents, are they separated?"

"They're separated in the sense that there is physical distance between them. But they're still married. Still madly in love. That is, when he's not trawling the world looking for a new family. He says it's not about us, that he loves us both unconditionally." Luke takes a breath. "It's such a noble word, *unconditional*. Brave. Blindly committing to situations it knows nothing about." He gets lost staring at the space in front of him, focusing on nothing in particular. I don't know where his head is. I'm not sure he does either. I wish I could lace my fingers through his and lead him back to the safety of my stairs.

"I used to get mad at my mom because she wouldn't make him stay. She would tell me I was too young to understand. But what was there to understand? He couldn't have loved us because he kept leaving us." He dusts his bottom lip with his thumb, and for a second, I wonder if he's going to start snacking on his nails. Because I would. Instead, he stands up, trots down the stairs, and starts pacing. I don't hold him back. I don't hold him back or try to make him sit because I hate it when I'm spinning and people try to make me be still.

"Then, three years ago, the summer I turned fifteen, he comes home, rolls up the drive in his camper, bearing gifts of ice cream cake and a replica Super Bowl ring. There's something different about this visit, though . . ." He turns to look at me for the first time since he started moving. "I mean, he's always happy to see us, but this particular time I remember thinking, *He's not just happy, he's relieved.*

"One week turns into two, two turns into three, and he's still hanging around eight weeks later." His eyes twinkle as he relives the memory. I like this part of the story.

"We didn't even do anything, just hung out at the old house like a pair of losers, eating Cheetos and watching the Cartoon Network. My dad is a nice guy, you know? Not like one of those phony family guys on infomercials, with the blindingly white teeth and side parting. I mean, he forgets to shave and has zero sense of style, but he's warm. He smiles a lot, sees the good in everything and everyone. He hurts for people he's never met, pays it forward like it's his religion. I think you'd like him." I nod because I think I would too.

"So my mom gets him this job at the airport, working as a TSA agent, and I get the biggest kick out of seeing him at the breakfast table every morning. Both of them grabbing coffee before they head off to work. Real Rockwell kind of moments, you know? I thought, *This is it; he's stay-*

ing for sure. Whatever crazy stuff was happening inside his head has vanished, and he's going to be able to stay happy here now." Luke stops moving, like he's bumped into a brick wall. I don't speak because I can see he's trying really hard to work through his thoughts, possibly push down some unwanted emotion.

He closes his eyes, inhales strength, exhales sadness. "The smiling happy faces made it easy to ignore him pacing around at night, skipping meals, all the sudden onsets of silence. I'd never seen him cry until the week before he went again, when I found him curled up on our kitchen floor, drawing circles in some sugar that he'd spilled. See, the plan was for him to come home and stay home. But the depression came back and started kicking his ass until he couldn't stand it.

"I love him . . . unconditionally. I mean, yeah, sometimes I see how miserable his calls to cancel a trip home make my mom. And sometimes, as you know, I lose my shit and yell at him over the phone in the middle of the night. But then I remember that I would give back those eight weeks, every single minute of every single day, if it meant never having to see him that broken again."

"I'm sorry," I tell him. I'm not sure if that's the right thing to say. I'm not sure there even is a right thing to say.

"Don't be." He pauses. "This might sound odd, but I

can't wish he were any different, you know? Like, I can't start wishing away pieces of his personality, because then he wouldn't be my dad."

The bridge of my nose pricks. I keep my eyes wide open because I know if I blink, I'll leak tears. Mom's said the same thing to me, about me, more than once, usually after I've apologized for acting like a freak.

"You must think I'm awful." Luke's chin touches his chest. "Shouting at him like that when he can't help the way his brain is wired."

"No!" I deny vehemently, clinging to the banister bars and pushing my face up to the gap. "Are you kidding? Some days I wonder how my mom hasn't killed me. We've only argued a couple of times since I got sick, and hell, we scream the place down. But no matter how loud we yell, we never love each other any less. I totally get it. It's hard from both sides. I understand. I really do."

"Wow." He chuckles through the following few moments of awkwardness, then comes back and sits down on the stairs beside me. "You know, you're the only person I've ever told about all of this." I feel honored. Privileged. I know how hard it is to part with private information. "He's not around often. I'm pretty sure that's left most of my friends thinking he's dead."

"They've never met him?"

"No. You're the first to even see him, which feels kind of odd." He looks up, looks down, picks at the seam on the side of his jeans before turning to me again. "It feels kind of good to get it off my chest too.

"Anyways . . ." he says, clearing his throat. He straightens his shoulders and coughs testosterone around the room. "He's coming back at Christmas. Has promised to stick around an entire week this time."

"That's awesome." I fix a fake smile and nod enthusiastically. The urge to cushion a potential fall with clichéd warnings about not getting his hopes up is strong, but somehow I swallow it.

I'm exhausted. I try to sit up straight, but my spine is made of sponge, so instead I slump forward, lean on my knees, and stare idly out of the porch windows. He does the same.

"You know those people who bring down a banging party by singing ultra-slow, bleeding-heart ballads on the karaoke?" I ask him.

"Yeah?"

"We should do that as a job, but, like, tell our stories instead of sing," I tease. He bursts out laughing. Like a yawn, I catch it, start laughing until my sides split open and all the misery that's been burning my lungs spills out onto the stairs.

"Well, Neighbor, it's been a ton of *fun*, but I gotta make tracks. Face the music." He's nearly two hours late for school already. I guess it wouldn't be fair of me to suggest he stay until we run out of words. Plus, I have a GPA that's in serious need of some inflation.

We stroll toward the door in silence, both trying to make the walk last longer by taking slow steps. Well, that's what I'm doing, and despite having longer legs, he keeps pace beside me, so I think it's safe to assume it's what he's doing too.

"I have a question," Luke says as he heads out onto the porch. I'm kind of impressed he can fight the friction enough to spin on the balls of his boots, but he does. "It's a hypothetical."

"Okay."

This might be serious. His lips pull into a straight line and I brace myself against the door frame, ready, for the past hour to be blasted to smithereens by what he has to ask.

"How does a person, let's say a guy, in this case, go about making plans with a girl who can't leave her house?" He lowers his chin, looks at me from under his eyebrows. "Hypothetically," he reminds me. It's lucky I'm holding on to something so I can't fall down dead. *Her heart just exploded* is what they'd have to engrave on my headstone.

"Well," I whisper, because this has to be a dream and I'm afraid talking too loud will wake me up. "*Hypothetically speaking*, he would probably have to ask her. Then, I don't know, maybe if the girl likes movies, they could watch one together?" I shrug, wish I were wearing a sweater so I'd have a sleeve to hide behind. I toe the brass runner at the bottom of the door.

"Hey, Norah, you wanna watch a movie with me on Friday?"

"Yes."

26

I SPEND TUESDAY WALKING AROUND on colorful clouds. Sort of. Occasionally my brain forces me to think about all the ways my date with Luke could go wrong, then my energy goes into trying not to fall off the clouds and land in a mangled mess on the ground below.

On Wednesday it takes me almost six hours to complete a math assignment. Luke is in my head (sans all the morbid BS about disaster dates), and I don't want to waste time trying to figure out angles of triangles. I want to listen to the *Love Life Live* acoustic sessions on 98.6 FM and think about the color of his eyes, the curve of his jaw, the sound of his voice.

Thursday goes like both of the above, except there's this low-level buzz of frustration simmering beneath my bones. I'm moody, irritable. I want to scratch off my scalp when the obnoxious guy on TV starts raving about politics with what seems to be nothing more than a first-grade education. Mom's response to my ranting and raving is "You've got it bad for this boy." I've no idea how she's deduced this. I was simply trying to explain that people who don't know facts shouldn't be allowed to contribute to important discussions.

My mood lifts around seven that night when I find a neatly folded note on the doormat and read a single line written in perfect cursive.

See you tomorrow, Neighbor.

It's Friday. Thank God. When did they start adding hours to weekdays?

I climb out of bed like a normal person, no rolling, flopping, or crawling. Straightforward steps, all grown up. I pull on jeans and a black, slightly fluffy, slightly sparkly sweater without wincing once. It's like New Year's Eve up in here. I'm making resolutions to better myself every five seconds.

I sit down at my vanity, something I haven't done in forever. The thing is antique, dark, way too big for my room. It's the sort of dresser you see on the set of a horror movie. That's what my gran said when she gave it to me. We both agreed it was magnificent.

Good Lord. I get a sharp shock when I first see myself in the mirror; it's like being snuck up on by a ghost. My enthusiasm for today wanes a little.

An increase in worry and a decrease in sleep have

been screwing with my face. Pretty sure my current diet of cheese and sugar isn't helping anything either. Like a sculptor, I pull at the skin on my cheeks, the sag under my eyes, the creases on my forehead, but I am not clay. No matter how hard my fingers try, they can't banish the Crypt Keeper from my reflection.

I open my dresser drawer. It's full of makeup samples that Gran used to send me every time K. Maine launched a new something-or-other. It's all unopened. Makeup takes a lot of effort for someone who only puts on real pants approximately fifty days out of the year. I'd been planning to sell it online, buy myself a new phone instead, but today seems like a good day to indulge. Plus, Gran used to swear that a smear of lipstick and a dash of mascara was magic because it never failed to make her feel more confident. Confidence is something I could always use more of. Especially when I have a date.

I root through the drawer, check labels, tear off cellophane, and streak various shades on the back of my hand. Who knew lipstick came in so many colors? I find five different reds, four pinks, three browns, two purples, and a stick of jet-black.

I line them all up in a neat little row along the edge of my dresser, select one, and test it against my cheek. It's times like this when I could really use a girlfriend to come over and help me figure out which shade suits me best. At this rate, I'm going to miss my date completely.

I'm pretty sure I break the record for time spent choosing lipstick. I've lost two hours, and after all the *umm*-ing and *ahh*-ing, I settle on the first color I found.

It had to be red. Red makes my eyes pop and my pale skin look less like a tragedy and more like art. Rose red. I'm not brave enough to wear the shade called Fire; it looks too much like blood and makes me think of vampires.

Thank God there are only two types of mascara. And as my life is no John Hughes movie, I put the blue color back in the box and paint my lashes black. Easy.

This time when I catch sight of my reflection, I'm startled for a whole new reason. A better reason. The Norah staring back at me in the mirror looks so much different from the Norah that was here before. This Norah looks vaguely normal, alive, not consumed by her mental health.

"Norah." Mom knocks on my door. I jump, lift my wrist, ready to wipe the lipstick from my mouth. I'm not sure why, but I feel like I'm five and she's about to catch me using her expensive perfume as furniture polish.

"Nor, are you awake?"

My door opens. She's coming in and I still haven't wiped away the red lipstick. It's bright and I'm worried that if I smudge it across my face, it'll stain the way cherry soda does. Panic pulls Mom's mouth open when she looks at my already-made bed and doesn't see me lazing around on it.

"Hey," she says when she finally finds me, all shock. I can't decide if it's because I'm wearing clothes or because I'm sitting at a vanity I haven't used since the day it arrived. "I thought you'd still be in bed."

"I thought you'd be at work," I mutter from behind my hand. I wonder if I can get away with sucking the lipstick off. Probably not. She's shocked, not stupid. Besides, I'd have to Google side effects of eating lipstick before I'd feel comfortable swallowing it. Thick lines of worry crease Mom's brow.

"I'm taking the day off. What's with the floating hand?" She heads into my room, limping. With a wince, she sits down on the bed and straightens out her legs. She's wearing oversize zebra slippers and I can't quite make out what's wrong with her feet.

"What's with the limp?" I counter, still hiding my mouth.

"Nothing much." Mom flinches, ever so slightly, but there's not a lot I don't see.

"Your hip hurts?" I ask. Mom rolls her eyes because my all-seeing anxiety never lets her have secrets for long.

"I guess I'm having a little trouble putting weight on it today."

I forget about my mini-makeover, drop my hand and flee to my cell at the side of the bed. "We should call the doctor. What if the hospital missed something? What if it's broken? Did you know people can walk around for years with broken bones? It's like that doctor said about your wrist—broken bones can set funny and cause years of endless agony."

"Gee. Thanks for that, Little Miss Sunshine." She snorts. Right. That was perhaps a touch morbid. "It really suits you, by the way."

"What does?" I grab hold of my cell. My agony until the sweet release of death drags you under comment might have been morbid, but the concern still stands. I'm getting ready to call a doctor.

"The lipstick."

"Oh." I shrug, channeling my embarrassment into scratching off a scab on the side of my thumb. "I think I feel silly. I mean, I didn't when I first put it on, but when you knocked, I wanted to take it off."

"Why?" Mom pats the bed beside her. I slump over, slosh through the murky puddle that is this morning's can-do attitude, and flop down beside her.

"I don't know." But I do know, and she knows it, which

is why she waits for me to elaborate. "Does it look like I'm trying too hard? I don't want him to think I'm trying to be flashy. And what if he doesn't like it, or thinks it looks bad? What if—"

"Stop." Mom grabs my shoulders, pushes her face into mine, and eyeballs me. "Go back to that second you first put it on. Can you do that?" I nod, a little too scared to do anything else. She makes me think of one of those angry guys on TV, the ones who try to sell beds at crazy discounted prices.

"How did you feel? Just you? Nobody else."

I close my eyes, cast my mind back to the instant I saw my reflection. It's like Gran said, I felt confident. My lips feel slick as they pull into a smile.

"I felt good."

"Then that's all that matters. You are beautiful, always. You would be beautiful if you got a giant butterfly tattooed across your face. Beauty comes from how you treat people and how you behave. But if a little lipstick makes you smile, then you should wear it and forget what anyone else thinks." That's exactly how she lives. Just ask her closet full of bright colors and crazy patterns.

I open my eyes, give her a hug, kiss her on the cheek, and stamp it with a big red rosebud.

"Now, about my hip . . ."

"Right. Call the doctor." I unlock the screen of my phone.

"Hold your horses, sweetie," she whinnies at me. "I don't need a doctor. I had it x-rayed at the hospital. It's not broken, just badly bruised. So you can quit worrying about the bones setting out of shape." I'm still ready to call a doctor. Bruising means bleeding.

"It is fine," she repeats. "What I need to do is rest it. Doctor's orders, which I've maybe ignored a little bit since I got back home." I don't yell at her. She's in pain so I let this one slide.

"Then rest," I reply. "No more puttering around the garden or popping out until it feels better . . ." She sees the second I remember what's supposed to happen today.

"Yep," Mom says.

"Ugh. I have a therapy appointment."

Forgotten again.

What is it about Luke that sucks away part of my memory? Is this normal? On the Metro, people talk about kissing. The kids who are lucky enough to have evaded detection by family members sometimes post about reaching second base. They talk a lot about where they eat and post the funny snippets of conversation they have, but to the best of my knowledge, no one has ever mentioned memory loss. Mental note: after my date, research the side effects you encounter when in the presence of good-looking guys.

So today I get a date with Luke, and, seeing as how Mom can't walk, let alone work a brake pedal, an impending free pass on therapy, maybe?

"Don't get too excited, missy . . ." Maybe not. "I really don't think you should be skipping a session right now. I'm going to call and ask Dr. Reeves if she wouldn't mind paying one last visit to the house instead." It's like spending all of your allowance on a triple-scoop ice cream cone with hot fudge sauce only to drop it before you get a single lick. Don't get me wrong, Dr. Reeves is great, but I could have done without the emotional trauma of a session today. Damn. So close.

Dr. Reeves won't mind. She'll come over, I know she will, because despite the fact that Mom pays her, I think she quite likes me.

27

Maybe we should wrap up early?" Dr. Reeves says. At least, I think that's what she says. Her words are warped, sliding into my ears but getting caught up and mangled in my mind mess. I'm too busy wondering where Luke and I will sit when we watch the movie tonight. Not too close, for obvious reasons. But not too far away either. Also for obvious reasons. Maybe I should suggest we sit at the table and watch the TV in the kitchen. But then, those chairs are super-uncomfortable after prolonged exposure.

"Norah." I've never heard Dr. Reeves raise her voice before. It startles me, makes me tune out the insanity and tune in to her instantly.

"I'm sorry. Really. I don't mean to ignore you. I want to hear what you're saying, but I'm finding it hard to concentrate on anything."

"I get it," Dr. Reeves says as she collects her sheets of paper and shuffles them into a leather folder. I look at the little black lion embossed on the front and get all dreamy because its shaggy mane reminds me of Luke's dark locks. "Please don't apologize. It's good to see you getting glassy-eyed over a boy." I flush and wonder if I could get away with wearing sunglasses on my date so Luke doesn't see. "But I'm starting to get worried about your scratches, and it's my job to make sure you're not a danger to yourself."

Whoa. Wait. What? Now she has my attention like she grabbed my chin and yanked it around to face her.

She's looking at my arms, but I feel like I'm laid on a gurney, legs spread, and she's rooting around down *there*, like a gynecologist, inspecting my scars with a flashlight.

"Scratches?" I bury my hands between my legs, convinced my little scars are what we're talking about. But that's impossible. I cut up there deliberately so no one will see.

"It's something both your mother and I have noticed you do when you're anxious."

Stop.

I'm confused.

Mom and the doc are smart, but this isn't the X-Men. I joke about it sometimes, but they're not really mind readers. And they don't have a super-ability to see through walls or items of clothing. Besides, I've only cut a handful of times, and the last time Mom was miles away, laid up in a hospital out of state.

She picks up on my confusion like it's fired off a flare.

"You don't know you're doing it," she says, a hooked finger starts stroking her invisible beard as she assumes her making-mental-notes face.

"Doing what?" My tone is laced with frustration.

When she's done analyzing, her hands come together in prayer position and she throws me a sympathetic smile.

"Sometimes, when you start to panic, you scratch patches of your skin until they bleed."

"So? Everyone itches."

"That's true, they do. Do you have an itch right now?" She flicks her eyes toward the table. I follow her gaze, see my finger scratching aimlessly across my thumb. My stomach lurches.

"Are you familiar with the term *self-harm*?" She's using Mom's your-rabbit-just-died voice.

"Yes, but no." I dismiss her poorly disguised suggestion with a snort. "I'm not doing that." I mean, I am, like, every once in a while. But she seems to be suggesting that itching is the same as slicing, which it's not. Maybe she's the one not so familiar with the term *self-harm*.

I'm done with this session. It's just gotten ridiculous. Too ridiculous. And that's coming from someone who, nine times out of ten, can emotionally invest in an episode of *SpongeBob SquarePants*. I wonder how mad Mom will get if

I just leave the table and go hide in my room. I wonder if she'll call off my date with Luke.

She wouldn't.

She might.

I start thinking about breaking stuff.

Dr. Reeves is talking about control, describing how I feel when I hold scissors to my leg. But it's not the same. Everybody scratches an itch. Sometimes scratches bleed. Self-harm is something I do in private—barely ever—to make myself feel better. It's intense and frightening. It's not having a quick scratch in front of folks. Right? Was notorious booger picker and small scab eater Tommy Martin accused of self-harm in the first grade every time he picked himself a snack? No. I really think she's making a fuss over nothing. Scratching is normal, and I don't appreciate her tearing strips off my already shaky sanity.

My legs are gearing up to go when I feel a sting in my thumb like I've been bitten by a fire ant. My nail's broken through skin. There's blood. My mind flashes back to last week and the well of scarlet pooling on my thigh.

It doesn't mean anything.

It doesn't.

I was just itching.

Everybody itches.

Everybody.

Except the answer to Dr. Reeves's original question was *no*. There was no itch. My eyes scrunch shut. I'm trying really hard to conjure a memory of a tickle, a fizz, a crawling sensation, something that would warrant the blood now crusting beneath my nails, but I get nothing. There was no itch, no reason to scratch myself senseless.

I jump up from my chair, hand stretched out in front of me, glaring at it like I've sprouted extra fingers. I want to get away from it but swiftly realize I can't. So instead, I head to the sink, flick on the cold water, and wash away the blood. I snatch the soap, squeeze a gallon of the green liquid onto my hands, then start rubbing. The new wound stings, but I keep going until I can't see marred skin through the thick cloud of bubbles. I rinse and repeat until my hands feel clean.

When I'm finished, I exhale a breath so loaded it shakes the leaves on the trees outside.

"You're laying this on me now? Right before my first date ever?" I whimper. Trembling legs carry me back over to my chair. I plop down, plant my elbows on the table, and bury my forehead in my hands. I can see my reflection in the glossy tabletop. No makeup in the world is strong enough to hide this revelation on my face. I'd need cement, a sandblast, a brand-new fucking face. I slam a fist down on my reflection.

"Norah, listen to me." Dr. Reeves is drawing a tree on the table again. With a single sideways glance I ax it down. "It's *because* of your date that I wanted to talk to you about this. Relationships are hard for anyone."

We're not even in a relationship, my mind argues, and I pout internally like a child. Of course I don't correct her because I'm smart enough to know that, when it comes to a mind like mine, labels are moot. Feelings are involved and that's really all that matters. Dr. Reeves starts explaining that butchering your body isn't uncommon in the fight to feel in control.

Like she's dealing cards, she lays three brightly colored pamphlets in front of me. They all depict smiling folks basking under a summer sun. They're bright, cheery, shiny: everything self-harm is not. It's a series called Coping Without Cutting. Subtle. I'm sure all of the kids feel comfortable reaching for these.

"Take a look," Dr. Reeves says encouragingly as she slides the first booklet a little closer to me. "Think of it like being prepared," she says. "You might not need it, but it can't hurt to know a little something about what's happening."

The author of the booklet is some guy called Adrian

Crowe. His name is written in Comic Sans because these guys are clearly down with the kids. I could breathe into a bottle of milk right now and turn it sour.

I peel back the first page, read the opening paragraph with my nose tipped so high I can smell the ceiling. I wish I could invest in the words instead of picturing myself being shut inside an asylum.

"They're autobiographical. These people talk about how they used different techniques to combat their own struggles with self-harm. This guy—" She taps Adrian's picture. He's old, maybe late fifties, with white hair and glasses. He looks like he's lived most of his life in a library. "He used to draw pictures on his skin when he got the urge to scratch. And this woman—" She opens booklet number two and we meet Roxie Gaines, a girl only a little older than me but infinitely cooler with her bright blue hair and black makeup. "Roxie squeezed the stuffing out of stress balls instead of hurting herself." Dr. Reeves abandons the show-and-tell, ducks down, and disappears inside her snakeskin purse. It's faux; I asked the first day we met.

"I got you something," she says, producing a brown paper bag. She tips the bag upside down, and half a dozen rainbow-dipped balls roll out. They bounce around on the table for a couple of seconds, but Dr. Reeves corrals them with her arms, and they come to a standstill. "Stress balls," she says proudly. "I was thinking you could discreetly carry one around in your pocket and do what Roxie did."

She picks up one of the rainbow-splattered rounds and squeezes it into a pancake. "The guy at the store told me they were almost indestructible." It's adorable to watch her test this theory, teeth clenched, tugging and pulling the ball in all different directions. Admittedly, I'm wondering if I could break one.

"Your turn," the doc says.

I pick up the ball that looks the most yellow. It's spongy but has a coating that feels like clay. I squeeze it, and I'm almost disappointed when my fingers don't pierce the outer shell regardless of how hard I push.

"Norah, tell me what you're thinking."

"I'm thinking if I take this, it will be like accepting what you're saying." I'm finding it very hard to believe that this whole time I haven't been in control of the one thing I thought I was.

"Is that a bad thing?" Dr. Reeves asks, taking more notes.

"That depends on whether or not I'm going to end up in a hospital." I can't look at her, so instead I roll the ball around in a figure eight.

"Why would you end up in a hospital?"

"Because hurting yourself is not exactly something

stable people do." I'm not fully invested in the idea that scratching and self-harm are the same, but I keep that piece of info to myself.

"People hurt themselves for lots of different reasons, but right now I'm confident that you're not trying to escape life."

"I'm not at all," I agree vehemently.

"Right. But I do think we need to reevaluate how you cope with stress. So what do you say, maybe we can give this a shot?" She's not really giving me a choice. All I want to do is erase this conversation with brain bleach.

I nod, can't say *yes* because scratching is a normal response, and I can't get past thinking everyone does it. I don't hate myself for it. It can't possibly be the same as self-harm. I don't always break the skin, and when I do, the marks don't even scar. In fact, they totally disappear within a week. I've seen more damage from squeezing pimples, so how is it self-harm?

28

W HEN I GET BACK to my room, the stress balls, along with the happy-shiny pamphlets, get dumped in the bottom drawer of my dresser, where I'm almost certain they'll stay until the day I die.

I'm tired and my bed looks so inviting, soft and safe, like a giant pile of feathers, willing me to come over and rest my head, which is suddenly so heavy my shoulders shudder under the weight. I want to burrow, sleep until next spring. This isn't good. I don't want to turn to sludge before tonight. I have to stay perky. Sunny. Excited. Shouldn't be a problem. I'm practically a pro at beating back sadness.

I veer left, drag unwilling legs away from my bed and plonk myself back at my vanity. The chair that came with it is anything but inviting. I think at one point it might have been used as some sort of medieval torture device, despite the expensive velvet upholstery covering the seat.

Only two butt-numbing hours until Luke arrives.

• • •

At 6:45, Mom lets me know that she's making herself scarce and scuttles off to her bedroom. Exercise and I are estranged, but I have fifteen minutes to fill and I can't sit still, so I do laps around my room while chewing the inside of my mouth into a mini–mountain range. At least I'm not scratching.

I squeeze my hands to keep them from shaking. According to 90 percent of the Internet, everybody gets nervous before a first date. But then I guess it's pretty safe to assume most of that 90 percent are worrying about making a good first impression, not wondering what sort of bacteria their date will be breathing into their airspace or trying to determine the odds of choking to death on a piece of popcorn.

I decide to avoid eating solids altogether . . . just while he's here.

Luke knocks on the door at 7:01, and I trip down the stairs, making a din like a running herd of wild wildebeests. I take the last step twice then race to the door, my arms only slightly bruised, my legs begging not to be used anymore today.

"Hi." Luke flashes me that grin, and my motor functions fail. "You look really good," he tells me. "You always look good." He tips his head, rubs the back of his neck, and I think I see a slight red tinge blossom on his cheeks.

"Thank you," I reply, feeling a little flushed around the gills myself but happy I stuck with the lipstick.

One of the things I kept freaking out about on Monday was the prospect of silence. My mind isn't always where it should be, which makes conversation hard to carry. I guess I was worried we'd find ourselves trapped in an atmosphere of not knowing what to say, but Luke doesn't let that happen.

He's talking about the two DVDs he's brought as we make our way to the front room.

"Where do you want me to sit?" he says, eyeballing the couch. It's a three-seater, so we can share it without me getting weird.

I sit on the left, he flops down on the right, and an immeasurable black hole opens up in the space between us. I'd never really noticed how far away the other side of the sofa was until now. We may need cups and string to communicate.

"So, what do you wanna watch?" Luke asks, his voice raised a little because he's noted the overcautious distance and is having fun with it.

"I don't want to catch boy cooties," I tell him. "You could have been anywhere, rolling around in anything, before you showed up here."

"This is true. Can I just note, I really admire your level of resistance to my raw animal magnetism," he says, all snark.

"I'm not going to lie." I huff an exhausted breath. "It's been tough."

We settle on a movie called *Zombie's Curse*. It's so loaded with cheese I start craving macaroni. We laugh a lot, don't talk much, but when we do, I find myself wanting to shuffle closer to him.

His hand rests on his leg. My eyes keep flitting over and finding it. There's a thick silver ring on his thumb, and his fingers keep tapping nonsensical beats against his jeans. Occasionally, his hand relaxes, flops off his knee, and lands on the couch like an upside-down spider in shock. That's when I want to grab hold of it. It's such an unexpected want, it scares me.

I was slipping into unconsciousness the first time Dr. Reeves ever touched me. It was a Monday, and I was trying to get across the parking lot to her office, already caught in the steely grip of a panic attack. Limbs like jelly, face melting off, lungs squeezing themselves into nonexistence, the usual. My body was heavy, too heavy for Mom to carry alone. That's really all I remember. When I came around, Dr. Reeves was timing the beat of my heart against the slow-in-comparison second hand of her diamond-encrusted watch. She was pressing two fingers hard against my wrist. Her skin was cold, which surprised me because she has such a warm smile.

By the time I crawl out of my thought stream, the credits are rolling on the movie. Worse, Luke is looking at me looking at his hand, which has made its way back onto his leg. My jaw drops.

"I . . . I . . ." I want to explain why I'm fixated on his lap, but I can't remember how to talk. My finger finds skin on my wrist and I start scratching until it stings.

"It's okay," he says, sitting up straight and sliding to the edge of the couch. "I promise. Whatever you're worried about, you don't have to be."

The need to explain myself subsides. I take a deep breath. Breaching the black hole, I edge a little closer to him.

"Norah Dean, is it possible you're curious about what it would be like to hold my hand?" he asks.

"No," I protest, my response slamming into his stomach like a fist. Just for a second, a blink, a flash, I feel like I'm on a diving board and his question is at my back, poking me in the shoulder, trying to make me jump.

"Wait," he says, holding up his hands, more panic than

person. "I wasn't suggesting that you should be. I mean, I'm not suggesting that you are. I'm sorry—" He's all jittery, and it's my fault. I'm so defensive. I shouldn't have reacted so quickly.

"No," I interject. "Please don't be sorry. You didn't do anything. I was . . ." I collect another lungful of air. "I was thinking about it." My heart gathers speed until it sounds like it's slamming into my eardrums, and then, without saying another word, I press my hand down on top of his. My fingers slide seamlessly into the spaces between his fingers.

"Is it okay that I did this?" I ask him, my eyes unable to meet his. Instead I stare at our hands. Study how perfectly they're slotted together, like pieces of a jigsaw puzzle.

"I don't know, is it?" I note how still he is, wonder if he feels like he's beside a wild deer and any sudden movement will scare me away.

I nod, but my mind is already starting to race. I'm thinking about all the things a person can touch throughout the day. And then that kid, the one who keeps coughing into his hand on the Monty's Cough Syrup commercial, is in my head.

We've been touching too long, I decide, and let go. My

hands suddenly feel sticky, like they're coated in sugar. I eyeball the bottle of sanitizer on the table but don't want my OCD to hurt his feelings, so I excuse myself, head for the bathroom to wash my hands. I'm terrified, but I can't stop smiling.

29

LUKE DROPS BY EVERY night after school for the next week.

We sit on the couch for hours and talk about everything and nothing all at once. Like on Wednesday, we start chatting about French, I quiz him on some Spanish homework, and then, I'm not sure how we make the leap, but we're talking about cheese. Cheese. We spend the next hour discussing cheddar as if the survival of humanity is at stake. He tells me his favorite kind is cashew-nut cream cheese. I've never tried that. Shocker. Maybe I will start making a list of things I'd like to try . . . on second thought, that might do more harm than good. I'm not even sure we have enough paper in the house to cover it.

The space on the couch between us stays the same, lingering like a chaperone at junior prom, forever ensuring we don't get too close. Not that there's any chance of that. He doesn't mention the handholding. Neither do I.

It's Friday morning, and, as per usual, Mom is reading the paper. Not the real paper; they're still not allowed in the house. This thing is a broadsheet called *You and Your*

Garden Monthly. The scariest thing in there is an article about a successful aphid massacre in Minnesota. I checked. With bated breath, I stir the oatmeal in my bowl. It's thick and creamy and smells amazing, but I can't swallow it down yet because something is on my mind.

"Mom."

"Hmm?" She replies from miles away in her planter's paradise.

Deepest of breaths. "When Luke comes over later, would it be okay if we watched a movie in my bedroom?"

The paper goes down and she eyeballs me from over the top of her wire reading glasses.

"Should I be worried?"

"No." I shake my head, whip my hair into a frenzy.

"Have you gotten comfortable with him touching you yet?"

"Sort of . . ." In retrospect, I could have probably said no.

"What does that mean? Exactly?" She folds *You and Your Garden Monthly* in half, sets it down beside her empty bowl.

"It means we take all our clothes off, and he turns into a koala, clinging to me like a tree while we watch TV."

Mom chokes on the sip of tea she's just taken. "Norah Jane Dean."

"It was a joke."

"Obviously," she says. "I'm just a little shocked you made it."

Her shock would be less, I'm sure, if she knew how hard I was working to keep a mental image of the aforementioned out of my mind. I take a half second to wonder if Luke would find my quip amusing. It's a joke at his expense, after all, having an abnormal girlfriend, one he can't touch.

"So what is 'sort of' comfortable?" Mom prods.

"I touched his hand last week, you know, before the fear kicked in."

Mom pushes her glasses back on top of her head. I foresee a disaster when it comes to pulling them free from her hair later.

"Does he get it?"

"Get what?"

"Your limitations?"

I'm not really sure what she's asking. "I mean, we've talked about it a lot."

"But does he understand?" Mom says, her Dr. Reeves impression almost perfect. I load my mouth with a spoonful of oatmeal and nod. Nope. I still don't have a clue what she wants to know, but a serious note in her voice suggests another ill-timed intervention, and I'm not sure I can handle two of those in one week. I'm still considering the scratching issue. "It's nice to see you smiling," she says, and I have a sneaking suspicion she's decided it's not worth pursuing this line of questioning. At least not yet.

"So . . . is that a yes?" I flap my lashes, throw my best grin in her face.

"Sure," she says.

I'm sitting at the top of the stairs, using my teeth to file down the corner of my thumbnail, when Luke knocks.

"I'll get it!" I yell, sprinting down the stairs, excitement level off the charts as I bunny-hop back up the last step before heading to the door. Mom laughs at me from the living room. She's been swallowed. All that's left of her is a pair of feet in penguin slippers hanging over the arm of the couch.

"Hi." I'm a little out of breath when I answer the door. Worse when I'm done soaking up his smile.

"You like vanilla ice cream, right?" he says, holding up a brown paper bag. "Not the vanilla-pod stuff. I remembered that thing you said about not liking black bits in your food. Assumed you were being literal." See. He does understand.

"Aww," Mom coos from inside the mouth of the couch.

Luke winces like he just coughed too loud in church.

"I didn't know your mom was home," he whispers. Lately, she's been doing a great job of making herself scarce.

"That's okay. We're going upstairs," I tell him and lead the way.

Tonight we're watching *Mad Mad Mary*, one of my favorite horror classics. I'm on my bed, legs crossed, and Luke is slumped on my sill. I didn't ask him to sit so far away; he just sort of gravitated toward the window.

"Who does that?" he says. His eyes are on the TV. My eyes are on him, wondering for whose sake he's bypassed the bed. I conclude he's done it for me, but out of nowhere, for the smallest of seconds, I wish he'd done it for himself. "Don't go up. Go out." The guy in the movie, the lead, runs straight past the door and takes off up the stairs. Luke starts reciting a list of mistakes the characters in horror movies make, a mental list I've made a thousand times before. It feels good to have someone to share with.

"Don't move to a house that's a million miles away from anywhere," I add.

"Yes." He almost chokes on a spoonful of ice cream. "Switch on the lights the second you hear a strange noise." I laugh so hard the urge to pee hits me. "I'll be right back," I say, climbing off the bed. He pauses the movie. I try not to get teary over how considerate he is.

One relieved bladder and two fresh squirts of Mom's

perfume later, I float back down the hall, so happy I feel like there should be bluebirds frolicking overhead and stems of sweet roses to stop and sniff. Anxiety is forced to trail ten paces behind me.

I stop when I get to my room because I can hear Luke talking and I don't want to gatecrash his call. "When?" he says into his cell. "Next Friday? Are you serious?" I see him through the crack in my door, pacing. Excitement has erupted on his face. "Yes. Awesome. Can you get me two tickets?" Pause. Face scrunch. Headshake. Someone pulls the plug on his smile. He runs a hand through his hair. "Actually, dude, I'm not going to be able to make it. I already have plans." He laughs. "What makes you think they're with a girl?" My heart leaps into my throat. "There might be." Pause. "She might be." He perches on my bed, reaches for the antique silver photo frame that sits on top of a wicker table. He smiles at the picture of me blowing out eighteen candles on my seventeenth birthday—had to round the candles up to the nearest even number so as not to upset my psyche. Lame.

"Trust me. You don't know her."

Anxiety catches up to me; I wobble when it slams into my back. Me. It's me that's pulled the plug on his smile.

"Nah. Don't worry about it. I'll catch them next time. Thanks anyway, man." He hangs up, tosses his phone in the air and catches it. He's all happy-go-lucky again as he heads back to his safe seat on the windowsill. I push my body up against the wall, count to ten as my finger carves out a crevice in my palm.

We need to talk. He can't start missing out on things for me. He can't do that. That's like climbing into a car with its brakes cut. Disaster imminent.

I head back into the room, watch my feet move, one in front of the other. Everything feels uneven, so I use the furniture to ferry me back to my bed.

"Norah. Are you okay?" He sits up, startled.

"Sure. You know me . . ." I dismiss with a wave the worried expression he's throwing my way. "Stability of spaghetti."

"Is the movie too much?" He gets off the sill, walks over, sits on the very edge of my bed. "We can watch something else."

"No!" I protest a little too intensely. "I mean, honestly, I'm fine."

"Okay," he says. "I'll quit bugging you." He stands up.

"You can . . ." A heat wave washes over me. "You can sit over here with me . . . if you want to."

"Sure." I revel in the way the bed shifts when he sits back down, more on than off this time.

The rest of the film plays out, but I don't tune in.

Between his proximity and trying to figure out how to mention his phone call, which I'm totally going to have to confess to eavesdropping on—ugh—my mind is a hot mess. I'll figure it out. I really wish Mom's question from this morning wasn't starting to make more sense.

30

WHEN LUKE SUGGESTED we sit and count stars the following Friday, I was suspicious. You normally find stars outside, after all. But then he showed up at my house with a projector.

We're lying on my bed like soldiers, arms by our sides, legs together, too afraid to touch, and watching space swirl around on my ceiling. It's impossible to count the stars, there are so many, flickering like diamonds on a black backdrop.

My iPod is playing on random. Rock chicks have been commandeering the airwaves for an hour, but then some dude starts strumming his guitar and, with a soft voice, begins singing about holding the girl he loves. My concentration abandons the stars and I focus hard on the lyrics of the love song, the love song with lines that, somehow, speak directly to my current situation.

The invisible barrier between us . . .

The ache in my heart . . .

The burn of constant curiosity . . .

"I got you something," Luke says, twisting his body

and leaning over the side of the bed. While he's reaching, his shirt lifts and I can see the bottom of his back. I swallow lumps.

I'm supposed to protest, I know that for sure, because I see it happen all the time on TV. Though I'm not sure why anyone would want to object to a present. That's a thing I'd like to figure out, but my brain is too busy inspecting the sliver of exposed flesh. Luke has freckles. I've never been close enough to his skin to see freckles before.

"Check it out." Luke lies back, and my stare charges toward the ceiling. He hands me a book. Not a book. A journal. The cover is coated in pictures. It's shiny. Silky smooth. My fingers skate idly over an image of the Arc de Triomphe, the Latona Fountain, the Eiffel Tower, and a half a dozen other famous structures in France.

"It's like a journal," Luke tells me, opening it to the first page. "But it has a travel planner in the back." He flips through more lined light blue pages, stops at a group of white sheets coated in plastic. "You can keep photographs in this part. Or maybe postcards. And then this section here is a directory, with every number you could ever need." I watch him flip through the rest of the journal. The excitement in his smile is immeasurable. "I thought you could use it when you go to school in France."

"I love it," I tell him. "Thank you so much."

I do love it. Really, I do, which is why I can't understand the bolt of hostility that shoots through me when he says *France*. He's so thoughtful, and I'm super-grateful, but my mind is unsettled.

Luke talks about Paris, about art, about maybe dumping his no-travel policy for a week to visit the Louvre and see the *Mona Lisa*. My head spins. He keeps asking me what I think. Asking me if I've ever seen this online? Or that online? Seen them online? Seen it online? Seen her online? Or him online? In conclusion, my life is all about things that can be found on the web, and *yes* is the only word I can contribute to this conversation.

The sound of Luke breathing beside me is melodic. I copy the rhythm, force my lungs to slow down.

He's just talking. Dreaming. Dreaming for both of us. I smile to myself, squash hostility with happy. Reclaim the normal night we're having.

The warmth of my room mixed with the low light makes me sleepy.

My eyes are getting heavy when Luke's pinkie brushes against the side of my hand. I stiffen. At first I think it's a mistake, but then I feel it a second time.

"Is this okay?" The bed shifts, he turns his head, and I turn to meet his face. He's drenched in starlight, practically sparkling. There's only inches between us. I can smell spearmint on his breath. My body bursts into flames.

We're not wearing matching sweaters or strolling through a fall landscape, but I imagine kissing him now would be perfect. I look at his lips. They're parted, just a little. It would be so easy to tighten the gap between us and press my mouth against his.

Except: petri dishes, full of little alien life forms that live on the human tongue. Then this morning, I was flicking through my Metro feed, and this one guy from Cardinal was talking about having mono. Mono spreads like wildfire in schools. Their school. His school. As much as I want to, I can't forget that.

His pinkie meets my hand now, draws circles on the side. Pins and needles explode in the pit of my stomach, and shivers, good shivers, the kind you get when something exciting happens, shoot up and down my spine. I can't pull away.

"Norah." I like the shape his lips make when he says my name. "Will you be my girlfriend?"

Blink-blink. "What?"

He smiles. "Will you be my girlfriend?" I float up and up and up, get lost in the makeshift galaxy on my ceiling. My heart feels like it's trying to box its way beyond my rib cage.

Yes. I think it so loud it's a wonder he doesn't hear it.

But this is me. Nothing is ever easy. I guess every story needs a villain, and never one to be outdone by something as silly as a heartbeat, my brain kicks back, harder. I come crashing down to earth.

And just like that, my bed becomes bottomless. I'm sinking through the floor, Luke's dreams and aspirations fall from the starry sky and slam into my chest.

I've been searching for an opening to talk to him all week. The idea that he should have been somewhere else tonight plagues me.

"Answer me something honestly first?" I say, propping myself up on my elbow. He frowns at me. I'd frown at me too. I'm brutally massacring his romantic moment. I don't mean to, don't want to, but practicality is pressing. There are questions in my head and the threat of gnawed fingernails is fast approaching.

"Do you miss kissing?" Granted, I'm kind of going in from an obscure angle, but I figure missing out on a concert/movie/trip to the circus/whatever is small fry, easy to dismiss in comparison to a kiss. He might be able to catch a concert/movie/trip to the circus/whatever next time. He's not going to be able to catch another girl's lips so easily.

"Where did that come from?" he says.

"Just thinking . . ." I shrug as casually as I can muster. "Do you?"

"Honestly?"

Casual quits on me. I climb off the bed, pace while I consider writing honesty off as overrated. No. I need to hear the end of this conversation. Mom was right; he needs to understand just how many limitations are hanging over him.

"Yes," I say.

"No, I don't. But I do think about kissing you every time I'm with you. I'm kind of looking forward to the day that's okay."

"What if . . ." I say, perching on the edge of my bed only to stand back up a second later because all my muscles have been replaced by jumping beans. "What if you're waiting a really long time? It's unreasonable for me to expect that from you, isn't it?"

"It's unreasonable for you to expect me not to kiss anyone else? You realize I quite like you, right? And that I have this crazy new built-in thing the kids are calling self-control?"

He's missed my point. He thinks I'm questioning his capability instead of the commitment. A swarm of bees wakes up inside my skull.

"I don't want to be with anyone else, Norah."

"That's not what I meant." I can't explain; my mind isn't putting sentences together properly.

"Wait. Is this about the party invite on my Metro wall?" He side-eyes me.

"Party invite?" I haven't been on social media since this morning. There was no invite then.

"You haven't seen it?"

"No."

He sits up. "Can I borrow your cell?" His is still being fixed.

"Sure." I grab it off the side table, hand it over, slightly embarrassed by its ancient appearance. My mom sells bricks that are more discreet.

"I thought maybe you were worrying," Luke says as he punches buttons. He shows me the screen.

It's his Metro page. The last post is a colorful upload inviting him to the Fall Ball at Cardinal High. Of course the invite is from Amy. *Committee Chair* has replaced the *Queen* in her user handle.

"You don't have to worry. I'm not going," he says. I think if he could, he'd pull me back down on the bed and wrap me in a hug. At the bottom of his invite, there are almost a hundred comments from dudes that call him bro and chicks that sign their names with an XO. They're all talking about how much fun this thing will be.

"You can't miss this party," I say, successfully suppressing all reluctance, though it does leave a bitter taste on my tongue. "You can't stop doing things because of me," I tell him. I perch on my bed but have to stand for a second time, because nothing says *serious discussion* like a game of musical chairs. "We're different. I have limits, you don't. We can't pretend that's not a thing. I'm afraid if we do, you're going to start feeling shackled to me . . ."

"That's not going to happen," he argues lightly.

"If we're not careful, that is exactly what is going to happen."

"Norah, it's one party. If it makes you happy, I'll just go to the next one," he replies, but he's stopped smiling. I think maybe he's starting to understand what I'm saying.

"What about your call last week?" I say it quietly, hope it lessens the impact. "I heard you talking on the way back from the bathroom."

The part where I've invaded his privacy seems to go unnoticed. His face crumples like he's been hit by a sudden stomach cramp. "I forgot about that."

"Would you have gone if you weren't with me?"

He straightens his shoulders. "But I am with you, and I love hanging out here with you. I love talking to you, and eating ice cream with you. I love watching cheesy horror movies and staring at the stars with you. *J'adore* that I can now speak eight whole words of French," he says, all smug. "Pretty soon I'll be fluent." I crack a smile, can't help it. "I'd rather hang out with you than go to any concert or party."

He's so sweet. So nice. It pains me to press on with this and shatter the sentiment. I continue pacing.

"Humor me for just a second?" I'm a little breathless, so he doesn't argue. I'm wearing holes in my carpet. "If you hadn't met me, would you have gone?"

He groans, falls face first onto my bed.

"Yes, probably. I probably would have gone. But—"

"And the party?" I interject. I have to get this out. Clear the air so we can move on. "You'd be going to that too, right?"

"I don't know; maybe. They're all pretty much the same, those things."

"But you'd go?" I repeat, jaw tight. For the first time since we met, he's looking at me like I'm about to go all Carrie White on his ass. I'm not; I just need him to see how bad this will be if he stops going out, stops hanging with his friends, cuts himself off because of me.

"Yes," he says. "I would."

"Right. So you have to go. Don't you see? You can't not go places because I'm not going."

"But I love your company."

"And I love yours. But if you stop doing things because I won't be there, you're going to end up feeling trapped here."

"Norah, come and sit down. Take some deep breaths with me for a minute?"

I do as he asks because I am feeling a little lightheaded. Not sure if it's panic or exercise making me feel this way, though. I sit on the bed and he watches me inhale and exhale. It hurts to see him bury his hands beneath his knees because he's trying not to reach for me.

"I'll go to the party," he says. "But I can come and see you immediately after, right?"

"Yes. Yes. You absolutely can. If I'm going to be your girlfriend—"

"Wait," he interjects, grinning from ear to ear. "You're going to be my girlfriend?"

"Yes. If you can promise me you won't hold back just because I can't do a thing."

"I promise," he says, and his pinkie, as light as a feather, draws a heart on the side of my hand.

31

It's FRIDAY NIGHT, and for the first time in forever, Luke isn't here. But I can't complain. If this thing between us is going to have a shot at survival, I have to get on board with not wanting to be where he is all the time too.

Which is easier said than done.

I'm usually the biggest fan of Max DeWinter movies. But, alas, not even Hollywood's latest teen heartthrob flexing his arms and running around in a disheveled white shirt can capture my attention.

"Quit it." Mom's hand crashes down on my bare thigh.

"Ouch." It didn't hurt, but the slapping sound makes a protest seem necessary.

She pushes on my leg, forcing my bouncing knee to a standstill. "Well, feeling a little like I'm in the path of a Mongolian death worm over here."

"A what?"

"A Mongolian death worm."

"That's not a real thing."

"Sure it is. Google it." She quickly dismisses her suggestion with a wave of a hand. "Actually, don't do that."

I laugh. "Don't worry, I won't."

She leans forward, grabs a sugar cookie from the coffee table, and starts licking the chocolate off the top of it.

"So, are you going to tell me what's bothering you?"

"I don't know what you mean," I say. My eyes find the television set and focus on Max firing a gun at some guy I assume is the baddie.

"Are you kidding? Mark DeSomething . . ."

"Max DeWinter," I correct.

"Right. That guy. He's been shirtless twice already and you haven't said a word."

It's official. I've become that kid who's best friends with her mom. We'll be wearing matching velour track-suits and investing in a tandem bicycle next.

"It's possible you know me too well," I say, giving her a wary sideways glance.

"Agreed. But until you're feeling better, you're stuck with me." She playfully socks me in the arm. "So spill. Did you and Luke have a fight? I'm not going lie, I was sort of expecting to find him vegging out on the couch when I walked in from work."

I guess I can complain a little, at least to my mom.

"He's gone to this school-ball thing." I pout, snatching a cookie off the table and crumbling it between my fingers.

"Oh dear," Mom replies. She exhales a sigh, and I catch the sweet scent of strawberry wine. Not for the first time since I got sick, I wonder what alcohol tastes like.

"He's going to be surrounded by gorgeous girls in glamorous dresses." I flop back against the couch, all drama, completely justified. "There's this one chick going. She's got her sights set on him. Big time." Last Friday, when Luke and I had our chat, and I forced him to go to this stupid thing, I was so focused on keeping the handcuffs off, I completely forgot about Queen Amy.

"Oh dear, oh dear."

"She's so pretty. We're talking music-video levels of good-looking. All tall and tan. Plus, she drives this supercool car, and she can leave her house whenever she wants."

"She can leave her house whenever she wants? Ugh. So unoriginal."

"Nice job, Tina Fey, you nailed it." Mom bows her head, and I jam an elbow into her arm. "Come on. I'm serious. She is the kind of girl guys kill for."

"Okay." Mom adopts a serious face and turns toward me, crossing her legs on the couch. "If she's all that, and he could be with her, why isn't he?" You know when you're about to get advice so obvious you can't think for a second why you didn't figure it out on your own? That's about to happen. I can feel it.

"She's a little rude, kind of bossy, sort of pushy. She's pretty relentless. Some might say abrasive. She knows we're a thing—she must, because he changed his relationship status on the Metro, and, trust me, Mom, she's all over his page, all the time—but she still insists on dropping hugs and kisses on his profile every morning," I reply.

"You mean to tell me Luke turned down this tall, tanned über-babe with a sweet ride just because she's got a crappy personality? Is he crazy?" Mom knocks it out of the park using her best eighties Valley Girl voice, complete with vocal fry. I roll my eyes so hard my vision cramps.

"I never said she was nice," I defend myself weakly.

"Maybe, but you're worried that nice, smart guy Luke, the boy who has been around here every night to spend time with you, is incapable of resisting Tall and Tanned just because she drives a nice car?" Mom shovels the now-chocolate-less cookie into her mouth, dusts off her hands, and reaches for her wineglass.

"It's more the idea that she can leave the house, go on dates, hold his hand. Give him actual hugs and kisses. The car is really just a bonus," I venture cautiously. Mom likes to pretend that the only reason I don't have any friends is that they've all been too busy to call—for almost four years.

"Nor, I may be getting older, my sight is definitely not what it used to be, but I can see that Luke is a good-looking kid. If he wanted someone like the girl you're describing, he'd have her already. You have to try and cut him some slack. At the very least, get your head asking the right questions, like why, if your mental health bothers him, does he keep coming back?"

That makes sense to me, but I can't make it stick. It rolls over the top of my head the same way water rolls off a duck's back. In my mind, Luke is at that party being reminded of everything he doesn't have while he's with me. I wonder how dazzling Amy's dress is.

A knock at the door makes both Mom and me jump. A wave of pink wine rip-curls right out of her glass and splashes on her shirt. She uses her fingertips to wipe it away.

"Are you expecting someone?" I ask.

"You mean besides Brad Pitt?"

"Then it's probably him."

"How's my hair?" Mom snickers as she climbs off the couch and heads for the door. She makes a ceremony of opening it and revealing our mystery visitor. "Ah. Norah, I think this Brad Pitt is for you."

"Hi, Mrs. Dean." Luke. I clamber to my feet, trip over

buckling Bambi legs as I make a dash for the door. The instant I see him, something in me goes slack. I sink, feel weightless, like I'm submerged in water. He looks dapper in his button-down with that stuff in his hair that makes it look wet. I'm so happy to see him. And then sirens screech in my head. Why am I seeing him? We agreed. He's not supposed to be here.

"Why aren't you at the Fall Ball?" My tone is clipped.

"I think I'm gonna go and catch the rest of this movie in my room," Mom announces. She kisses me on the fore-head and then trots off upstairs.

"I was," he says. "But it was boring, so I bailed early." I check the clock that hangs above my grandma's glass cabi-net in the hall. It's only 8:05. He left his house at 7:15. Cardinal is ten minutes away. He only stayed at the party for thirty minutes.

Oh, well. At least he didn't break his promise, right? And he went. I did my part, didn't hold him back. Plus, when your self-esteem has been as pummeled as mine, when there's a guy standing on your front porch with a face made for film and a smile that makes you believe in magic, it's way too easy to convince yourself that he hasn't rushed home just to hang out with you. Like he said, the party must have been boring.

"You wanna watch a movie?" In his right hand he's

carrying a brown paper bag with the Mamma's Maid Ice Cream Parlor logo printed on it.

"Hmm, maybe. But I gotta warn you, my company doesn't come cheap," I tease.

"Oh yeah? What's it going to cost me?" His voice drops low, and a bomb explodes in the pit of my stomach.

"One whole carton of ice cream," I say, flapping my lashes so hard a breeze starts blowing.

"I'm in luck." He holds up the brown bag. Fears of him feeling shackled die. I stand aside and usher him in. I can't wait to show him the monster movie I recorded.

Sometimes a thing that happens in cheesy horror movies is sex. I usually skip past those parts. Not because I'm a prude. It's all that sweaty skin pushed together; it totally screws with my mind.

I could see it coming from a mile away. I should have suggested we turn it off when the two leads got trapped in a basement and started talking about taking their clothes off to avoid pneumonia.

"Wow, that's . . . erm . . ." Luke tips his head to the side as the sex unfolding onscreen takes an acrobatic turn for the worst. I sink like a stone into my seat. "Whoa! A head wound waiting to happen, that's what that is." I laugh, despite my agonizing demise. Luke turns to me, clocks my

cocooned body, and reaches for the remote. "We can probably skip past this part."

"Thank you," I say when he hits fast-forward.

Except the half wolf/half man and his female costar
keep going and going, only now it's happening at super-
speed.

"Hot damn," he exclaims and starts pressing buttons
on the remote so fast it's a wonder his fingers don't catch
fire. Anxiety releases my body from its tight furl, and I
burst into hysterics, my limbs loosening to liquid propor-
tions. I render up so much control I start slipping, like
butter off a baking tray. My butt slides down the leather
couch, and I hit the floor with a bump.

"Shit, Norah." In a blink he's kneeling beside me. "Are
you okay?" He reaches out, hands hovering close, but not
quite close enough to touch. I look at him through floods
of tears. Happy tears. Hilarious tears. I've never laughed
so hard I've cried before. I can't talk, so I just nod. He
shakes his head, starts chuckling. He gets comfortable on
the carpet beside me and I'm glad I used Mom's expensive,
coconut-scented shampoo.

"My stomach hurts," I tell him, rubbing muscles that
have been asleep for way too long.

"I bet. You'll have a six-pack tomorrow."

"I don't know why people do sit-ups when laughing is so much fun."

"People are crazy." He excuses them with a shrug.

"What about me? Do you think I'm crazy?" I'm half teasing, half testing him.

"I think you're beautiful. And smart. And funny." He gets an A plus. I flush, my insides going gooier than our ice cream leftovers. In my head I'm rolling around in green fields; my sky is pink, the sun is made of gold glitter. But then, a gray storm cloud rolls in, smothers my sweet sky with thunder.

He didn't say no.

"I . . . I . . ." I stutter. It's a small voice, but it cancels out his compliments in one swoop.

"What's—" A bang, like a gunshot, cuts his question in half. My bones leap from my body and my heart trips. I brace for the apocalypse, an infestation of zombies, a tumbling meteor, World War X breaking out right here in Triangle Crescent.

"Norah, it's okay. Look." I didn't notice Luke stand up, but I find him by the window, the curtain peeled back. He's looking at the sky. "Fireworks," he says as three more bangs cut right through me. I jump again and my teeth catch my tongue.

"It's not July Fourth," I say, like he doesn't already know this, like *I* don't already know this.

"Come take a look." He's all excited. I feel afraid. "Wait. Our first fireworks display. We need a better view." What I need is the couch and the coffee table to help me stand. He speeds off into the hall; the lock on the front door clicks, and I hear the bolt grind as he pulls it back.

Has he gone? Did he forget that I can't follow?

I lean left until I can see the front door. It's wide open and he's just standing there, leaning up against the jamb. Outside is like a light show; every bang creates a new color. In my head I see the photos on Amy's Metro profile, consider that if she were here instead of me, she'd take total advantage of this situation. Probably snatch his hand, drag him outside, curl up against him while they watch the sky. Fireworks are romantic. I've seen that exact scenario unfold on YouTube kissing videos. The thought carries me cautiously toward the porch. I fall in beside Luke, too wobbly to stand, too caught up in acting normal to suggest we close the door in case one of those babies gets loose and flies straight for us. My knees buckle, and I sit on the floor, legs crossed, on the inner side of the step.

"Are we okay to watch?" he asks. I think of the party he's not at, the measly few minutes he spent with his friends on a Friday night.

"Sure." I owe him at least ten more minutes of normal. Just keep breathing.

But something doesn't feel right. My mind is attempting sabotage, refusing to find the beauty, the fun, the excitement in watching what are essentially pretty explosives.

Luke sits on the floor beside me, plants his feet on the porch, talks about how he hasn't seen fireworks since last year.

"What about New Year's?" I only ask because I distinctly remember that night being one of the loudest. I spent it cowering under my comforter, eating potato chips and mainlining rock music.

"Fell asleep before midnight watching a *SpongeBob* marathon. Forever one of the cool kids."

He turns, winks at me, then spins back to look at the sky. He makes me smile.

I fix my sights on his profile. His jaw is so sharp, I think if I ran a finger over it, I'd cut myself.

"I'd like to go to Times Square one New Year's," he says. "Just to see what all the fuss is about."

"Yes." I sigh. I mean, right now I couldn't think of anything more terrifying, but I'd be lying if I said I hadn't thought about being there before.

"We should go." Luke is suddenly so animated, it's a

wonder the fireworks aren't watching him. "I bet we could get a couple of free flights off my mom," he tells me.

Interesting, but irrelevant. I laugh a fake laugh; there's nothing funny about my desolate future.

He turns to look at me; I wonder if my face has fallen as much as his.

"What? You don't want to go? Or maybe you don't want to go with me?" Did he take a bump to the head when I wasn't looking? Maybe the noxious fumes the fireworks are spreading have gotten him a little confused.

"I can't leave my house. I think it's safe to say the chances of me jumping on a plane to go and watch fireworks are nonexistent."

"Oh God, no. I didn't mean . . . I'm sorry . . . I wasn't meaning this year . . . I just meant . . . whenever, one year, any year, you know?"

"Maybe." I stare at my polish-perfect pedicure. It only took me six hours to get it right.

"We don't need to put a date on it. Who's to say this time next year you won't be globetrotting? Come spring, you could be in Europe." My heart smiles; it's not strong enough to show on my face. "But . . . you don't believe any of that's possible?" he ventures carefully.

"No. I mean, yes. I'm not sure. I know it's probable . . ."

I pause, don't know how to finish my sentence without sounding like I'm feeling sorry for myself.

"But . . ." he prompts.

I shrug. I have no idea how to tell him I feel helpless. That I can't seem to find the strength or energy to fight myself daily for an infinite amount of time and make the doc's neural pathways stick. That I'm afraid. That I'm just . . . stuck.

"You're brave, did you know that?"

He must have me mistaken for someone else. "You have all these fears, your body endures all this pain and heartache, but you keep going. I think that's really brave."

I shake my head. My mind is telling me that he's wrong. Brave is swords and shields. People who are fearless in the face of adversity. Warriors for social justice. Brave is not me. But my heart registers the way he's looking at me now, and my shoulders straighten. I feel shiny, normal. Something flips over in my stomach and I find myself looking at his lips.

"I think I see you a little differently than how you see yourself," he says.

"I like how you see me," I tell him in a whisper. And then he leans forward, closes the gap between us, and pushes his lips against mine.

My biggest fear comes from a place I'm not expecting, as his breath, warm and sweet like peppermint, fills my mouth. I think about all the stuff I researched, every alien thing that popped up on my computer screen in a petri dish. I wonder if Luke had a drink at the Fall Ball, shared a cup with someone who had a cold sore. I consider how many cheeks his lips touched when he arrived, and then how many more cheeks those lips touched before reaching mine. I even spare a second to remember the boy at Cardinal who's suffering from a case of mono. But the fear that asserts itself the most is his motive for doing what he's done.

I spring back like he's spat acid. Make like a crab across the floor and wipe my mouth on the sleeve of my sweater.

"Norah. I'm so sorry." He reaches out, grabs my hand, and I rip it free from his grasp. "Shit," he says, clutching his fingers like he's just been burned. "I'm sorry. I didn't mean to do that. Any of that. I wasn't thinking. Fuck. I'm so sorry."

Warmbreathpetridishesbugsbacteriaalienlifeformscold-soreskissescheekslipsmonomotive. Motive. MOTIVE.

It's how my head is working as I pull myself to my feet using the banister. Faster and faster, like a malfunctioning merry-go-round. No stopping. No slowing. No breathing. My mouth is numb.

Luke keeps saying *Fuck*, running his hands through his hair, an I've-just-seen-a-car-accident-unfold expression emblazoned on his paling face.

"How could you do that?" I ask, tears streaming down my cheeks, words sliced and diced as they fall through chattering teeth.

"I don't know," Luke says, all flustered, watching the floor as he paces back and forth.

"You don't get it," I spit. "I thought you did, but you don't."

"I do." He makes a beeline for me, hands outstretched. My knees are trembling too much to move; the best I can do is flinch. He stops a foot short of my face when he sees my body jerk and plants his hands hard in his pockets. "I hate that," he says. "I hate that I've made you feel afraid."

"Then why did you? You didn't have to. Or did you?" Motive. Talking about flying to New York, buying me a journal for France, sitting here watching the fireworks like a normal couple. He thinks I'm beautiful, smart, funny, but he never actually said not crazy. I wonder if he only stayed at the ball for a few minutes because he felt like I used to watching my Metro feed on a weekend. I wonder if he sighed when he left a roomful of bodies swaying against each other, arms and legs free from scratches, for a girl-friend he can't even kiss.

He didn't leave the party because he was bored; he left that party because it was a slap in the face.

My head is having its own ball. Adding things together like this is Clue and we're trying to uncover a killer.

"No. Norah, please."

I could breathe life back into the dead with the amount of adrenaline running through me. "Is that what this is about? You said you didn't miss kissing, but you do, don't you?" It doesn't matter what he says. I can't hear him for the rush of blood in my head. Besides, the answers have already been decided in my mind.

"It's not about kissing, Norah. It's about you, about how I feel about you. I got lost for a second."

"Bullshit. You don't just forget I'm this, that I have all these things wrong with me."

"That's what I'm trying to tell you. I did. I do. I don't always see it, but I always see you."

"You see normal. And that's not how this works. You should have stayed at your ball. Found a girl you can have fun with, one who doesn't hold you back, break down when you try to touch her." I wipe my mouth a second time; I'm not even thinking about germs anymore.

"I'm confused. Is this about me kissing you or about your own insecurities?" He's lucky I can't touch him because I would slap him so hard right now.

"You need to leave," I say. My guts turn inside out.

"You don't mean that," he replies. His heart is thumping so hard I can see it throbbing in his throat.

"Yes, I do. Go. Leave me alone." I try for a yell, but it comes out small, a tremor tearing through it.

"Norah, please . . ."

"Leave me alone."

For a second I think he's not going anywhere, then, like a torpedo, he disappears out the door.

32

Norah,

*I'm so sorry. I made a huge mistake. Please
forgive me.*

Norah,

*You were right. I didn't understand, but I'm
learning. I bought some books to read. I'm going
to figure this out.*

Norah,

*Did you know that approximately three million
people in the U.S. suffer from some form of OCD?
I didn't know that.*

Norah,

*I started reading about agoraphobia today. There's
this association called Limitless. They have an
online support group for people to share stories and
strategies.*

Norah,

I miss you. I kissed you because I couldn't help it.

I shouldn't have done that, but that's all there was to it. Please don't push me away. I have everything I want when I'm with you. I shouldn't have crossed that line, but I swear to you, it wasn't because I needed to.

33

"Norah, honey." Mom creeps into my room, as quiet as a mouse. "How are you feeling?"

"Dead inside."

"You're not dead inside." She pulls the comforter from over my head, and my skin fizzes at the sudden *whoosh* of fresh air. I wonder why she asked if she was just going to tell me I'm wrong. "You promised Dr. Reeves you'd get out of bed today."

"It's only . . ." I look at my watch: eight thirty. I moan, snatch my covers, and bury myself back beneath them. God. She's brutal when she's trying to save me from myself.

"I was hoping you'd come downstairs and have some breakfast with me. I made pancakes in the shape of rocket ships." I flip the cover down, consider blowing her off for the fourth time in as many days, but she looks so helpless. Her shoulders are definitely more slumped over, and I suspect that has something to do with the amount of stress sitting on her back.

"Sure," I reply.

"Really?" she ventures cautiously so as not to spook my already-made-up mind.

"Yeah. I could eat a pancake." Maybe. At least, I know I definitely can't stomach any more snot shakes, and I have to do something to sustain myself.

She flits toward the door, rolling up her sleeves. I suspect this is because the aforementioned rocket-ship pancakes have yet to be made, and she was just using their existence as a way to coax me out from under my sheets. "They'll be ready in five—"

"Mom?" I call before she can leave the room.

"Uh-huh?"

"Did we get any mail yet?"

She waits a second, takes a deep breath before dropping the bomb. "No. I'm sorry, honey." I should stop asking. It's not fair that I keep making her deliver sad news, bad news, no news.

I've left it too long.

"Maybe he'll write tomorrow," she says. "I bet he's been all kinds of snowed under with his finals."

It's been two weeks since Luke last dropped a folded yellow note written in perfect cursive through the mail slot. It's been almost four weeks since he kissed me.

"I wish you'd talk to me," Mom says. "It's been a long time since I couldn't figure out what you're thinking."

I don't know how to talk to her. Don't know how to talk. Can't figure out what I'm thinking. Not sure I even want to. I was being hyperbolic when I said I was dead inside, but I am stuck in some sort of limbo wasteland. I let my head take Luke's kiss to a dark place, and it's been lording it over me ever since.

I'm always a slave to my thoughts, always at the mercy of what I'm not, what I can't be. But he brought expectation here, shone a light on life, and something that's been sleeping woke up inside me. I can't figure out how to lull it back to sleep, can't figure out how to nurture it into something normal.

Before, I was simply-average Norah. Then I was too-sick-to-function Norah. Now I'm drifting somewhere in between.

"I love you," I tell Mom.

"I love you too, baby," she says.

She leaves, and I reach under my pillow, grab the journal that Luke gave me, and turn to the Notes section.

My heart throbs.

It's there. I did write it.

I thought maybe I'd imagined it, was sort of hoping I had.

The List.

Last night, somewhere between exhaustion, low blood

sugar, and more emotion than a signed senior yearbook, I started writing a list of all the things I want to do before I officially hang a *Do Not Resuscitate* sign on my life— well, I *started* drawing the Leaning Tower of Pisa, but that turned into a sketch of Rouen Cathedral, which turned into doodles of hearts, and then thoughts of kissing, and suddenly here it is: the accidental list.

I run my fingers over the lines of ink, feel the barely there indents the pen pressure has left in the paper. I don't remember the final draft looking this long.

I've only written down ten things, but the actual construction of the list took six pages to get right. Well, this is me. It's not as simple as writing a letter to Santa. It took a while to prioritize, arrange my to-do items in order of importance. Finally, after the tenth attempt, I had it all figured out. At least, I had the top six figured out. I think.

1. Get my high school diploma
2. Go to France (with Mom?)
3. Smell the roses in our garden
4. Try some cashew-nut cream cheese
5. Learn to drive a car

My insides feel like they're being crammed into a jam jar. Spelling out all the things I can't do tears my soul to pieces. I knew it would. A tear drips onto my nice, neat, perfectly assembled final draft and smudges the ink of item number 6 into an unreadable blur. The words vanish, but I know exactly what was written.

6. Kiss Luke.

34

It gets to five and I'm watching a woman on television turn a pair of old net curtains into what she says will be a "traffic-stopping tunic." I'm not convinced. I wonder if maybe she's high on fabric-glue fumes, because she's smiling a smile that outstretches space. But then, I suppose she exhibits this same level of delirium every week, even the times she's not in range of a tube of Crazy Paste. Maybe crafting just makes you happy. Maybe I'll feel like less of a failure if I can turn wax crayons and rose oil into a bunch of scented candles. Or make costume jewelry out of a bulk buy of gemstones. A small business venture to give my life purpose. That's how my gran started. The story of her mixing yogurt and sand to make a facial scrub during tough times is legendary.

Meh. My enthusiasm is in broken bits and I can't even muster the energy to stick that back together, let alone craft a pair of pretty earrings.

I jump when my phone rings, not from fright. It's excitement. It shoots through my stomach like a falling star, only to burn out when I check the screen and discover it's not Luke. Not that there's a reason he would be calling. I guess it was just a thought because it's Friday night. Or what used to be ice-cream-and-mind-numbing-movie night.

"Hey, Mom."

"Hey, sweetheart. How are you feeling?" She sounds rushed. I can hear her sifting through sheets of paper.

"I'm good," I lie, pulling the sleeve of my sweater over the new scratch on my arm. "Are you okay?"

"Ugh. You remember me telling you about the new guy, Justin?"

Ah, Justin. The office rookie who can't decipher his ass from his elbow and smells like weed every time he comes back off his break.

"Yes."

"He's only gone and mixed up a ton of inventory slips."

I hiss a painful note through my front teeth, though I don't really know what this means. I'm just leeching off her tone.

"Yeah. The guy has placed orders for almost a million dollars' worth of building material that we don't need. Ugh." Her palm makes a slapping sound as it hits her forehead. "My boss is going to kill me if I don't fix this mess."

"Can you fix it?" I hesitate before I ask. It's hard to decide how serious she is when I can't see her face.

"Norah Dean," she tsks. "This is me you're talking to. I can fix anything." True. Turns out this morning we didn't have any eggs to make the pancakes she promised, so she used banana instead. They were actually pretty good.

"Right." I smile. Not serious, just a little stressed.

"Will you be okay fixing your own dinner?"

"Absolutely. You want me to make you something?"

"Don't worry about me." She groans. "I've got a feeling this is going to take all night. You'll be all right alone?"

"Puh-lease," I scoff. "This is me you're talking to. One night is practically child's play these days."

"Smart-ass," she teases. "I'll be by my phone the entire time. Call me if you need anything, anything at all, okay?"

"Cross my heart." I go through the motion, despite the fact she can't see it.

"What's my extension number?" Mom asks, testing my memory because she hasn't been able to leave her usual laundry list of emergency contacts on the fridge.

"Mom, I know the number. I didn't forget."

"Good. Then you should have no problem reciting it back to me right now."

I reel off the number. "Now, how do I reach 911 again?"

"Har. Har."

• • •

Microwavable macaroni and cheese. It's what's for dinner. I pierce the film lid twelve times and blast it with radiation for twenty seconds longer than the instructions say I should. You can never be too careful when it comes to undercooked anything.

I sit down at the table and fork my way through the gloppy white sauce. Every bite makes my insides clench and then gurgle, but I power through, remind myself that I have to eat to stay alive.

Despite appearances, it's not the worst meal I've ever had. Mom gets me this brand of mac and cheese especially because they don't put ground pepper in it, which saves me from the indignity of having to sift through mountains of melted cheese just to fish out the almost invisible black bits.

The clock claws its way to 6:00 p.m., and I'm forced to mute my Metro feed, because if I get one more notification about how much fun people are having with their Friday night, I'm going to break the shit out of my phone.

After I'm done eating, I head down the hall. I'm checking the lock and the bolt on the door for the eighth time when I hear voices. My heart hammers in my ears. Luke.

Don't look. Don't look, don't look, don't look, don't look, I think as I make my way over to the porch window. It's just a window; it shouldn't hold so much sentimentality for me, but it does, and when I peek through the curtains, tears sting my eyes.

Luke is standing in his driveway with a blond girl, some chick with a nose ring, and this dude wearing a Death's Head band tee under a tuxedo jacket.

Another party. Another dance.

That's why my phone's been blowing up. The guys are all wearing tailored jackets. The girls are decked out like a couple of Christmas trees in dresses that twinkle under the dying sun. Smiles all around, excited chatter; I feel like I'm watching a coming-of-age sitcom. Luke climbs in the driver's side of his truck. Blond girl climbs in beside him. His date? Maybe. The other guy and girl dash off and jump into their own car, one that has streaks of orange flames painted up the sides. I startle when Luke's truck growls to life.

I will him to look up, to look over at my house. I beg, plead, pray, but without taking a single glance this way, he reverses out onto the road and speeds off, closely followed by the car.

I turn around; heavy eyes survey my empty house. Still. Silent. Alone. I'm transported to a cold place. A lonely back alley that's never seen a single ray of sun, that forever collects rain. I feel any color that my skin was holding on to roll right off and pool around my ankles.

This is my fault.

I broke something beautiful.

I cut away the one thing that made me feel like I wasn't just waiting for death, and I did it because I let my mind run riot.

He was right. I wasn't angry because he kissed me. I didn't tell him to leave because he made a mistake. We came undone when I let my insecurities take control. Because I was obsessing over everything I wasn't, and everything I thought he wanted.

I should have listened to him. Trusted him.

Anxiety wraps itself around my lungs like frozen vines. It squeezes and squeezes until I can't breathe. I'm falling, fast, and there's only one way I can think of to stop it.

My legs feel like they belong to someone else as I climb the mountainous staircase. I'm sobbing by the time I reach the top. The world is turning so quickly. I just want it to stop. I want my heart to stop hammering. I want thoughts to leave me alone. I've been thinking for so long. My brain is blistered. It hurts to use my head right now.

My muscles are mush as I stumble into the bathroom, thump on the light, and snatch the side of the sink to steady myself.

My reflection makes me feel sick. I grip the basin so tightly my knuckles pop. I wonder if I cut deep enough whether I'll be able to keep my mind from mixing me up indefinitely.

"You sabotaged me! Why won't you just leave me alone?" I scream, then reach for the scissors. My wrist catches a carton of Q-tips, and they fall from the cabinet, rain down on the floor. It makes me think of summer with my gran, blowing dandelions in her garden and dancing in the floating seeds.

God, I miss that girl, the one who could twirl barefoot in the garden.

I sink to the floor, scissors in my hand. I haven't seen the last cut I made. I've felt it sting against my jeans, but the second that stopped, I pushed the incident to the back of my mind. It's easier to live with yourself if you do that.

When I run my fingers over the space, I find it. It's slightly raised, still healing. The thought of infection spares it, and I move to the older scar below. Scissors poised, my head on upside down, I pull my skin tight.

My eyes scrunch shut and more tears squeeze out. Luke's face, when I put my hand on top of his and he started grinning like a kid on his way to Candyland, is burned into the backs of my eyelids. I can touch him. It won't kill me. If I could have stolen myself, slowed my head down for just a second, we'd be together right now, watching a movie.

I want to tell him I'm sorry. I want to tell him I'm insecure. I want to tell him that I am hard work, that my head is a mess, that my sickness was making even the smallest thought explode that night. I want to tell him his kiss scared me but I can't stop wanting a second one. I want to ask him to teach me how to touch.

I want to show him my list.

I want to tell him I've been dreaming of doing things.

I want to tell him, more than anything, that I miss him.

I close in on my thigh with the blade, but then something happens that's never happened before. I meet with resistance, like there's an invisible barrier between skin and scissors. I can't make them touch, can't make myself do it. Wiping snot on the back of my hand, I stroke the sharp edge with my thumb. I'm not sure what I'm looking for, a force field, a puppet string being pulled. Something. But I find nothing. So it must be me stopping myself. I can't even begin to fathom what that means right now.

Weeping turns to tearless sobs as I curl up in a ball on the bathroom floor, waiting for my heart and head to slow down. I hug my knees so tight they're almost touching my chin. The scissors stay in my palm. I keep them close to my chest because I'm not sure I don't need them yet.

35

Iᴛ sᴛɪɴɢs ᴡʜᴇɴ ɪ ᴏᴘᴇɴ my eyes. The bathroom light
is luminous, bleaching everything it touches bright white.
My body jerks awake. I cash in on the burst of energy,
clamber to my feet, and lurch toward the door. I survey the
bathroom, wonder how I got here. My bearings are AWOL,
rolling around the floor like spilled marbles. For the longest second I can't remember anything. It's only when I feel
something in my palm and unfurl my fingers to reveal scissors that I remember I came up here to cut myself. But I
didn't. Couldn't. I stopped myself. Something I've never
been able to do before. Just to make sure, I reach between
my legs, swipe my thigh with my fingers. They come away
clean.

I drop the scissors in the trash can as I leave without
a moment's thought. I'm too busy thinking about reaching
out to Luke.

I trudge across the hall, float toward my bed, and flop
down. I pull on my headphones, turn up the volume on

the *Greatest Love Ballads* album I downloaded last week, and open a new message tab on my phone.

Saying sorry is hard.

And the soulful song lyrics being crooned into my ears aren't inspiring at all.

Finding a balance between explanation and emotional blackmail is causing friction and creating a storm inside my head.

Exhaustion burns my eyes, and typing out a text is getting tough. I'm making more mistakes than sense. I blink, and it takes minutes instead of seconds to recover my sight. I really need to go downstairs, turn on all the lights before it gets too dark.

I don't make it.

After a second blink, I wake with a start. There's a brief moment of panic because I can't hear a thing. Then it registers that I still have my headphones on. I pull them off and sit up. My head feels like it stayed behind on the pillow. Ugh. I should not have gotten drunk on love songs. Emotional hangovers are the worst.

Beyond midnight has crept into my bedroom and covered everything in a blanket of pitch-black. At some point during sleep, my cell escaped my clutches. I reach out, pat my comforter down in search of it. When my fingers hit the screen, the thing illuminates, blasts a laser beam of light into my eyes and scorches my corneas.

That'll definitely help your headache, I chide myself silently.

Green and purple spots dance in my vision as I check the time. Two a.m. Whoa. Exhaustion got me good.

I need orange juice and a cold compress for my head. With the enthusiasm of a corpse, I abandon my phone, roll off my bed, and slump out the door. I've lived in this house for seventeen years but still use the wall to guide me to the light switch.

I drag my fingers down the wall, run them over photographs of me, Mom, and my grandma, all dressed up in our Sunday best especially for this shoot, which took place on a Wednesday the summer I turned thirteen.

The last summer I ever really *lived.*

The last frame my fingers find is the gaudy gold one that displays my "Congratulations, You Graduated from Middle School" certificate. The light switch is just above it, right before Mom's room.

I'm about to slap it on when I notice the faintest glow of silver moonlight seeping out of a crack in Mom's door.

That's weird. The door is open. Why is the door open?

Mom's door is never open. We have a pact. She's never broken the pact, not once since I got sick.

Okay, brain, calm down. We've been here before.

This little talking-to works about as well as it does when other people try it on me: not at all. The cogs of my mind are already turning, throwing out thoughts that make my blood run cold.

It could be Mom. Maybe she's home and forgot to close her door; she has had a lot of her own brain fog to deal with. It's possible she slipped up this one time. But then, if she's home at this hour, she'd be in bed. And if she's in bed, why aren't her curtains closed?

Because she's not in bed. She's not in her room.

I glare at the door handle, see Mom closing it before she trotted off down the stairs and left for work.

I remember.

I remember getting twitchy because she just headed off to work without washing the brass finish smell off her hands.

My knees knock together. But if Mom closed the door, and I didn't open it . . . Then, right on cue to confirm my suspicions, there's a bump, and a single note from Mom's silver jewelry box rings out. It only does that when it's open and the crystal ballerina begins her pirouette. I feel a sharp jolt as my entire world comes to a screeching halt. My whole body starts to convulse.

There's someone in my house.

I dry-heave.

Call Mom. I reach down to my waistband, but my cell isn't there because I left it on the bed. I look over at the way I just walked; the corridor stretches beneath my feet.

Fuck.

I don't know what to do. My eyes roll into the back of my head, make me blind for a second.

Mental slap.

There is one thing I absolutely cannot do, and that's pass out.

My body aches as my muscles go into spasm. I roll my jaw, try my best to shake my shoulders loose. I have to breathe. Get some oxygen in my blood and try my best to stop my heart from tripping over itself to choke out beats. I can hear it in my ears. It might sound hypnotic if I weren't so scared.

I have to move, get away from this door before whoever's in Mom's room comes out and finds me. Going back to my room would be a mistake. If whoever is in there is robbing us, they're going in my room next. I know they haven't been there already because everything is untouched. A robber would have taken my phone, the TV, my iPod, but it was all still there. Shit, my gran bought me headphones that are worth more than a small car.

Bathroom is out too; there's nowhere to hide in there. And I stopped being able to fit inside our linen closet when I was six.

Logic says I go downstairs. Impossible. I've got weights strapped to my knees. But I have to find a way or risk meeting the intruder face to face. And then what? What if they're armed? What if they kidnap me? What if they kill me? Is my survival instinct really that broken?

I'm wasting too much time on what-ifs.

I have to move before I shut down. The only parts of my body that are still working sufficiently are my arms. I crouch down, lower my butt onto the carpet, and push myself toward the top of the stairs. It's just like rowing, except there's more friction. A lot more friction. The resistance-fueled scrape of my skin against the worn green carpet that lines our hall stings worse than when you catch your arm on a boiling kettle. It's like having your legs exfoliated with an electric sander.

My toes test the floor in front of me, silently tapping out my path like a white cane. When the solid surface disappears, I know I've reached the first step. I push myself down; my body hits the second step with a sharp jar. I mentally promise my spine to be more careful with the next one.

I keep going, hit the halfway point at the same time I hear Mom's door squeak. It's dark out here, not as dark as it was before my eyes adjusted, but still pretty well drenched in night. I pray it's enough to keep my presence concealed and scoot toward the banister, where there is slightly more shadow.

The intruder leaves my mom's room backside first. It's probably better if I don't see him, but that prepared-for-everything part of me has to know which room he goes into next, has to know what he looks like in case the police ask. I have to know for me too. When this is all over, I'm going to need to be able to put a face to the person that broke into my home and ruined my safe circle forever.

I blink away tears and wipe them off my cheeks. The intruder turns, and I startle, fight hard to hold a squeal back behind my teeth. The jackass is wearing a skeleton mask. Vomit rises up in my throat. I lift a trembling hand, slap it silently over my mouth, and swallow my gorge back down, along with a tidal wave of sobs. When he moves along the hall, his jacket makes a scrunching sound. I notice his jeans, or rather the skulls stitched on below the side pocket . . .

My mind races back to the moment I first saw them. Oh, shit.

I've got to get out of this house. This is the Helping Hands Guy. The one that stood in my kitchen a couple of months ago, ogling my nearly naked frame. I remember his dark eyes climbing up my body like a cockroach.

Bullshit he had a key. Bullshit he was following company procedure. There's no way my mom would let anyone have a free pass to our house. I should have known that, should have been able to see through his lies. I don't let my mind question whether or not he'd planned to rob us that day, because if he had that would mean I interrupted him. God, he must be pretty angry at me for that.

I watch him disappear toward my bedroom, and then I carry on sliding down the stairs until I hit the bottom step. I can't take it twice. I don't have time. I wonder if he figured out what was wrong with me. He'd only have to ask his boss.

I'm suddenly afraid he'll catch on to my escape attempt if he finds my room empty. My heart tries to choke me.

I slide onto the floor on my hands and knees and crawl toward the door. My teeth slam down on my tongue when something bites into my palms. There's a popping sound.

Several popping sounds. I freeze. Try to swallow back more tears and a mouthful of hot saliva.

At first I can't figure out what it is. Something is slicing into me and my best guess would be I'm crawling through a field full of sharp paper. But when I lift my hand, I see it, glistening in whatever moonlight has managed to sneak in through the porch windows. Broken glass. My head snaps around to survey Gran's Georgian glass cabinet. He must not have been able to pick the rusty antique lock because he's totaled the front of it, and I'm bleeding all over the debris.

No time to dwell. The door is only a few feet away and my eyes are rolling again. I hold my breath, think of my bed, my soft warm sheets, my favorite book, Mom and me talking about television, Luke's smile and the way his skin feels against mine.

The pain doesn't stop, but the popping sound does. Somehow, I've made it.

My hands are soaked ruby red. They shake like the tail of a rattlesnake as I reach for the latch. It clicks, and I pull back the bolt. The door is unbroken; he must have found another way in. I pull it open a fraction, let the moonlight pour in. A rush of fresh air engulfs me, and it never felt so good.

But now I have to make it across the driveway. It might as well be an army assault course. I pause, squeeze my teeth together so tight my jaw feels like it's going to snap. The sweat surfacing on my palms exacerbates the sting and sets my cuts on fire.

I can't do it. Fuck. I can't do it.

This is my new hell. This is definitely what being damned feels like. I think *Fuck* a thousand more times. It's a mistake to run a hand through my hair, but I do it anyway, splashing blood into my blond.

I hear the faint bump of a jackass stumbling into something upstairs. God. I hope he caught his shin on a sharp corner. I hope he smacked it down to the bone on my gothic vanity and that it hurts so bad his stomach starts turning. But then I guess if he's hurt himself, he's probably going to be even more pissed off.

I really gotta go. He could discover me at any second.

I crack the door further so the gap is wide enough for me to fit through.

I don't have a heading, but I'm looking at Luke's house. His truck is in the driveway. I was hoping there'd be a light on, but the place is bathed in blackness. The Trips' house is dark too. Triangle Crescent is sound asleep. I wonder if any of our neighbors will wake to discover missing valuables and lakes of shattered glass.

Luke's house is the closest option. And he brings me ice cream without black bits because he knows I don't like them. He gets me orange juice when my legs aren't working. He brings the stars to my bedroom so I can lie beneath them. He talks about my future, even when I'm not sure I have one. He makes me feel safe.

I need to feel safe again.

My legs are still as stable as jelly, so I have no choice but to move forward on my hands. Placing my palms one at a time on the ground, I give a brief thought to all the sneakers, boots, sandals, and shoes that have tread their crap on this porch over the years. It makes me whimper. All that bacteria I'm dipping my open wounds in.

My shoulders emerge from the door and everything grows to twice its original size.

Come on, Norah. You can't stay here.

I pant out a breath, scrunch my eyes shut and then open them in the hope it will clear my vision. It doesn't.

I lift my palm, move it forward slowly, and do the same again. And again. I tune out the squelching sounds until my sliced-up knees have joined my hands on the infection-imminent porch.

The night is cool. It feels big, infinite, impossible to think the sun can overcome it. Every muscle tightens, as if my insides were being strangled by elastic bands. Sniveling,

I make my way down the steps, wishing they'd stop moving and make this easier.

With my dignity still trapped inside the house, I flop off the porch and collapse on the concrete driveway. My left hip smashes against the ground, and I bump my chin so hard my teeth slam shut, almost severing my tongue in two.

I look up, spit blood.

Luke's front door is still a million miles away. How is it possible I've moved so much and it's not gotten any closer?

There's a *thump-thump-thump* from inside my house. I've stomped up and down those stairs enough times to recognize the sound. He's coming.

I push through the pain, get back up on my knees, and crawl toward the boxwood hedge as fast as I can. I go deaf, can't hear anything as I haul my ass over the bush and launch myself at Luke's front door.

I slam my fists into the glass and hammer hard. My other hand works the doorbell as I look back over my shoulder.

There's a skeleton standing on my porch.

"Please, Luke. Open the door." I try to scream, but fear is holding my vocal cords hostage and it's a timid shout at best.

The skeleton turns sharply, then leaps off the porch. I think maybe he's going to make a run for it, but then he starts marching toward me.

I thud on the door. Thud so hard it's a wonder my fists don't go through the wood. "Luke!" This time I do scream. It rips from my throat like a liberated lion, shatters wineglasses, makes the atmosphere shake, leaves dust in its wake.

A warm beam of orange light breaks like sunrise from behind the door. I hear the dangling of a chain and the door flies open.

I don't take him in, don't say a word, just throw myself at his chest and press myself airtight against his torso.

"Norah. What the fuck?" he says.

"There's . . . there's . . ." It's hard to talk through sobs. I'm choking on a river of snot and tears. "Someone's in my house."

"Norah, where's your mom? Is she still in the house?"

I shake my head no. That's all I manage before the feeling in my lips disappears and my face melts right off. He wraps one arm around my shoulders; the other snakes around the back of my legs.

"Luke, what's going on?" I hear his mom ask as he lifts me up. I sink into his arms, all my muscles sighing simultaneously.

"Call the cops and an ambulance," he says. I press my head against his heart, feel its angry beat beneath my cheek.

"I got you," he says. "You're safe."

The sound of his breathing carries me off into blissful unconsciousness.

36

GENTLE FINGERS STROKE my cheek, and my eyes flicker open.

My body is all crunched up, bent around like a jelly bean. Mom is looking down at me, smiling. She presses something spongy against my mouth, and my lips latch onto it, suck water from it until the thing is bone-dry.

"Go easy," she says in tones softer than silk. "Too much too soon will make you sick."

I don't focus on anything but her face. Still, dread circles overhead like a flock of starving vultures.

"Where are we?" I ask, but we both know I already know the answer to that. The smell of industrial-strength disinfectant is corroding my nasal passages. The sheets covering me feel like fiberglass. I'm in the hospital.

"Baby, try not to panic."

Panic. Right. That would make sense given my current situation, but my body seems to be behaving. I can feel the flutter of something in my chest, maybe fear. Not the same kind of fear I've been sharing headspace with for the past four years. This is different. Weaker. It stays hidden. I'm not sure it has the drive to push through to the surface.

I lift my eyes, spot my hand wrapped tightly in white bandages, a yellow IV line poking out of the top. I follow the tubes attached to it, up and up, until I find two bags of fluid, half empty. One is clear, the other milky. Safe to assume that explains the sudden change in anxiety levels.

"Mom?"

"It's just a painkiller and some sedative."

"No." I shake my head, reach for the needle, but my other hand is bound in dressings too. It's refusing to go in the direction I tell it to. At first I think the extra padding is responsible for restricting my movement. Then I realize it's not the bandages at all. My body is ignoring me.

A drunk whimper flops from my lips. I focus hard on my fingers, try to psychically beam my instructions straight to the source, but they refuse to acknowledge me. It's the medicine. It's circulating in my system, killing off my control like an evil little nanobot. My breathing hitches.

"Sweetie." Mom restrains my hand with the slightest of touches. "Listen to me: you've been hooked up to this thing for almost two days. Two days and nothing horrible has happened. It's helping."

"I can't . . . I . . ." My head goes foggy and some monitor starts beeping a single obscene note. It sounds like a microwave when it's finished a cycle and wants your attention. Is that my heartbeat? Should it be beating that fast? Should it . . . I can't finish my thought; I don't remember what it was.

The beep works like a Bat-Signal, brings a nurse thundering through the swinging door. Her hair is bright orange, dreadlocked, and she's wearing scrubs covered in superhero cartoons.

"Good morning, sunshine." She flashes her pearly whites at me and all I want to do is ask her what's good about it. I give it a second of thought but can't find the energy to rouse my inner ass.

Mom scoots back, and the nurse takes her place, hovering over me. The badge fixed to her ample bosom says *Carmen*. There's a bottle of green sanitizer attached to the side of my bed. I watch her pump it several times until a string of clear liquid squirts from the nozzle. It goes white and turns to foam when it settles on her palms. She rubs it all over, just like I do, making sure to get all the hidden spots between her fingers. You'd be surprised at how much of your hand doesn't get washed if you don't spread your fingers. Then, to my horror, the nurse, a complete stranger, touches me. Without blinking, she reaches down the front of my hospital-issue gown and pulls something sticky off my chest.

"Don't think you're going to be needing these any-more," she says, her knuckle clipping the edge of my breast on the way back up. She saunters over to the trash can, drops the sticky things in it, and hits her hands with an-other squirt of sanitizer from a bottle hung by the door.

I look at Mom and know my face is pulled in all differ-ent directions when she winces.

"Just take a deep breath," she whispers to me. The nurse comes back. Takes what looks like a pen from her pocket.

"Look straight at that back wall for me, sweetheart," she says. Turns out the pen is not a pen but a flashlight. She illuminates the end and shines it in my eyes.

"Okay. Well, that all looks good." Her nose wrinkles when she smiles at me. "I'll go and chase down that pre-scription. And then hopefully we can get you back home before the day is out."

"Home," I repeat. The one place in the world where scary things couldn't get me is no more. *Home* is a word that should conjure images of thatched cottages, flower-beds, and white picket fences. All I see now is skeletons and shards of glass bejeweling my bleeding skin.

"That's right," the nurse replies. "There's nothing like your own bed." She chuckles to herself as she exits the way she entered, in an emergency-type rush.

"They caught him," Mom says, doing that thing where she reads my mind. "Luke called the police, and they managed to catch him while he was making a run for it. Is it okay that I'm telling you this?"

I think *no,* but say yes.

"Ours wasn't the first house he hit. The guy used his job to scout locations and seek out vulnerable people. He's going to prison for a long time."

I think she means for this to make me feel better, but I feel nothing.

Almost nothing.

"Is Luke okay?"

"Worried sick about you. He hasn't stopped calling." She turns, points to a table in the corner of the room. It's adorned with two big bunches of yellow and purple flowers. "And he keeps sending you daisies and carnations."

The flowers are beautiful. I close my eyes, remember how tight he held me when I fell into him. I wish he were here.

"I told him you'd call him as soon as you could." And I will.

"Tell me what you're thinking about," Mom says when the silence starts to stretch. She perches on my bed, reaches over and rubs circles on my hip.

"I don't even know." My brain feels like it's trapped

in a vise and every time I try to figure something out, it squeezes tighter and tighter around it.

The intruder. My injuries. Leaving the house. Having to stay in the hospital. Taking sedatives. Strangers touching me. My plate is too full. I have mental indigestion. My life is on its ass. It's a face in full shadow, a stranger at a bar, a reflection I don't even recognize anymore.

I'm being forced to challenge ideas that have kept me safe for so long. There's an entire library of information in my head, and suddenly I can't decide if any of it is worth reading.

"Get some rest," Mom says, leaning forward and kissing my forehead. "We'll get you through this. It'll all be over soon. I promise."

In Recovery

Back before the black-and-white pages of frightening reality were banned from our house, I went through this stage of reading nonfiction. Celebrity autobiographies mostly, but there was this one rags-to-riches story about a woman named Audrey Clarke. Audrey owned a small grocery store in Brooklyn during the Great Depression.

As the misery of that decade rolled on and on and on, she ended up losing most of her store stock to looters. Debt collectors took what was left after that, including her clothes. By the time the Depression ended, she had no house and no business left.

She was sleeping in a neighbor's toolshed when she turned to writing to fill her days. Her books were good. She made quite a bit of money from eager publishing houses in the end. Lived out her life in a very affluent neighborhood, playing golf on the weekends and collecting classic cars.

I liked reading Audrey's story because never, not once, did she entertain the notion that she had been beaten.

There's this one thing she said that keeps popping into

my head as I swallow down my serotonin-reuptake inhibitors and watch that damned blackbird jumping around on my windowsill.

Your mind adapts to what worse is. Suddenly, that thing that seemed so terrifying at first is dwarfed by the next challenge that comes your way. But you adapt again and again and again, until you find yourself fearless.

I never really understood what she meant until it no longer felt necessary to be afraid of swallowing a tiny tablet after I'd crawled through broken glass. Literally.

"Stop tormenting that poor blackbird."

My bones leave my body briefly. When I turn around, I find Luke in my doorway, hands in his pockets, pulling his jeans so low they sag off his hips and I can see the elastic waist of his shorts. I swallow back a sudden influx of saliva. A cord headband pushes his hair off his face. His eyes make me think of oceans; his smile belongs in a gallery.

My best friend. My boyfriend.

"I wasn't tormenting it. It was tormenting me," I say in my own defense, grabbing my bag off the end of the bed.

"Don't forget your balls," he says with a wink, pointing to the two rainbow rounds on my dresser.

"Check me out," I say, tossing the balls up in the air.

"Good job," he tells me as I juggle. The thing about constantly carrying around circular objects is that you turn into a circus clown. On the plus side, it's been almost a month since I last broke skin scratching. Dr. Reeves and I agreed that biting my nails was still allowed.

For now.

Luke cracks a grin and the temperature of my room rises to Florida-in-July degrees. Then he does this new thing we've been working on a lot lately . . . he holds out his hand.

"Your chariot awaits, my lady." I hesitate, stare at his fingers, his palm. He has what a fortuneteller might call a long life line.

"Did you . . ."

"Wash my hands first? Yes."

He fixes a stare on me that makes me tingle from tip to toe. Acceptance of the strange is his superpower.

Before I have time to think myself out of it, I slap my hand into his. The medicine I've started swallowing delays my crazy just long enough for me to complete the action before deciding it's going to destroy me. Once it's done, and I can see that it won't, Dr. Reeves says all I have to do is focus on slowing my heart rate. Easier said than done for a woman who's never been in close proximity to Luke for longer than five seconds. I guess that's about to change.

"Are you sure you don't mind coming with me?" I ask as we make our way out of my room.

"Are you kidding? After all the things you've said about her, I can't wait to meet the good doctor." He means it. I might have questioned his enthusiasm when I first floated the idea of him coming with me to therapy. But he hasn't stopped talking about it for the past two weeks. I cozy up to his arm. Because (a) I'm addicted to the winter-spice aftershave he wears and (b) we've started down the stairs and I can feel a flutter of anxiety in my chest.

"You okay?" he stops and asks when we hit the second-to-last step. Deep breath. I nod; my jaw feels a little loose and I don't want it to start jerking if I try to speak. Mom appears from the kitchen, giving me her my-little-girl-is-all-grown-up eyes over the top of her Best Mom in the World mug.

"You can do it," she says.

"You've totally got this," Luke affirms.

It makes me smile. And with that, we head toward the door.

But not before I take the last step twice.

Author's Note

Norah's story began as a rant, an angry exploration of how stagnant my life had become. For while this book is a work of fiction, Norah's challenges are very much a reflection of my own struggles with mental health.

It wasn't a story I ever planned on sharing. The things that go on inside Norah's head—inside my head—were a secret, because sometimes I behave in ways that feel strange and are inexplicable. Sometimes it feels like my own mind is trying to destroy me. Sometimes, I feel like I'm too strange, like no one could ever understand me, least of all myself. But my way of understanding things—including my thoughts—is to write them down.

Watching this story unfold was an odd experience. There's so much going on in my brain, I forget skirmishes I've fought, or instances in which I've had to overcome challenges—and all the small, seemingly irrelevant things I have to do battle with daily. But suddenly it was all there on paper, and it seemed so . . . huge. Norah is a poster child for self-sabotage: she makes mistakes, she breaks, she fails, and she hurts, but she doesn't give up. She's a warrior, slaying demons every time she swallows food when she's afraid of choking, killing malevolent beasts with every morbid thought she banishes. Norah triumphs—it comes at a cost, but she does triumph. And I figure that is a story worth sharing.

While I based a lot of Norah's treatment on my own treatment, therapy is carefully calibrated and tailored to each individual. What works for Norah may not work for her readers—and vice versa. There is no miracle cure for mental illness, but you can make it manageable. If you struggle as Norah and I do, there are people with experience, insight, and strategies who understand and who want to help. You just have to ask, and I hope you will.

Acknowledgments

Anne Hoppe, your editing skills are of the highest caliber; you have shaped this book into so much more than it was before, but beyond the technicalities of storytelling, I want to thank you for being such an amazing person. I was worried about this story, about how nonsensical it would seem to someone who hadn't experienced my mental health at its worst, but you made it so easy to be honest and open. Thank you for loving Norah, and for allowing me to take the lead with her story so we could nail the perspective and share her experiences with anyone out there who may be facing the same struggles.

And Mandy Hubbard, much of the above applies to you, too. You are a Jedi. Thank you for encouraging me to tell this story. And thank you for answering all my ridiculous freak-out emails. As I write this, we're still twelve months from release. Can you imagine the conversations we're going to have? Apologies and endless gratitude in advance. You're a trooper.

Massive thanks to everyone at Clarion and HMH. Hayley Gonnason, Meredith Wilson, and Tara Shanahan thank you for your tireless efforts to get *Rose* into the hands of readers. And to Christine Kettner: Thank you for creating such a gorgeous jacket that perfectly reflects this story. I'm beyond grateful to be a part of this publishing family.

I'd like to say a huge thank-you to my mum and dad for their endless love and undying patience. I know these past ten years have been tough. I feel so lucky to have you.

To the best older sister and little brother a person could hope for, Lisa and Nicholas: Thank you for always taking care of me, standing up for me, and supporting me, especially when it comes to my mental health. (Liam, this applies to you, too.)

To my best friend and mentor, Rach. You already know. There will never be enough blank pages for me to put into words how grateful I am to you. I'm forever part of your team.

To my amazing beta readers and critic partners, Megan Orsini, Claire Donnelly, Nicole Tersigni, Candice Montgomery, Dawn Ius, and S. E. Carson—I'm still waiting on planet Dictionary to come up with a word that expresses the outrageous level of gratitude I have for you guys and your writing skills. Thank you for making me a better writer.

To Louie, Suzanne Van Rooyen, and Jennifer Shannon: I love you guys. Thank you for always being on hand with words of wisdom, encouragement, cake, and kindness. This book broke me a lot; I couldn't have written it without your support.

To the awesome members of #WO2016, and my fabulous Twitter family: You make the drawn-out days of no words and floods of tears bearable. It's a privilege to always be around such a broad network of knowledge and skill.

Last, but by no means least, Professor: Thank you for saving my life . . .